BOY IN THE MIDDLE

BOY IN THE MIDDLE

Patrick Califia

CLEIS
PRESS

Published in the United States by Cleis Press Inc., P.O. Box 14697, San Francisco, California 94114.

Printed in the United States.
Cover design: Scott Idleman
Text design: Frank Wiedemann
Logo art: Juana Alicia
First Edition.
10 9 8 7 6 5 4 3 2 1

Grateful acknowledgment is made to the following publications in which these stories previously appeared: "Who Casts the First Stone?" appeared in *Set in Stone,* edited by Angela Brown (Alyson Publications, 2001). "Above All the Lights" will appear in *Men of Mystery,* edited by Greg Wharton and Sean Meriwether (Haworth Press, 2006). "Date Rape" appeared under the title "Better than Date Rape" in *Best S/M Erotica: More Extreme Tales of Extreme S/M,* Volume 2, edited by M. Christian (Venus Book Club, 2004). "Boy in the Middle" appeared in *Best of Both Worlds: Bisexual Erotica,* edited by Sage Vivant and M. Christian (Haworth Press, 2005). "Flannel Nightgowns and White Cotton Panties" appeared in *Master/Slave,* edited by N. T. Morley (Berkley Trade, 2005). "Gender Queer" appeared in *Bed: New Lesbian Erotica* edited by Victoria A. Brownworth (Haworth Press, 2005). "Learning the Alphabet" appeared in *Blood Lust: Erotic Vampire Tales,* edited by M. Christian and Todd Gregory (Alyson Publications, 2005). "It Takes a Good Boy (to Make a Good Daddy)" appeared in *Doing It for Daddy* edited by Pat Califia (Alyson Publications, 1994). "Tamping the Dirt Down" will appear in *Best Gay Erotica 2006,* edited by Richard Labonté (Cleis Press, 2006).

Contents

Introduction:
Pansexual Passion

I began writing erotic fiction as a deliberate maneuver to break out of a destructive cycle in which I would write poems or short stories, read them over with distaste and dissatisfaction, and then destroy them in a fit of self-loathing and anger at my own (perceived) lack of skill or talent. I picked a forbidden topic that I hoped would carry me through the thorny barriers that blocked any ability to relax during the process of creation, enjoy my own work, or own it with jubilance or just quiet gratitude. If I was unable to create realistic characters or write believable or gripping dialogue, surely I could accurately portray one of my own sexual fantasies. I never intended to show this story to anyone. And that story, "Jessie," spent a few months in my desk drawer before I read it to a friend. It was years later that it finally appeared in *Coming to Power* and, later, *Macho Sluts*. It remains a favorite for many readers, perhaps because it has the fresh feel of something brand new and brave.

The story drew mixed reviews from everyone who encountered it. Naiad Press publisher Barbara Grier requested a manuscript copy for her privately held lesbian archives, and told me, "You know, there's nothing like this. I've been reading lesbian fiction for decades, and it stands alone. But it's absolutely unpublishable." Perhaps because I wanted to prove her wrong, and perhaps because the choice of sexual fantasy as a topic had gotten me through the gauntlet of self-hatred and doubt that had shredded my other fiction, I kept on writing about sexual fantasy. The slow growth of a leatherdyke community generated new material for my fiction and also created an audience for it. That audience was augmented by sex-positive feminism and a new, pansexual and politically-aware, BDSM tribe.

In this book, "The Only One Who Can Save Her," "It Takes a Good Boy (to Make a Good Daddy)," and "Who Casts the First Stone?" can be added to the list of my lesbian erotic fiction. (As you might expect from a story that has the word *stone* in its title, this last piece explores the relationship between masculinity and butch identity; the main character from this story also appears in a story in *No Mercy*.) I realize that some readers will be turned off by a transman who writes about women having sex with one another. I suspect, however, that many of the same women who will say that about my work, now that I have begun my gender transition, would also say that male-to-female transsexuals are not women, and that a female-to-male transsexual like myself can never actually be a man.

That's the problem with gender essentialism. I certainly share many organs with the characters in these stories, and I haven't forgotten what it feels like to put a female body up against the body of another woman. I had as much fun, and got as turned on, writing about the lesbian vampire and her lover in "The Only One Who Can Save Her," as I did with other pieces of fiction. I hope you will too.

Back in the mid-1980s, it certainly would have helped me to "sell" my work as politically valid if I had kept myself on the topic of woman-to-woman sex. Feminists, especially lesbian feminists, "knew" that the pornography that men had created was toxic to us. It was based on misogynist stereotypes of women and false male fantasies about what lesbians looked like or did with one another. Any woman who enjoyed this toxic sludge was a pawn of the patriarchy. And the truth is that most commercial depictions of lesbian sex were dreadful then. There was a valid need for women who desired other women to make their own images of sensuality, and for women writers to describe our love and lust in a language of liberation.

But...but...the truth was that my own sexual fantasies were mostly about men dominating women. (This book includes two unabashedly wicked tales of female submission to male masters, "Flannel Nightgowns and White Cotton Panties" and "Making Honey.") And my real sex life included male as well as female partners. And what about my own conflicted and inventive relationship with my own body? How often did I see myself as a woman when I had sex with someone whose genitals resembled my own? Not very often. During a time when the penis represented everything that was wrong with the world and half of our species,

I spent a lot of money and time coming up with ways to appropriate the phallus and subvert it for my own dual-gendered purposes. With a stubbornness that was perhaps self-destructive, I set about incorporating at least some of this material into my fiction.

Macho Sluts. Melting Point. No Mercy. Each of these books included a combination of sex acts, genders, and erotic roles. Some of the stories were set in worlds other than our own, and included nonhuman but intelligent and sexual beings. The content was primarily women-only sex, followed by man-to-man sex, and a little male-female interaction. (In fact, I wrote so much fag porn that there's a whole book of it out now, *Hard Men*.)

There are two stories about man-to-man sex in this book. "Learning the Alphabet" takes us into the backstory of my novel *Mortal Companion*. The vampire protagonist of that book, Ulric, takes over the suicide mission of a grief-stricken goth boy. And in "Tamping the Dirt Down," two brothers wrestle, literally and figuratively, with the legacy of their abusive and recently expired father. In "Above All the Lights," the hero comes a few steps closer to living his homosexual desire.

During the decades in which these books were created, a new style of group and public sex had emerged that fit my style much better than being solely a lesbian ever had. The boys-only fisting parties that had stretched to include Cynthia Slater and her female lovers had evolved into special events with a queer aesthetic that encompassed "straight" as well as gay and bisexual couplings and other impassioned combinations of bodies, hearts, and minds. They were called pansexual parties. Pan for short, and I think He would be proud to see His name evoked once more to bless licentiousness.

I began calling myself bisexual about five years ago, during the same months in which I started taking testosterone, using the name "Patrick," and asking people to address me with male pronouns. It was a long overdue adjustment in my public persona, a delay that had been motivated by fear and also by my own adherence to the ideals of a certain kind of feminism that grew out of women-only institutions. I still think that there's something inherently radical about being a dyke. I believe it's important for women to be able to get together with other women, with no need to worry about male intrusion or voyeurism. It made me sad and scared to leave a culture behind that had done so much to shape my personality. It was a world I had always fought with and deplored, as well as admired and struggled to build. But I wasn't going to die as a revered elder of a tribe of Amazons in black leather jackets. Amazons only cut one of their breasts off. And I needed to get rid of both of mine.

To borrow a phrase from Anaïs Nin, I have been a Spy in the House of Love for most of my life. My body and my spirit have never been easy with one another. I have no idea what it is like to grow up happy that you are a man or at ease with the fact that you are a woman. I don't know what it's like to welcome the changes that puberty brings, to relish a sense of being more grown up. I have no idea how the world looks to people who see their masculinity or femininity as an easy and congruent attribute of their hormones and their own self-image. But I've been a good student of the men and women who are not two-spirited. I've gathered my intelligence in such a comprehensive and thorough fashion that they assimilate my stories as their own. Perhaps I've been able to steal these faces, words, and wisps of feeling because I've wished, so very hard, to be able to dance through life as a woman. Or as a man. One or the other. Excluding the Other. Not both. Or neither.

So here is a book that celebrates several forms of passion. It is diverse, perverse, and bold. Not all of the sex within these pages is same-sex, but it is all queer. The word *queer* has grown far beyond the parameters of homosexuality. It encompasses a wide range of self-aware deviation from the norm. Gender outlaws as well as gay men and lesbians, bisexual people as well as male-female couples who fornicate rather than mate—all of them are queer.

The master in "Boy in the Middle" is a queer-identified bisexual who is also transsexual. His threesome with a genetic female masochist and a boy who is also a transman highlights the complex flavors of passion that incorporates both masculine and feminine, male and female, energies and bodies. I've already mentioned other stories with transgendered characters—"Above All the Lights" and "Who Casts the First Stone?" The story "Gender Queer" belongs on that roster: in it, a more experienced FTM master introduces a guy who has just begun to come out as trans to the pleasures of gay male sex and S/M.

I've gone out on a limb including so much material

about transgendered people in a book that is intended for readers who are both trans and unigendered, but it is more important to me than ever to make a full range of underrepresented people visible in sexually explicit fiction. Fortunately, there are already a few successful anthologies out that focus on the differently-gendered experience. Of course, there is no way for one book to include every possibility. (None of my FTM characters have had genital surgery, for example.) This project has to be ongoing, and we need to hear from many different people who have their own unique experience with original expressions of gender in their own lives or the lives of their partners.

This is important because transsexual people have virtually no accurate reflections of their own experience in mass-market pornography. There is a genre of photo magazines or movies that feature male-to-female transsexuals (MTFs) who have breasts and penises. These women are called "pre-ops," even though some of them don't want to have genital surgery, or may simply never be able to afford it. There are a handful of movies featuring FTMs, most made in the last ten years, none in wide circulation. Our bodies are generally perceived as defective (sadly, often even by ourselves). Erotic images of us are in the same category as fetish photographs of amputees—images of sick people made for an audience that is even sicker.

But are we really handicapped or incomplete? I think it would be safe to say that we are frustrated. I wish my clit was long enough to penetrate my partners. Testosterone has made it more impressive, but it's not going to protrude that much, no matter how good the blowjob is. But doesn't every man wish his penis were larger, got hard quicker, stayed hard longer, et cetera? You don't have to be a transwoman to wish your breasts looked more like a brassiere model's, or feel ambivalent about your pussy. Granted, the frustration of transpeople with their bodies is several magnitudes greater than the negative assessments genetic men and women might make of their own bodies.

This is the problem with the medical model for understanding pleasure and gender—it sees any variation from the majority's experience as a disease. Transgendered people have been defined by our *symptoms*, not by our strengths. The editor of a mainstream magazine of stroke stories once refused my offer to write a story about FTMs with the statement, "Oh, the poor half-and-halfs. Nobody wants to read about them. I don't think I want to see anything about *that*." Yet this is a lesbian who prefers butch women—women who are so butch they at least fall close to the FTM experience. Her own bed has seen many of the same experiences and feelings that she, as a gatekeeper, excludes from her magazine and thus from wider circulation, wider knowledge.

I don't think transgendered people are mistakes. The saddest thing I ever heard in my therapy office was when a transsexual client told me that being "gender dysphoric" was, "a curse. I mean, nobody would ever ask to go through that, would they? And nobody would ever wish that upon their child. It's a tragedy. A horrible problem with no solution."

I can't agree. I believe I chose to be here, on this planet and during this lifetime, as a transgendered person. I believe we've been a part of many human cultures, and we're not always treated as mentally ill or handicapped people. Sometimes we're seen as priests or entertainers, prostitutes or sacred dancers, foster parents or potent warriors and hunters. Today, we wrestle with the same existential questions that plague everybody else—why am I here, what am I supposed to accomplish in this lifetime, what is right and what is wrong, how can I find love, what sort of pleasure can my imperfect body give me, how do I find community, what face do I want to wear when death takes me?

When fiction is well written, these are the questions that take precedence, not the specifics of sexual orientation or gender identity. I have been privileged to educate and be educated by a readership that takes a radical stance on issues of sexual freedom and gender equality. This book is a vacation from the hard work of seeking equal rights for sexual minorities. If your preferred flavor is vanilla, this volume of erotica will probably disappoint you. For everybody else, it's a sweet, mean, uncomfortable but delicious ride to your own or somebody else's orgasm. It's a sort of black leather pajama party.

Come as you are.

With bright and dark blessings,
Patrick Califia
San Francisco
June 1, 2005

Who Casts
the First Stone?

Then he brought me to the door
of the gate of the Lord's house
which was toward the north; and, behold,
there sat women weeping for Tammuz.
                                   —Ezekiel 8:14

The mirror behind the mahogany bar of the Pearl and
the Peacock showed Tammuz a too-familiar face. In
the center of the bar, between the tall rows of ver-
mouth, gin, vodka, Scotch, rum, and bourbon, there
was a large, thick panel of silver glass that bore hir
image in profile, then (as s/he rotated on the bar stool,
lit cigarette in hand) full-face. There was that thick
dark hair that resisted being combed back, off hir big
forehead. There were hir eyes, too small, dark as a
dog's. The thick-lipped, mobile mouth and the promi-
nent broken nose made hir look coarse. S/he turned hir
head to the left and right, disapproving of the jowls

that had appeared long before age could excuse them. Beneath this caricature, hir incongruously tiny, square hands brought the cigarette up to hir lips, which pursed to blow smoke rings. *Your lady walks out, self-hatred walks in. Business as usual.*

"You haven't heard a word I said," pouted Lotta Trouble. Lotta was a foot taller than Tam, a vision of bleached-blonde Hollywood glamour. Despite her nickname, she was a kindhearted person, probably worried about her stolid date's state of mind. Tam squared hir shoulders, which were as broad as any man's, thank God, and turned to face the bouquet of feminine beauty who graced hir arm this evening. Lotta was the poppet s/he chauffeured around in between lovers—provided the hussy was not going out with Tam's ex. A striking male-to-female trans-sexual, Lotta loved to tell people her pussy was "made in Morocco," even though the work had been done by good old Dr. Stanley Biber of Trinidad, Colorado. A fairly lonely person despite her gregarious nature, Lotta enjoyed going places with Tam. They'd tried having sex once, ages ago, but it hadn't been a great success because Lotta didn't particularly like butches. She doted on girls who shared her penchant for long afternoons at the hairdresser, dark shades of lipstick, high heels, and short, tight dresses.

"I know everything you've said," Tam growled, and ordered them both another drink.

"Are you saying that I repeat myself?" Lotta retorted, raising her dangerous right eyebrow. The perfect cone of her platinum beehive hairdo reminded Tam of a missile that was about to go off.

2

"Honey, we all repeat ourselves after four drinks," Tam drawled. It might be time to quit drinking. Again. S/he offered Lotta one of her own long, girly cigarettes with little flowers at the base of the filter, and waved a light at the tip of it. *How can she stand that much menthol and that little nicotine?*

Their drinks arrived, and Tam took a sip after hoisting hir bottom-heavy glass with a conciliatory grin. "Here's to your beautiful self," s/he said in hir gravelly voice. Lotta relented and returned the smile. "Yes, honey, you can call my attorney on Monday. He'll take care of that eviction notice." To Lotta's surprised stare, Tam replied, "I told you I was listening." The drink was very strong. Tam had not ordered a double. Given the abstemious pour that was common in dyke bars, even this one, which s/he owned a share in, Tam looked up to see who the bartender was and what the hell *she* was drinking.

There were two people behind the bar, a slightly older redhead who was always whistling show tunes soundlessly to herself and a towheaded kid with a stocky but athletic body and the plain, open face of a farmboy. Of course, farmboys did not generally wear eight-gauge rings in their noses. Tam knew that redheaded Cory wouldn't let her elbow slip. Who was this new person, who was staring at hir and rushing over with a bowl full of peanuts and *another* bowl full of pretzels? Had someone broken with protocol and pointed out Tam as one of the owners?

Lotta had tasted her own drink by now, winced at its robustness, and followed the direction of Tam's gaze. Tam felt hir companion discount the baby-dyke bartender as a potential source of sexual stimulation and reject the peanuts with horror for their high-fat content. "So have a pretzel instead," s/he told Lotta, who replied, "They stick to my teeth, angel." What would it be like to be a high femme, unable to avail yourself of butch creature comforts like a sharp, sturdy toothpick?

Tam accepted the snacks with the barest of nods, as s/he also accepted having their drinks lifted and the bar carefully cleaned. In the course of the next half hour, s/he noted that the bartender also brought them extra napkins, changed their coasters, emptied the heavy cut-glass ashtray every time Tam simply waved hir cigarette over it, and dusted all the bottles at their end of the bar.

"Somebody is trying to get your attention," Lotta said, resting her hand on Tam's shoulder. Her sharp oval nails were a purplish shade of red, and she'd dusted them with gold glitter before the polish dried.

"Jealous?" Tam asked, not looking at the busy barkeep.

"Let's just say I know when my presence is not wanted," Lotta replied good-humoredly. "I think I'll go powder my nose."

She tucked her sequined gold evening bag under her arm and stood, turning carefully to orient herself toward the ladies' room. Tam stole a lascivious glance at her shapely bottom, outlined in black spandex and framed by a maroon patent-leather bustier and the ruler-straight lines of her stockings. S/he felt the kid behind the bar watching hir watch Lotta's ass and feeling really unhappy about the randy gleam in

Tam's eye. Tam knew Lotta would not be back for at least an hour and a half. The Pearl and the Peacock had a very nice pool table, and Lotta had survived as a gender-ambiguous youth in Dead Truck, Oklahoma, by doing more than one kind of hustling.

What should s/he do about this offering? An experienced top, Tam was not slow to pick up on the maneuvers of a bottom who wanted some personal attention. But the bartender was not hir usual type. No curves on that ball. Still, it was a three-day weekend, and Lotta could not be exploited to fill up every lonely minute. Within Tam's chest the sharp fragments of hir broken heart moved unexpectedly, causing pain to shoot up to the corners of hir eyes and down the fingers of both hands. The last femme, who bore a remarkable resemblance to Bettie Page, had left Tam, as they so often did, for a man who had less money but a lot more respectability to offer. Tam thought again about the clinic at Stanford, a syringe full of oily amber testosterone, the sculpting blade of a scalpel. Would it solve hir problems or simply add new ones?

S/he could reach no conclusion about this dilemma. Taking hormones would give hir a beard, another layer of muscle, perhaps pull hir already-low voice down another octave. It was hard to admit, even to hirself, how excited s/he got when s/he thought about being able to feel those changes in hir own flesh. Imagine a beard that did not reek of spirit gum; imagine being able to put on a shirt and tie and look at hir profile without wincing. But s/he hated men almost as much as s/he hated the pendulous ample breasts and hidden, inward-looking genitals that marked hir as female. Where would s/he go? Who would s/he fuck? Planet Lesbos was a small world, with no room for someone who looked even a hair more masculine than Tam already did.

A memory tugged at Tam's consciousness, threatening to add more hurt to the bonfire of pain in hir chest. S/he had not thought of Wilson for how many years? That would have been in hir midtwenties, a decade ago, when s/he was living in London, attending a snotty, ivy-clogged, limey university to study the history of fine art. That was before Tam figured out that The Academy would never allow hir to make hir own art.

S/he had encountered Wilson at the Palace, the first lesbian bar where Tam became a regular. In fact, hir early experiences at the Palace had a lot to do with what sort of dyke Tam had become, second only to hir affair with the ash-blond sophisticate who taught music and drama in hir high school. It had been pretty easy to do Miss Lowenstein. She had picked Tam out the first day of class, and waged one of the sneakiest courtships Tam (in retrospect) had ever seen. She gave the baby dyke and nouveau fag leading roles in the school play, concocted a fiction of a dating relationship between the two of them, and then spent a lot of time "rehearsing" alone with the butch girl while the cocksucker slipped off to do guilty business-suit daddies in the bus station.

It was as easy as paint by numbers, Tam thought, smiling. Miss Lowenstein would press her hands to her lips and say something like, "I can feel your desire. It scalds me. I know you want to kiss me, and I'm afraid I won't be able to stop you." How stupid would you have to be to ignore a cue like that? What were some of her other pronouncements? "If you put your tongue between my legs I won't be able to contain my excitement or my shame." Then there was, "Please don't violate me with your cruel, clever hands, or I'll never be able to enjoy normal lovemaking again." It could have been hot, but these protests sounded rote, even to a novice skirt-chasing bulldagger.

Tam had known better than to ask why the coaching was all one-way. S/he thought s/he knew why hir lover never touched hir. It was because s/he was ugly, that was all. Tam's own mother never embraced hir, could barely be civil, and was visibly relieved to have hir out of the house for longer and longer periods of time. S/he also knew better than to try to continue the affair once s/he graduated from high school. When the window between ages sixteen and eighteen closed, Miss Lowenstein was courteous but circumspect. She did use some of her art school connections to wangle Tam a scholarship overseas, and for that, the young butch was deeply grateful.

It was with nothing more than this youthful indiscretion behind hir belt buckle that Tam braved the gates of hir first dyke pub and forked over an exorbitant cover charge, which s/he was never asked for again after that first night. The Palace was down by the waterfront, and when the tide was out you could smell river water and the rotting wood of the docks as you approached the bar. The tiny front windows were rendered opaque with gray paint, and barred besides. Inside this grim and dingy establishment, no bigger than a living room and dining room shoved together, the clientele was (or pretended to be) a great deal more upper-class than the neighborhood. Butches wore black or gray wool trousers, white button-down shirts, and sometimes coats and ties. Khaki cotton trousers and V-neck sweater vests were acceptable in the summer. Femmes appeared in conservatively colored secretarial dresses that covered their knees, and sometimes wore little hats and gloves. A girl who turned up once in jeans and a striped rugby sweater had been turned away, as had a giggling mob of mini-skirted, thrill-seeking coeds with long hair that had been ironed straight, go-go boots, and vinyl jackets printed with op-art geometric designs.

Cops could not do a better job of shutting out the social unrest of the '60s than George, the prim elderly owner of the Palace, who had been an ambulance driver during World War II. It was George, not the neighborhood bobby or Scotland Yard, who decreed that there would be no dancing at the Palace. Too shocking, too lascivious, a pair of women openly dancing with each other in public. This was not Paris, you know. Of course, this rule was breached every time George was not around and the bartenders were plied with enough gin-and-tonic.

The Palace had a fiercely maintained hierarchy and conservative notions of proper social sex-roles for "gay girls." Femmes came and went, to and from the straight life, it was presumed. If an AWOL femme, no matter how beautiful or notorious, came back to the bar a few years later, she had to start all over again, and she couldn't come back at all if the woman she'd dropped for a man was still a regular. A butch could also disappear, especially if she was in a relationship, because everyone knew the bar scene would break up any couple. During this sabbatical, however, her legend would be kept alive by cronies eager to prove that role-playing was more severe and authentic in the good old days of what's-her-name. These raconteurs kept the young bucks from getting too big for their tweeds.

The only person other than an alcoholic waif known as Floozy who had a rude *nom de dyke bar* was Tam. S/he was known as the Ugly American. The rest of the butches, Brits all, knew each other only by their painfully Anglo-Saxon surnames. As if they were residents of a public school for boys. (Tam never, incidentally, saw Floozy going home with anybody.)

Wilson was the kingpin of this bar's habitues. Tall and somewhat horse-faced, she had untidy short sandy hair and smoked thin black cigars that stained her fingers. This slovenliness somehow produced an aristocratic impression. But then, to Tam, it looked like Englishmen never combed their hair. Wilson was rumored to be an heiress or perhaps a barrister or a physicist. As a matter of fact, she was a cabdriver, and the fact that Tam knew may have been one reason Wilson took hir home one fateful and formative night. To shut hir up for good. Tam had a highly inappropriate crush on Wilson, who was embarrassed to death by this unorthodox butch-on-butch passion.

One of the hallmarks of status at the Palace was the right to tell a story free from interruption or comment, no matter how drunk one's peers (or oneself) might be. Wilson liked telling anecdotes in a Cockney accent, which Tam had quickly figured out was like telling jokes about (to put it nicely) the "colored people" down South back in America. On this particular evening Wilson had been telling a story about Floozy's arrival at the Palace under the mistaken impression that it was a gathering place for *tykes*, haw haw. Tam arrived and just the sight of hir rattled Wilson so much that she snapped her mouth shut and then said irritably to her guffawing cronies, "Why must we always be going on and on about that illiterate slattern?"

Floozy was only ten feet away when Wilson uttered this scathing sentiment. Looking like a big china doll, she had been listening to the story with everyone else, trying to keep an identical expression of amusement on her face. Her big blue eyes and nicely curled hair made a pretty picture, but Floozy was so quiet and passive that Tam thought she might be one of those very lonely mentally ill people who are thought to be merely different.

"Sylvia's due here at ten with her mate from work," Wilson told Tam, thumping hir on the shoulder. "Why don't you squire her girlfriend about for the evening? I've met her. She's not hard to look at. Doesn't wear too much cheap scent like most stenographers. They'll be here any minute. Sylvia knows better than to be late when she has a date with me."

Tam extracted hir gold pocket watch, acquainted hirself with its face, and tucked it comfortably back into the pocket of hir herringbone pants before answering. "It's ten-forty-five," was all s/he said, pulling down hir wool vest.

Wilson gave a great gasp of exasperation and waved her hands in the air. "Will you never give this up?" she inquired, clearly annoyed. She took two steps over to Tam, took her by the shoulders, and spun her about. "Look at that bit of fluff," she hissed, indicating a brown-haired girl in a mauve suit who was sitting alone at the other end of the bar, making rings on the countertop with her wet glass. "Or those birds over there," she insisted, jabbing Tam in the kidneys to make sure s/he did not miss two giggling gamines, a blonde and a redhead, both in black cocktail frocks. "*These* are the objects destined to receive and enjoy your perhaps somewhat ham-handed attentions," Wilson said, each word a staccato beat of disapproval. "Not me, Tam. For God's sake. Get a grip on yourself."

Tam removed hirself from Wilson's grasp and turned around, dusting off hir arms. "I don't believe I have the pleasure of knowing what the fuck you are talking about," s/he said, trying to sound casual and offhand. Little bitter tears stung the corners of hir eyes but would never well up and fall to hir cheeks. S/he knew they were undetectable.

Why *did* s/he feel hir stomach jump whenever Wilson was around? Why did s/he stroke hirself at night, imagining Wilson's strong arms locked around hir, their lips hungrily exploring one another? Why did the pretty girls who made eyes at hir leave hir feeling cold and hard as a pillar of granite? At this point in hir Palace engagement, Tam had broken a couple of hearts and one hymen. She thought she knew the femme heart and spirit inside and out. None of her conquests had made more than a tentative effort to discover the texture of the skin behind Tam's underwear or pajamas. Even in bed, Tam felt the need for protective armor. But in hir dreams of lovemaking with Wilson, both of them were skin-to-skin.

Perhaps a hint of these deviant fantasies showed on Tam's big transparent face. Wilson gasped with exasperation again and threw herself back onto her bar stool. The unfortunate Floozy picked exactly that moment to reach for her drink and upset it. Wilson leapt out of the way long before getting splashed, but Tam could tell from the belligerent set of her jaw that Floozy would pay for this insubordinate error.

"My, my, Floozy, aren't you a spastic creature?" Wilson drawled. "I believe I must ask you for a rag with which to mop up this mess." Snapping her fingers, she attracted henchmen to the left and right who came prowling after her, unsure what she was up to but eager to help. If poor Floozy had stood her ground and demanded a towel from the bartender, she probably would have escaped with nothing worse than a verbal dressing-down. But she saw the approaching butches, felt their menace, squeaked, and backed away from them.

Two of Wilson's friends grabbed Floozy by the arms and held her while two other strapping butches grabbed her feet and lifted them into the air. Wilson was between Floozy's legs, neatly unrolling her panties. She latched on to Tam and dragged hir close to the victim as well; took Tam's fist in her own hand to jam it hard against Floozy's mons. A little pair of pale yellow cotton panties hovered just above the girl's flailing knees. Tam could not help staring at her cunt, which seemed nearly bare since Floozy's pubic hair was thin and as blond as the hair on her head. The slender pink inner lips stood well away from the nearly flat outer lips, making them look fragile and helpless. It was obvious Wilson wanted her to fuck Floozy, albeit briefly, while the gang provided cover.

Was Wilson's prey wet with unwelcome excitement? Was she dry as fear? Tam did not want to find out. This situation violated all of hir rules about rough sex. (For example, rule number one about being *asked* to provide a hard ride.) S/he couldn't do it. Tam shook hir hand out of Wilson's fist and stepped back from the huddle.

On the spot now, Wilson had to get some sort of reaction out of Floozy to provide a triumphant end to the spectacle. Tam knew the tall Brit was far too fastidious to stick her fingers into Floozy's pretty but (by Wilson's own dictate) slutty and therefore unclean parts. So she contented herself with actually removing the girl's panties, while Floozy kicked and protested with more strength than Tam had ever seen her demonstrate. Once Wilson had them in hand, she mimed wringing them out, said, "These are useless," and threw them back at the girl.

Floozy, now in tears, went running to the loo to put her knickers back on. She passed Tam on her way and gave the Ugly American a venomous look. Tam realized then that Floozy had been nursing a crush on hir, a crush that had now turned to wormwood and gall. S/he sighed, knowing too well the sinking feeling of having acquired yet another enemy. Tam told hirself s/he probably deserved Floozy's wrath. It wasn't like s/he had rescued the poor girl from harm or public humiliation. All s/he had done was sexually reject her. If you were going to be chivalrous around damsels in distress, Tam told hirself, you had to be prepared to go all the way or become an object of scorn forever.

Feeling vindictive toward Wilson for putting hir on the spot, Tam slid a few steps closer, leaned on the bar, and made a big production out of consulting hir watch again. "Eleven o'clock on the dot," s/he said.

"Shut up and have a drink," Wilson said in an ugly tone of voice, and lit up a cigar. Figuring that was as close to an invitation as s/he was going to get, Tam dug in next to the object of hir unorthodox desire and took over the task of paying for her booze. By the time another hour rolled by, Wilson was feeling no pain, and Tam had carefully introduced the topic of girls who stood a chap up, and what such cavalier behavior deserved as punishment. In the middle of Wilson's flowery speech about this, Tam interrupted her (for the second time that evening) to say s/he wanted to go home. Wilson offered to drive hir, if only so she could continue to bend hir ear. Tam steadied Wilson with a hand on her upper arm, and by the time they got to the cab, the fresh air seemed to have cleared the tall woman's head.

Grinding the gears in the old taxi, Wilson cheerfully rattled down the dark and randomly placed streets of Ye Olde London-Towne, not asking for and not needing directions once she had Tam's address. It was a half-hour drive, long enough for small talk to run out and the fumes of Guinness to evaporate. Tam judiciously kept the atmosphere bright and cheery with a joke here and there, interspersed with sips of brandy from a pocket flask. S/he timed things so that Wilson was in the middle of yet another anecdote when they arrived at hir building. The goddess of spare change and one-night stands was with Tam tonight, because a parking place stood empty. Wilson took it without prompting, and Tam took her arm again, escorting her to the stairs.

Halfway up the three flights to hir apartment, it occurred to Tam that Wilson had not finished the last humorous tale and was perhaps not as drunk as she seemed. She was taking the stairs soberly enough. Maybe she was not oblivious to Tam's hidden agenda. This doubt bloomed into full-fledged anxiety when they left the stairwell, confronted Tam's apartment door, and Wilson took the key away from hir to let them both in.

Suddenly Tam's back was against the wall, and Wilson was pressed up against hir. S/he dimly heard the door close, slammed shut by a kick from the tipsy Brit. The mouth that s/he had spent so many hours staring at in the bar, lost in a haze of resentful aching fantasy, was pressing against hir own. Wilson kissed hir hard and fast, and Tam found hirself granting admission to a cigar-smoked, brandy-pickled tongue. The sensation of slick pressure quickly overrode the gamey taste of Wilson's ravishing kiss. Tam felt small and foolish, out of breath and in trouble.

"Not bad," Wilson admitted, and began unbuttoning Tam's shirt. Tam saw hir hands come up to stop her, and willed them back to hir side. But Wilson had seen the gesture of refusal, and stopped worrying at Tam's shirt front. "This *is* what you told me you wanted," she reminded Tam, and studied hir from beneath half-closed eyes.

"Yes," Tam admitted, and Wilson had hir shirt open and off hir back in less than a minute. S/he reached for the waist of Wilson's shirt, intending to pry it out of her waistband, but the other woman was towing hir toward the bedroom, somehow preventing hir from undoing her clothing.

They stood at the foot of Tam's bed, which was pushed into the corner to make the room seem a little bigger. Wilson put her arms around Tam and kissed hir again, while undoing the wide white strap of hir bra. Tam was not used to having hir shirt off in front of another person, but Wilson's quick fingers were all over hir large breasts, enjoying them. Tam thought Wilson was breathing a little quicker, and felt a pang of sick ambivalence in hir stomach at the thought of someone getting aroused by the size of hir chest. It made hir feel as if s/he wasn't really there, couldn't afford to stay connected to this body. S/he couldn't help being aware of the boyish shape of Wilson's torso. The one hand s/he put between Wilson's shoulder blades told hir that the other butch didn't feel the need to wear a brassiere.

Wilson stripped Tam completely, tipping hir onto the bed to finish taking off hir shoes, socks, and trousers. Then she just stood there and looked down at hir. Tam wanted to cover hirself up, but forced hirself to keep hir arms at hir side and ignore the chill. *It's just my body,* s/he told hirself. *It's okay, it's just my body.* But the greasy feeling of being inspected like a mutton chop in a glass case was inescapable. A small child's voice wept, *This is not me*, while a stern adult declared, *Yes it is. Deal with it.*

To Tam's relief, Wilson began to undress as well. She took off her button-down shirt, revealing a white undershirt, and her men's dress shoes and trousers, under which she wore boxer shorts, which she kept on. Tam had done the same thing in bed dozens of times, but feeling Wilson lay down on top of hir with fabric between them made hir heart wilt. Still, she could not keep hir legs together when Wilson's long thigh insisted on going up against hir crotch. Both of them knew Tam was wet, yet Wilson dallied, once again lavishing a great deal of attention on Tam's nipples and breasts. There was something very odd about seeing hir nipple in someone else's mouth, Tam thought. It would feel great for a few seconds, then shame would clamp down, and the suction would become excruciating. *Wrong.* S/he had to constantly fight the impulse to push Wilson's head away from hir torso, push her whole body out of the bed.

But this was the person s/he had longed to hold and make love with. So Tam put hir arms around Wilson and rubbed her back, massaged the muscles in her shoulders, ran hir hands a little lower, and clasped Wilson's butt. The other butch took this as an invitation to grind into Tam's hips, using her leg to create pleasure (and then discomfort and crushing). Despite hirself, Tam was getting more and more excited. S/he was also getting more humiliated and angry.

Then Wilson touched hir clit. Spread hir damp, thin, clinging inner lips apart and touched the opening. "Does that feel nice?" Wilson asked in a cozy little whisper, agitating Tam's clitoral hood.

It was the same way Wilson would talk to a femme. Tam knew it. Hir ears burned, hir face was on fire. But Wilson would not proceed without some encouragement. That cynical horse face was poised above hir, silently asking the question over and over again and secretly reveling in the inevitable answer.

It did feel nice. Why did it feel so wrong to say so? "Yes," Tam got out through gritted teeth, and Wilson rewarded hir with a series of intimate caresses that made goose bumps break out all over hir arms and a flush spread across hir chest and throat. Tam was past caring (well, almost) that this expertise was probably visited in identical form upon every woman Wilson happened to get spread-eagled upon a bed. Hir body felt ungainly yet seraphic. How could hir heavy thighs, big belly, wide ass, and fat arms contain so much joy? It was as if hir dying flesh contained an angel and this celestial being's enjoyment had permeated and subsumed Tam's mortal dross.

"What do we have here?" Wilson whispered, and the jokiness of it put Tam's teeth on edge. The long fingers brushed the opening of hir cunt, found it very wet, and circled around it, taunting. "Let me in," Wilson said, and grinned triumphantly when Tam's hips moved beneath her teasing fingers. It was as bad as having to ask for it out loud. She put a finger in, said, "Don't be lonely," and added another. To Tam, this felt enormous. S/he wanted Wilson to slow down, to let hir catch up with this unfamiliar feeling and figure out how to enjoy it. But Wilson said, "You're not going to be a two-finger fuck, are you, darling?" Suddenly there was unbearable stretching and pressure. Hurt. More hurt! Tam thought s/he might throw up or piss. Wilson was lost in her own world, eyes closed, lips pressed shut, moving her forearm far too quickly.

She wants to get this over with, Tam thought, and felt so much despair that s/he beat on Wilson's shoulders with both hands. The other butch took this for encouragement and pushed harder, causing Tam to yell and struggle. Wilson obviously mistook this for an orgasm and paused, looked unbearably smug, and stroked Tam's clit with her thumb. She left her other fingers in place just barely inside the opening. Tam had both of hir fists clenched now and was close to fury or tears or both. But Wilson had somehow settled into a pattern of touch that felt almost exactly the way doing hirself felt. Tam caught hir breath and was carried up and away, into climax and out of it.

Wilson studied hir, looking cold and clinical, and did not stop touching hir. She held herself up on one arm, so that her hand and one leg were the only points of contact between them. To Tam, the distance between their two bodies was like the great gulf that does not allow the dead to speak to the living. And yet there was union, fusion of a sort. Wilson eased her fingers a little deeper into Tam, and her thumb continued to tap and wiggle on what had become a sensitive spot indeed. Again there was a feeling of being lifted, shaken out in unbearably bright light, then returned to earth. Now Wilson was moving back and forth inside hir, timing fuck and clitoral strokes together, and Tam felt something else, another kind of come, pushing at the gates of hir perception.

"Tell me you love it," Wilson suggested.

Tam almost called her a bitch, but bit hir tongue. S/he could not bear to go on living without finding out what was about to happen. S/he had to know, had to experience the impending explosion, no matter what it cost. Who knew if this craving and contracting would ever come again?

"I think I'll love it," s/he said, trying to be honest. Not wanting, perhaps, to give Wilson everything before she had earned it.

Wilson's jaw tightened. "Not good enough," she decided. "Come on, Tam, you've been sniffing my arse for weeks now. If this wasn't what you wanted, you should have kept your dirty little thoughts to yourself." Her fingers did something unusually clever, some little maneuver that made Tam wince and cry out, this time from pleasure. "Beg. Me. To. Fuck. You."

"Please," Tam said, speaking before s/he could acknowledge how bad giving in would make hir feel later. "I am begging you to fuck me, Wilson."

"Very pretty," Wilson replied, and set to it. To give her credit, she did not slam into Tam to create another noisy crisis that was a mockery of real gratification. She backed off, slowed down, and built Tam up from the foundation, one thick wet dive after another, thumb constantly busy, pushing and teasing, polishing and drilling. Tam felt incoherent babble spill out of hir mouth, as abundant as sexual juice. When it arrived, the experience s/he had sold hir honor for, it was a tragedy with several acts and scenes. It seemed to go on forever. Muscles contracted in places where s/he did not know s/he had muscles. Wilson grimaced and kept on going, as if she had something to prove. Tam growled and sang, struck out blindly, and drowned in blushing delight. When it was over, s/he felt as if s/he would never be horny again.

Wilson sat up, wiped her hand on the sheet, and reached for her clothes. She had her pants on and zipped before Tam could recover enough to reach for her. S/he was surprised by the intensity of the desire s/he felt to suck Wilson off, to spread her legs and bury hir face there. Having turned down more than one femme who whispered the offer of a blowjob, Tam felt a rush of guilt. *Have I ever made anybody feel this worthless?* s/he wondered. *It's like having sex with a man.* Well—not the orgasm. That was something s/he'd never experienced in hir half-dozen attempts at heterosexuality. But the caustic shame, the one-sidedness of it all…that was too familiar.

"It's been great," Wilson said insincerely, peeling Tam's hands off of her. "Really. A giggle and a half. But I absolutely must be going. Ta ta."

Tam found enough of hir moxie to get a fresh grip on Wilson's hips. S/he levered hir bulk off the bed and held the other woman by the back of her trousers with one hand while s/he unzipped them with the other. Wilson was saying sharply, "Here, now, this will never do," when Tam's little hand wove through the fly of her boxer shorts and collided with a mushy wetness that rivaled hir own. Wilson's flushed, distorted face was a study in red rage and denial, her lips twisted as if she'd just swallowed poison.

The tall butch used every ounce of strength she had to escape from Tam's grasp. Retrieving her shirt and shoes, she said, "You know, Tam, you wouldn't be half bad if you fixed yourself up. Lost some weight. Got your hair done. No vertical stripes or polka dots, of course. But with cleavage like that you'd take the Palace by storm, you would. Cheers."

Then she was out of the bedroom. Tam heard the front door of the apartment slam. Wilson was probably getting dressed in the hallway, and s/he would almost certainly receive an eviction notice from hir Christian Scientist landlady tomorrow. S/he did not care. S/he lay back down on the bed and drew the sheet up between hir legs, so that it swaddled and protected hir injured girly softness, and then s/he wrapped the blanket around hirself as snug as a mummy's bandages. S/he felt a little wonderful. S/he felt even more awful. S/he tasted something bitter in her mouth, and knew it was regret.

The problem with having sex with other people was that both of you remembered what had happened.

It was a whole year before Tam could walk into another dyke bar or touch another person with a sexual thought in hir head. When s/he finally did break hir fast, it was with a tiny Irish femme whose red-hot temper matched her hair. Thrown out of university for cutting class to smoke dope and weld large pieces of metal together in the demented shapes of giant warring machines, Tam found hirself living with this gentle and generous girl. Wearing nothing but a little gold cross around her neck, Bridget swept the studio every day. She also cooked big dinners for Tam and mended hir socks, and had the decency to live side by side with hir hidden pain without ever mentioning it.

Bridget had been taught by old-school femmes how to take care of her butch, her manly not-a-man. Without asking or being asked, she slid her hands underneath Tam's clothing just far enough to make hir shiver, not far enough to trigger the fear and disgust that would lead to rejection. Lying underneath Tam, moving in a facsimile of intercourse that eschewed any penetration, she used her soft but strong little thigh to surprise hir with an orgasm that, if it was not as strong as Tam knew a climax could be, at least had no overtone of rape.

This amazing femme also introduced Tam to the delights of strapping it on. After hir girl had taken a thorough pounding, Tam would lay back on the damp, rumpled sheets, exhausted and sweating, while Bridget simultaneously manipulated Tam's phallus and clitoris. If the dick sometimes came off and Bridget's confident, knowing mouth pressed against Tam's flesh—if Bridget's wise fingers sometimes found their way inside Tam, to enhance hir pleasure—it was something that did not need to be discussed or named. It was something Tam did to make Bridget happy. In the ten or so years since the end of that affair, Tam had not found many femmes with her knack for walking through the minefield of butch pleasure.

The last time Tam saw Wilson, it was in a photograph in the *Gay News*. She was in a tux, holding hands with a girl in a bridal gown, getting married to Floozy. Tam never visited the Palace again.

The authorities eventually discovered that hir student visa had run out. It was probably no coincidence that this happened at the same time that Tam was losing hir Irish flame to the ugly politics of her troubled homeland. Tam shook hir head. It still felt dangerous to remember the faces that went with those times. The faces and the guns, the pipes and nails and fuses. Better to just imagine everyone shrouded in a balaclava. The thwarted British empire could hold a wicked grudge.

Coming back to the present was a relief. Tam shook hir head and drained hir glass. Yuck. The ice cubes had melted, and the diluted contents of the heavy glass were lukewarm. S/he had not noticed the fresh drink that stood, unordered, beside the dead soldier. Lotta was nowhere to be found. Perhaps she'd tried to waken Tam from hir brown study and called a cab when s/he proved unresponsive. The solicitous new bartender was polishing the beer taps, and Tam thought briefly that she would wear off the finish.

If nothing else, I'll be preventing a case of carpal tunnel, Tam thought, and put out hir cigarette. "Stop that," s/he said in a voice that was clear but calculated to carry only as far as the bartender's ears. Beneath a backward hunter green baseball cap, those twin receivers had indeed been reached, and rapidly turned tomato red. "Put that down," Tam continued, not rushing things but not leaving any time for escape either. The bartender dropped the folded square of rag she had been using to polish the taps. "Stand right there," Tam added, pointing to a place slightly to one side of the taps, which would otherwise block hir view.

The object of hir attention stepped quietly to her right, two steps, aligned her navel with Tam's index finger, and stopped. "Hands behind your back," Tam specified, just a touch irritable, and was rewarded with a military snap into a posture that was the opposite of really taking one's ease.

"Let's have a look at you now," Tam said comfortably, and proceeded to examine hir subject in minute detail, more to see if the woman would crack and ask a question than to gather intelligence. She was wearing a black T-shirt, baggy cutoff jeans that were barely held up at her hips by a studded belt, and green Doc Martens. In addition to the massive steel nose ring, she sported a tiny gold ring in her left eyebrow and a conservative quantity of earrings, only two in each lobe. After a suitably uncomfortable silence, Tam said, "So you play sports," with a rising inflection that asked a question.

"Softball."

"Position?"

"Catcher."

That figures, Tam said to hirself. S/he could easily visualize this solid person with her low center of gravity presenting a brick wall of defense at home plate. Fly balls and sliders would be hard-pressed to escape her.

"Your name is?"

"Jimmy. Sir?"

"Sir will do," Tam acknowledged. "Where are your keys, sprat?"

"In my gym bag."

Tam decided to overlook the missing honorific. "Put them on. We're leaving." Tam could tell Jimmy was overjoyed but afraid to walk off the job. "Cory," s/he called, "there's no problem if Jimmy drives me home, is there?"

"No problem," Cory said, not meeting Tam's amused gaze, and went back to whistling "The Girl That I Marry" without actually forming a single note of it. Jimmy located a lime green duffel bag behind the bar, extracted a small bundle of keys on an evergreen clip, and hooked them to the right side of her belt with just enough fumbling to tell Tam she didn't wear them there very often. Then she grabbed a pair of skates and slung them over one shoulder. She apparently did not have a jacket.

"Gotta make sure my date, uh, my friend has a way home," Tam suddenly remembered. "Wait here, boy." She got up, surprisingly steady on her feet, and tried to locate Lotta. The barroom was *L*-shaped. Just past the turn, Tam found Lotta in rapt conversation with a severe beauty who was wearing what seemed to be a nineteenth-century day gown. There was enough lace on the dress to mummify Marie Antoinette.

"Tam!" Lotta gushed, reaching for hir hand. "Come and meet Cybil!"

"Okay, darlin'," Tam replied, "but I came to let you know I've got a nibble on my line." S/he slid some money along the table. "Can you cab it home?"

"I shall take responsibility for her safe return to her domicile," Cybil said, sounding as if she found Tam delinquent and a ruffian. Maybe her hair was just scraped back so hard she only had one facial expression, that of a Sunday school teacher who's just been handed a frog. *Finally met a girl who's more high-maintenance than a Harley*, Tam snorted to hirself.

"Sounds like the start of something beautiful," s/he re-torted sarcastically. When s/he saw Lotta's hurt face, s/he felt small and petty. S/he bent to kiss hir friend and whispered, "Thanks for looking after me all night," and left after Lotta squeezed hir hand and gave hir a good-bye smile.

Jimmy was waiting patiently with no visible squirming, but a couple of customers were getting aggressive about her just standing there when they wanted refreshment. "Go to 7-Eleven," Tam advised them, and waved Jimmy to hir side with one yank of hir cocked thumb. The boy ducked under the end of the bar, coming up smoothly on Tam's right side. It wasn't until they hit the cold air outside that Tam remembered where s/he had parked the red 1968 Mustang convertible. "Wow, you have a really old car," Jimmy said, sounding as if she was not sure it would actually run.

The kid probably skates everywhere or takes the bus. I doubt she knows the difference between a carburetor and a muffler, Tam thought, and felt a wave of exhaustion. "Get in," s/he said curtly, opening the passenger-side door. "No, you are not really driving me home." As Jimmy got into the car, the neck of her T-shirt gaped, giving Tam a view of a spiky black graphic that had been tattooed right over her spine. *Yowch!* Tam could hear Jimmy's skates landing on the backseat.

Once s/he slid into the driver's seat, Tam fished around until s/he found the handcuffs on a length of chain. The cool weight of the metal brought hir back to a state of pleasant anticipation. One end of this device went around Jimmy's wrists, and the other end was welded to a bolt sunk in the floor of the car. "Welcome to the Batmobile," Tam said, and got them headed toward hir place, a loft that used to be a carpet warehouse and wholesale outlet. "I like bondage, heavy flogging, and fucking girls up the ass. What do you like?"

Jimmy laughed nervously.

Tam waited, but that seemed to be the whole message. "Come on, I've gotten more information off an answering machine," s/he said impatiently. "You're not some fucking prisoner of war. So spill your guts, or tell me where you live so I can take you home."

"Please—aw, please, don't do that," Jimmy begged. But still she did not answer hir question.

An unwelcome light began to dawn. "Now don't you fucking tell me that you've never done this before," Tam said with considerable disgust. "The 101 course is *not* what I had in mind."

Jimmy had taken off her baseball cap and was twisting it into some painful-looking shapes. "No, I *have*," she insisted. "I've done all of those—things— you said. But…"

Tam reached for another cigarette, thought better

of it, and unrolled the window instead. Suddenly there was a bad taste in hir mouth, and s/he quickly turned hir head to spit at the center divider. "But you haven't had any of those things done to you," s/he said quietly, cursing hirself for an insensitive clod.

"Maybe," Jimmy admitted, voice quavering. "But I'm not a wuss. I can take it. I know I can. Are you really going to take me home?" She sounded like she might cry.

That's what I'm good for, Tam told hirself, with a silent ironic slap on the back. *Making girls cry. What a hero. What a big shot.* "Oh, I probably should," s/he drawled. "But it's a little late to pick up another trick, don't you think? We're probably stuck with each other." S/he reached over to Jimmy and pulled her head into hir lap. The handcuff chain made a few notes of steel music, bumping against itself. "Why don't you just lay there and see what I smell like, and think about sucking my dick," s/he suggested, and accelerated to beat the yellow light that stood between the Mustang and the freeway on-ramp. Jimmy's breath was a soft warm pillow on her thigh, like the exhalations of a sleeping puppy.

Tam's neighbors were few and far between, and usually pushing a shopping cart full of their belongings or jealously guarding a bottle in a brown paper bag. So s/he didn't exercise too much caution about brandishing kinky paraphernalia in public. As it so happened, there was no one on the street that night. S/he went around to the passenger side, dimly aware of the engine heat that radiated from the hood, sprang the trick link that released the handcuffs from the chain, and hustled Jimmy over to the metal grill that guarded the service elevator up to hir loft. "Lift that thing," Tam ordered, and kept hir hand on Jimmy's upper back to feel the muscles moving there. "Get in, get in, get in, get in," s/he snapped, suddenly impatient to be in the thick of it and past this awkward gray zone between public and private, the real world and the all-absorbing realm of pain and domination.

But first they had to cross Tam's work area. S/he was creating steeds for an apocalyptic carousel—realistic, life-size molded plastic four-footed animals with pieces of machines, insects, or reptiles grafted onto their bodies, transplants they did not welcome or understand. Tam could tell Jimmy was overwhelmed by the work, freaked out by the scale of it and the bizarre images, the suffering it implied. The frieze of "death masks" along one wall didn't help matters any. (They were actually wax impressions done during orgasms, then turned into more durable bronze casts and painted.) Not willing to give a lecture on modern art, Tam dragged hir quarry past the studio, not deigning to explain one whit of it. "Pay attention to this," s/he ordered, and shoved Jimmy into the bedroom. "Skin it," s/he said rudely, indicating boots, shorts, and T-shirt. Shivering, Jimmy obeyed, looking around in wonder.

Tam found most dungeon accouterments unimaginative and retro. What was it with all that wood; all those four-by-four beams, Saint Andrew's crosses and whipping benches, racks and pillories, medieval aesthetic up to the eyeballs? "I didn't like the Inquisition the first time around," s/he was fond of saying. What s/he had instead was an assortment of highly polished bondage devices crafted out of aluminum, steel, and titanium, and padded with neoprene. Jimmy found herself leaning forward slightly against a stack of silver tubes. They looked like they would collapse and roll away if you put any weight on them, but they were actually very strong and held their shape. The side of the device that touched Jimmy's naked body was cushioned with thick black rubber. The handcuffs came off, but Jimmy didn't have much time to rub the red marks on her wrists. Tam rapidly threaded a strap through one of the tubes and cinched it tight, anchoring the boy by her waist.

"So your safe word is *stop*," Tam announced, and went to get hir paddling gear down off the wall. "I don't want to take a chance on you forgetting the code. Just be straight up with me about what you like and what you don't like, and we'll do just fine." Jimmy's tattoo had turned out to be a sword with an interesting handle that looked like the logo for a heavy-metal band, with elaborate Celtic knot work inside it. That image reminded Tam that there was a lot of bare skin in the room, and s/he turned up both of the space heaters and pointed them at the bondage stand and its guest.

"I was going to ask you if you'd like to do a couple lines with me, but I guess you're in a hurry," Jimmy said, trying to sound casual. Her voice was shaky, however, and so the slap that Tam gave her was not full force.

"Sir," Tam reminded the boy. "You're the one who started with the Sir shit, so don't be forgetting it. I only hurry when there's no pussy on the table, Jimmy. Sex is too important to rush." S/he laid an armful of whips and paddles, mostly made out of metal, plastic, and rubber, on the bed. This was a round mattress held aloft by a spiral of aluminum that did not look strong enough to sustain its weight. The most recent ex had laughed and told Tam it looked like a cake plate, so it was just as well that she was gone, baby, gone, luv is gone.

"Sir," Jimmy said, then added, "Is there anything else I should know?"

Tam sorted through the pile of brightly colored Delrin rods and spiky plastic straps. Unfortunately, there just wasn't a man-made substance that was appropriate for warming up a novice like Jimmy. "You should know that I don't like coke or crystal," s/he replied, extracting a suede deerskin flogger from the heap. *And I don't like either one being sold in my bar.* It had a chrome-plated handle that felt good, smooth and unyielding in Tam's getting-serious hands.

"Probably 'cause you never shot it," Jimmy said wisely, and added "Sir," without too much of a gap.

"So what I want to know, Jimmy," Tam replied, "is are you a dirty little junkie?" It was one of those things you sometimes said in a scene without knowing you were going to speak. To punctuate the question and cover up hir own surprise, Tam landed a good solid blow across Jimmy's shoulders. The deerskin whip didn't sting, but the combined weight of all its tails was enough to knock the breath out of somebody.

There was no response. Jimmy's eyes were closed, and her whole body was tense, as stiff as an ivory dildo. So the boy was planning to take this like a man or a Marine, tough it out by strength of will alone. Tam shook hir head. *If that was what I wanted I could have come home alone and pounded a hole in the wall.* S/he threw the flogger over one shoulder and closed in on Jimmy. The black strap divided that solid body in two, making her butt look very inviting. So that was where Tam put hir hand, on those chilled white cheeks, massaging and squeezing them. S/he put hir other hand on Jimmy's face, where the slap had landed, and turned it just enough to receive a kiss. Tam knew s/he looked like a thug who would slobber his way through an embrace, but hir large mouth was actually a very sensitive and carefully calibrated tool. Tam's mouth made promises it knew how to keep. S/he let hir lips talk to Jimmy's fear and resistance, draw the starch out of the younger butch's shoulders and legs.

Meanwhile, Tam's right hand was dispensing propaganda about the joy to be found in getting spread wide and plundered. S/he had gotten in between Jimmy's legs and was barely able to reach her clit. Tam let hir three middle fingers press in a semicircle around it, agitating the delicate nerves, while hir thumb found Jimmy's asshole and pressed gently, back and forth, erasing resistance. Between these two points of contact, moisture stained Tam's hand, begging hir to pay attention to another hole.

Jimmy was kissing Tam back now, licking at hir tongue, daring to want and be wanton. Tam let hir hands wander all over Jimmy's body, warming her flesh and outlining her skin. S/he was aware of a shift in Jimmy's posture when the back of hir hand grazed her nipples. Jimmy had big breasts, with very sensitive dark brown points. "I never could figure out why butches have all the cleavage," Tam whispered in her ear, and followed that with some judicious use of hir tongue. S/he knew that Jimmy could feel hir own breasts pressed up against her side. Then s/he bit Jimmy's neck hard enough to distract her while s/he carefully brought the boy's henna-colored nipples to attention. "Just let it feel good," Tam advised. "Nobody's going to do anything to make you feel bad here. I just want to make you feel good, that's all, not put you down or trash you. I know what you need. So let me give it to you, for once. Just this once you can relax and get what you need, Jimmy."

The deerskin flogger was the baseline for the whipping that followed. Tam used a whip with round latex lashes and the beautifully colored sticks as hot, exotic spices to wake Jimmy up when she got too far into a trance of rhythmic thumping. And s/he used hir hands to rouse the skin surface, attack the deeper tissues, tickle the downy hairs on Jimmy's back and thighs. It didn't take Tam long to figure out that Jimmy really hated to get hit on the ass, so s/he left it alone. Until the very end, when Jimmy was half-crying and half-coming, petted and lashed, kissed and bitten, pounded and stroked into a state of receptivity and willingness that was inspiring to behold. Then Tam came close to take possession of Jimmy's mouth again, moving in from the other side this time, letting hir tongue flatter and wheedle, hinting at the next border to be crossed, the next barricade to be surrendered.

"I want you," Tam growled, shaken hirself by how true it was. "I want all of you. And I don't want anybody from the past to be here with us." S/he touched Jimmy's ass as lightly as possible, traced its roundness, reminded her of its hunger and emptiness. "Let me cane your ass," Tam said. Nothing more appealing than a top who begs, even if s/he's asking for the one thing you swore you would keep for yourself.

"I don't know if I can," Jimmy panted, and Tam picked that moment to finally let hir hand slip between the bound girl's legs and outline the slippery quivering aperture that longed to be stretched and tested. S/he laid it on the clit too, bringing Jimmy up on her toes with bliss after burning bliss, so close to coming that her teeth chattered and her eyes were wet.

"Just six strokes," Tam promised, backing off on the clit, but leaning harder on the mouth of Jimmy's cunt. How close s/he was to sliding in, how mean s/he was being to hold hirself back! "So you can own yourself again. I just want to give you back your body, Jimmy. Let's try. Just try for me, okay?"

Maybe there was a faint nod of Jimmy's head. Tam said, "If you ask me to stop, I will," not sure that she would be able to keep that vow, and picked out a flexible length of black plastic that had a bit of snap to it.

S/he made the first stroke a kind one, and saw Jimmy tell herself she would be able to deal with this after all. The next one was a bit more of a challenge. Jimmy wavered, thought about calling the whole thing off. The next one was truly painful, and Jimmy shouted. Tam went back for another kiss. This time s/he didn't hesitate to fuck hir captive, sliding into her between pleading words, reminders of how important it was to do what you said you would do, shameful lies about how the sexual frustration of not being able to go on would hurt Tam up close and personal. Jimmy was delirious, unable to understand how Tam could do all these things that felt so amazing and still not let her come. "Do you want me to go on?" Tam asked, fucking her a little harder, and when Jimmy cried, "Yes!" Tam got a fresh grip on hir postmodern cane and laid all three of the remaining stripes on in rapid succession. S/he did not hit Jimmy quite as hard as s/he could, but it was enough to make Jimmy blind with fury.

While Jimmy cursed hir ancestors, Tam shucked hir own boots and pants and strapped on a medium-thick dick that was long enough to get into a big girl. S/he released the strap around Jimmy's waist and got a good grip on her hair. Jimmy found herself being propelled onto Tam's bed, facedown, and rapidly realized she had a whole new set of limits to worry about.

"Please don't fuck me in the ass," she said, clawing at Tam's harlequin bedspread.

"Now what did I say in the car?" Tam asked, thoughtfully tracing the cane weals and surveying the spray of marks on Jimmy's shoulders. There were only two places where the edge of the cane had broken the skin. But Jimmy's back would blossom blue and purple overnight, the bright bruises that were a novice's reward. The sword's hilt and blade were virtually unmarked, as they should be, over Jimmy's spine.

Tam thought it was a fine piece of magic to have a gorgeous weapon like that one, guarding your back. The lovely smell of the boy's sweat made Tam want to bite her again and again, in a frenzy of gnashing teeth. But another depraved act had been placed first on the agenda.

"That you like to—that you like to do that. But I can't," Jimmy said, unable to even name the unnatural act of sodomy.

"Why don't you let me worry about that?" Tam asked, and urged Jimmy forward on the bed, up on all fours. S/he came close behind, and rubbed the lewd tool against Jimmy's clit and the hole just below it. "You want to get fucked, don't you? I know I want to see you take it."

"I don't get fucked very often," Jimmy confessed, and Tam felt a blaze of anger. *Some things never change.*

"Then tonight is your lucky night," s/he said reassuringly, and gave Jimmy's cunt a little nudge. Above their bodies s/he held a bottle of lube, and a thin drizzle of clear liquid fell onto that point of contact. Back and forth, a half inch at a time, Tam advanced hir cock and worked the lube well in, till Jimmy's naturally slick self was buffered by a good layer of additional help. "Reach back here and jack off for me," Tam said, in the same companionable voice s/he would use to ask for a sandwich from the picnic basket. "That's right, do your little dick for me, Jimmy, let's see how hard you can get that thing. So do all the girls you tie up and fuck call you daddy, mister green baseball cap?"

"Maybe," Jimmy drawled, laughing and jacking off.

"Then I must be grandpa," Tam replied, and got another, bigger laugh. "Do you know how good it feels to get inside you, boy?" Jimmy visibly relaxed every time Tam used male nouns and pronouns, carried into a safe realm of pleasure, far away from the danger of her own body. "Looks so hot," Tam added, hips jamming. "Looks so fucking hot, you have me rigid in between your legs, fucking you, it's huge, I want to come so bad and I know I can't come just yet." And it was true, though Tam wasn't sure why. When s/he saw hir cock pushing into Jimmy, it looked and felt right, exciting, and if s/he kept this up long enough, s/he probably would have a sort of orgasm. It was not the same as the come Tam got from working directly on hir clit, but it was nonetheless satisfying, as if leaving spunk in somebody else's body was the way s/he was meant to come.

Jimmy let out a wail that was hard to interpret. Was she afraid Tam would come before she could get off, or was she dying to get off and afraid if she waited any longer, an orgasm would elude her? Tam used the time-honored method for handling such a dilemma, telling Jimmy, "Boy, you better not come until you ask me first. Don't you dare get off till I tell you that you can."

"I'm so close, Sir," Jimmy panted.

"Does this help?" Tam asked, and moved some of the lube up to her asshole. Jimmy was apparently too excited to remember her earlier panic about buttfucking. Besides, a finger on the outside was nowhere near as menacing as a cock pointed at your tailbone. "Just what the boy needs," Tam said, throat dry from breathing hard over hir work. S/he had a finger in Jimmy's ass now and was wiggling it around, a dirty-minded worm, bringing this verbal fag fantasy to life. "Daddy's big thick dick up his butt, pounding that come right out of him, fucking him so hard the cum just shoots—"

"Nownownow please now," Jimmy yelled.

"Well, okay then, show me, do it, make it really good for Daddy," Tam chanted, and felt a wave of hir own pleasure carry hir along with Jimmy through what looked and sounded like three good blowouts in a row.

Tam came out slowly, careful not to irritate tissues that were already sore, and tipped Jimmy onto her back. The big red-brown nipples were flat now, post-orgasmic, and the red flush was fading from her chest and throat. The whole room smelled like sex and lube, and Tam realized the space heaters had been on for so long it was like a sauna in there. S/he got up to turn them down, removed dick and harness, and climbed back onto the bed to cuddle Jimmy and tell him he was a good boy.

"That was amazing," the boy said, hiding her face in Tam's armpit. "You're amazing."

"Oh, 'tweren't nothin' special," Tam teased. "Just the best time I've had all year."

Jimmy propped herself up on one elbow and traced Tam's lips with one finger. The sudden intimate contact made Tam uneasy. *How weird is that, considering what else we've done?* "So are you going to keep your clothes on all night long?" Jimmy asked, glancing at Tam's undershirt and shorts. "I mean, I'm not sleepy yet, I could maybe—"

"Maybe what?" Tam asked sharply, sitting up. Where were the damn cigarettes? Wait a minute, s/he was trying to quit. S/he slid off the bed and went to pee and get a drink of water. Tam had to walk back carefully. S/he had scraped hirself, trying to wipe away the evidence of hir lusty response to Jimmy. The boy was curled up on the parti-colored bedspread, looking sad as a lost dog.

"Do you want me to leave?" she asked bravely. "I have my skates, I can get home if you want to sleep alone."

Tam looked around the room, taking in the dis-carded implements on the floor, the bondage stand that had traveled a couple of feet from its original placement, the clothes here and there, the atmosphere of wonder and transformation. For a few hours, this room had hosted a trip to another place, a nicer and more honest place where the harsh rules of the real world did not apply. Jimmy had trusted hir a great deal. And now she was trying to make it easier for Tam to betray that trust and get off the hook, back into the shitty game whose only prize was one more wall, a thicker breastplate over the heart. Another stone on the cairn of delight's deep grave.

Tam sat down, facing away from Jimmy, and peeled the undershirt off over hir head. Then s/he bunched up hir shorts and shucked those as well. It was one of the hardest things s/he had ever done, but s/he knew s/he had to make it look natural and easy.

Let Jimmy go away from this room with the knowledge that things did, in fact, change. Tam lay back, taking it slow, not looking down at hir own body, and smiled to reassure both of them. The hands that Jimmy put on hir were warm and reassuring, and the face that s/he looked up at was kind, without guile. The fact that their bodies were so similar was helpful, Tam decided. If s/he could look at Jimmy and get a twinkle in hir eye, perhaps s/he could at least tolerate hir own flawed physicality.

"What would you like me to do?" Jimmy asked. "I just want to give something back to you. You've been so good to me."

"Help me find my goddamned vibrator," Tam said, pawing at the side of the bed, in quest of the extension cord. Jimmy leaned over hir and came back with the Prelude. Tam switched the little machine on and positioned it to one side of hir clit, using the other hand to move that sensitive organ around, sometimes pressing it against the buzz, sometimes holding it further away. Jimmy hovered, and Tam knew s/he had to put her to work. A dog needs a job. "Suck on my nipples," s/he suggested, with no clue about how that would feel.

There ought to be a word to distinguish between a touch that felt fine, like Jimmy's, and a touch that felt awful. Respectful? Intuitive? Competent? On target? All Tam knew was that Jimmy's mouth was a heavenly place, and hir nipples felt right at home inside it. It was almost as good as s/he imagined getting your cock sucked for real would be. Hir excitement built sharply, but s/he had waited a long time to try to come, so Tam knew it was a real possibility that s/he would just skate the edge of an orgasm forever and ever, and not be able to actually get off. S/he turned off the vibrator, afraid of going numb, and Jimmy was smart enough to stop sucking at the same time, as if she knew the feeling would be too intense without its accompaniment.

Instead, she tentatively put her lips against Tam's mouth and moved them a little, asking if it was possible to give hir a kiss. Tam was frozen, startled, but Jimmy continued, and so s/he came gradually to life. The kiss was straightforward, a caress exchanged by equals, with no one keeping score. Tam felt hirself melting, becoming a better, more courageous person, less obsessed with self-judgment. Jimmy's kiss went on, like a good book that makes you grateful for its length because you do not want to leave the spell it casts. Her tongue was only briefly cautious, then she fed so much of her own desire into Tam's mouth that s/he suddenly understood why somebody would call Jimmy "Daddy." For some reason, it was nice to be reminded of other aspects of Jimmy. Instead of being threatened, Tam felt even more of hir resistance vanish. Perhaps it was because s/he could now believe that Jimmy was really enjoying doing hir.

When Tam sensed that a little blood had returned to hir parts, s/he switched the machine on again. The rounded nub of the vibrator's attachment, specially designed to massage the clitoris, was slick with hir juices, doing a fine job, making Tam tense hir jaw. But it would take a little more stimulation to make this work. S/he took hir hand off hir cunt long enough to urge Jimmy's hand down between hir legs. "Fuck me," Tam said. Jimmy slid into hir, after putting some lube on her hand. At first there was only burning and awkwardness. Jimmy's fingers felt thick as sausages. Then the boy settled into a circular pattern of in-and-out, not too far in either direction, just enough to make Tam's vaginal muscles want to grab her hand and contract around it. "Just like that," Tam said, leaning a little harder on hir clit with the vibrator. "Don't speed up or slow down, don't change anything, just...like...that."

Jimmy bent over Tam's chest and took the nearest nipple into her mouth, sucking it hard, loving it with firm strokes of her tongue. "Omigod!" Tam heard hirself bay, and then the grunting and groaning began, the involuntary noises that accompanied release from sexual tension. The orgasm was a good, complete one, not one of those little squeakers that leave you high and dry, feeling cheated. Tam rolled with it, groaned into the full majesty of it, let it shake hir throat and belly and thighs. *Delicious. Life can be so delicious.*

After Jimmy had a pee, they got into bed together under the black-and-white sheets, spooned one against the other like freshly polished sterling silver utensils. The sleep that followed was even deeper than the rest the Czar shared with his poor family in unknown, unhallowed ground. Before it hit, Tam thought, *I want a weapon that fills people with this much happiness. Then we'd have the last revolution we'd ever need.*

Above All the Lights

Hollywood is corrupt from the ground up, but it's the world's largest (or at least the best-documented) playground. So you should just close your eyes to the game's wicked ways and play, play, play. Or so they say. "They" being people I've never met, those who are actually in charge of everything. I'm not sure what scares me more—the nefarious heartlessness of "them" or the possibility that *nobody* is in charge.

I was too far away from the epicenter of Movietown, USA, to be a major player anyway. My office did not look down upon Mann's Chinese Theatre and its forecourt of stars' names and handprints, or the offices of a major studio. Instead, it looked down upon a high school where the rich and famous sent their progeny. These were kids who did not have to raid dad's liquor cabinet, steal mom's cocaine, or wreck their parents' automobiles. They had plenty of booze, drugs, and cars of their own. I should know. I used to go there.

Who was I to interrupt the law of supply and demand? Nobody special. Maybe that's why I was hell-bent on picking up litter along a highway that was strewn with broken bodies. I focused the telephoto lens on my camera and took another picture of a car that had just pulled into the parking lot. It was lunchtime, and the car was not driven by a student, a teacher, or an employee of the school. Nevertheless, it was there every day, punctual as the Malibu tides.

I made sure I had thoroughly documented the license plate, then took leisurely flip-book photos of the driver and his customer, who brazenly handed over a large stack of cash and pocketed fistfuls of tiny plastic bags that were probably not filled with pea-sized lumps of bathroom cleanser.

Last week's photos of these transactions had already been sent to the police. Nothing had been done, which I had expected, so I had retained the ugly receipt the post office gives you when you send something by certified mail, just in case the man in blue wanted to claim he wasn't getting his deliveries in a timely manner. This week's pictures would go to a couple of local newspapers along with a copy of that receipt. Maybe nothing would happen again. In which case, there was always the Associated Press and the *New York Times*.

What did I think of the War on Drugs? Not a hell of a lot. What did I think of someone who sold drugs to kids, even if they were kids his own age? Ditto. Silly, I know, but in these days of economic downturn with few paying customers, a man's got to have a hobby. Consistency being the hobgoblin of et cetera, et cetera.

Speak of the devil. Here comes honest work. The door to my reception area had just opened and closed. That anteroom would not delay my caller long because there was no receptionist. I wondered, and not for the last time, from whence film noir detectives got their buxom and irrationally devoted secretaries. (From the pool of starlets who had not yet learned to give blow-jobs as good as Marilyn Monroe's, I know, I know.) But the last thing I wanted was a blowjob from a buxom blonde, and wasn't that part of my problem?

If anybody knew that better than me, it was not the guy who barged through the door to my inner sanctum and then fell into the chair across from my desk as quietly as an autumn leaf descends to become part of nature's mulch heap. He's one of those big guys who are honestly not fat, who move on the balls of their feet like quiet hunting cougars. I think he has to pretend to be as noisy and bluff and hearty as the men he does business with. Mama, don't let your babies grow up to be realtors. It was my old classmate Sheldon Fawn. He has everything that his daddy once had and then some. That would include his daddy's last mistress, who is now Mrs. Sheldon Fawn.

Her last encounter with the paterfamilias had resulted in a fatal heart attack or something very much like it. I had been summoned to keep that mess out of the papers and off the police blotter. That had cost me my job on the force, which was quite a blow, considering that the job had cost me an inheritance. But Sheldon believed in trickle-down economics, so I got invited to way too many of his stag parties. Okay, so I *can* get it up for a hooker who charges five grand for a night of her time. All men are dogs. Say woof and swallow that cheese.

"Shelly!" I said, full of bonhomie but unable to pronounce it. "How's life among the slumlords, Bambi?"

"Shut up," he said, and helped himself to a cigar. The only reason he'd given me a humidor full of them in the first place was to make sure he'd have access to them when he came to the office. Unlike his wife, who had no reason to be prissy about other people's oral fixations, I let him smoke it. I liked seeing that fat brown cylinder in his overprivileged puss. White man sucking up carcinogens. Geronimo's revenge. Oscar Wilde's too, because sometimes a cigar is *not* just a cigar—as Sigmund Freud knew perfectly well.

"Are you working hard?" he asked, eyeing me through blue smoke and eyes I wished I did not know were a sultry blue as well. "Or hardly working?"

"Can't be hard and work at the same time," I said briskly.

"That's not what I heard," he said, and we went *haw haw* together. Nobody here but us testicles. My stomach was tense. The worse the joke, the nastier the job a client is about to hand me.

"So," he said, blowing smoke at the ceiling, "we've got a little problem, Harris."

"Do *we?*" He was oblivious to my sarcasm. My position in his life was one of delicate ambivalence. I had (sort of) weathered the scandal that got me kicked out of school, but because I had been accused of letting one of the school's top jocks suck my dick, I was a safe person to come to with the indiscretions of other members of our class. But I was no longer really a member of the club. If I were, my reception area would not be furnished with plastic patio chairs from Wal-Mart, perfect for alfresco blue-collar dining. I suppose I could have gotten something that was still cheap but not so god-awful ugly. But that was what my business was all about: ugliness.

"Smitty has been videotaped in compromising circumstances," he said bluntly.

"They say compromise is the basis for all lasting relationships," I mused. Shelly gave me a bland look that said, *you're crazy but I could still get you to buy a condo*. I tried to recall when Smitty Martingale had been elected to the city council. Did you know that Martingale is short for Goldfarb? Good, you're not supposed to.

"Do you want his money or not?" Sheldon Fawn demand-ed in the same tone of voice that he used to tell me to put his dick into a whore.

"Yes," I said, as I had so often before, and pulled out the keyboard tray on my desk. "What did he do?"

"He got videotaped with a he-she and now he's being blackmailed by its pimp."

"It?" I was suddenly all business as well, showing my teeth and raised hackles. Nobody comes to the defense of the criminal element more quickly than someone who is supposed to apprehend and punish them for their evildoing. Shelly gave me an affable but apologetic smile and even waved some of his own smoke away. Boundaries had been drawn and mutually acknowledged.

"So you want me to get the tape back," I hazarded

a guess. Sharp as Occam's razor. Which come to think of it would make a damned fine name for a detective agency. If really smart people ever needed bottom-feeders like me.

"That would be nice. For a start."

I raised one eyebrow. Banks give away toaster ovens to new customers. I distribute quizzical facial expressions to all comers. Because your first impression is your last impression, or so they told me in charm school.

"Some people don't know how to play by the rules," he explained. "I don't deal in chicks with dicks, but if I had fucked up as bad as this pimp has, I'd be run out of town on a rail no matter what was my stock in trade. You get my drift."

I rolled my eyes, having last heard that idiom in a John Wayne movie. I resisted the impulse to say, "I used to be Snow White, but *I* drifted" in my best Mae West. Forcing my voice into the bass register of a porn film, I thundered, "You want me to find the black-mailer, retrieve the tape, and get him to leave town."

"The further away he goes, the better," Bambi said, and put out his cigar. He tossed a fat envelope on the desk, and while I was still staring at its thickness, trying to estimate how many hundred-dollar bills it took to make a stack that high, he got up, adjusted the waistband of his slacks in a vain attempt to camouflage a fart, and left.

I stuck my face in the cash and fanned it like a deck of cards. The air quality suddenly improved. There was way more there than the price of a plane ticket to New York City. Or Paris, for that matter. Did Shelly (or Smitty) imagine this was the price of a broken leg or a bullet to the head? If so, they had overpaid street value and underpaid downwardly mobile little old me.

My mendacious school chum also left me a typed list of some other information that might help me to track down the blackmailer. There was a head shot of the hooker as well, a pretty woman who was one of those unique-to-California ethnic combinations: black and Japanese, shaken up with the aristocratic offspring of the lost Aztec empire and Spanish conquistadores. As they say in Tokyo, Domo arigato, Charles Darwin, and pass the salsa verde. I gave Bambi's cheat sheet a read, feet up on my own desk, then clambered onto those same size twelves and shuffled off in quest of a hamburger patty with no bun and a salad. After that, I would come back to the office and take a nap on the cracked but still comfortable leather sofa. I would have to wait until after dark to really go to work.

If you'd like to know what will be on the Paris runways next spring, take a postprandial walk with me along the ho stroll of West Hollywood, otherwise known as the TV Channel. This year, the girls-of-color-who-used-to-be-boys were congregating along Hydrangea Boulevard between Camellia and Rhodo-dendron Streets. It was a few months until another election would roust the police, who would simply chase them into a new locale a few blocks over. Sort of like a dog trying to catch a seagull. But to complete this metaphor, we'd have to find a seagull that is paying off the dog to leave him alone. And a dog that liked to fuck seagulls.

Every one of these girls looked like a supermodel.

But the fashion industry has room for only one or two black stars per year. I was a little overwhelmed by the profusion of miniskirts; fishnet stockings; halter tops; black patent leather, high-heeled boots; gold lamé; elaborately styled wigs; cat's-eye makeup; dangling earrings; and short-shorts. They were underwhelmed by me. Foot traffic is never welcome. A man who can't afford a car will try to get his head at a bargain rate. Doing the nasty in the great outdoors would be a big step down for these front- and backseat fillies. Only the lowest crack whore will forego the mean shelter of a windshield. Whenever I approached a group of them, they turned their backs and walked away, asses swaying invitingly, shoulders stiff with disapproval.

I took out a twenty and held it on top of the photo I was trying to match to an actual person. That got me a little more respect. "Why do you want to find this girl?" the first hooker I came up to demanded.

"She's my long-lost sister," I replied.

"Bullshit," she snapped. Her head began to bob and weave upon a neck like a black swan's. This is the African American woman's way of giving warning, much like the rattlesnake's ominous buzz. I was in no mood to be dressed down like a boyfriend who had bet the rent money on a pit bull who'd lost his balls. "Can the righteous indignation," I said. "Do you know the sister or not?"

"Not!" She snatched at the twenty.

"So who might know her?" I asked, clamping my thumb down on the cash.

She threw her head back and tossed a quick look at

a girl in a red kimono that covered more of her body than the outfits of the girls she was apparently supervising. "Taneena," she said grudgingly. "Her old man likes slant-eye bitches."

"Tch-tch. Where's your respect for diversity?" I chided, handing over the twenty.

She pocketed it and snapped her fingers at me three times, tracing a Z in the air. "For this chump change you don't get to lecture me about multiculturalism, white boy," she declared. There was not a trace of the ghetto in her voice. She sounded like a college English literature professor. Then, when she was sure I had gotten the point, she reverted to the cant of the street. "Get outta my face."

It was actually the twin cheeks of her high, perky, and utterly salacious butt that I had to turn my back upon. I did so rapidly, before the impulse to spend all my cash on a chance to fuck her up the ass got the best of me. Fucking smart asses doesn't discourage them. They just learn to mouth off when they want to get screwed. Ask Shelly.

Taneena didn't try to avoid me. With the composure of an experienced First Lady in charge of her old man's stable, she took the photo and said, "This girl is one of my family all right. You want to date her or somethin'?" The veteran of several busts, she knew perfectly well that I was no undercover vice cop. Or client.

"Yes," I replied. "I'd like to talk to her."

I expected to get a little bit of a runaround, but Taneena only pretended to be hurt. "I'm not pretty enough for you?"

"Baby, you're so pretty that your old man has got your booty locked up tight, doesn't he? The only part of you I could have is your mouth."

She laughed at me, licked her lips sensuously, and laughed again. "You want to fuck Lotus, you going to have to pay a lot more than twenty dollars," she warned.

"I got three hundred in my pocket just for twenty minutes of her time."

"Ooo eeee, twenty minutes! We got Marathon Man here with us tonight. Marathon Man is in the house. Give it up!"

We shared a giggle and I waited patiently while she chastised a plump girl in translucent lingerie to get off the curb faster when a car slowed down. "I want to see those big titties of yours fly through his window the minute he roll it down," she declared. "Work what you got for your birthday, Delanya, or Daddy gonna want his implants back."

"So what corner is Lotus prowling tonight?" I asked, getting Taneena back to the business at hand.

"She in the crib," Taneena said, as if any child should have known that. "Knox says if you go on the street with your face all beat up you won't get nothing but the freak trade. So he keeping her home."

"But she'll still see me?"

"Call him up and see. 1-800-FORT-KNOX." She sprang into the center of her little pack of trainees and administered a slap to an ass encased in copper-colored silk. "What you mean, you won't date that man, Sugar Bear? You here to make money, girl, not find somebody to marry. If he got his dick and his

54

wallet out, you best try to take that money away from him. I don't care if he's an old man. Old men got more money than young men anyway. Sugar's no good if it stays in the bowl, bitch."

Realizing I was in the way, I dragged my attention away from this psychodrama and stumped back to my car. There I had a swig of bottled spring water, which presumably came from the same sort of spring from whence our tap water is derived, and dialed the toll-free number. "Fort Knox," somebody growled. The voice was as deep and musical as Barry White's, but more menacing than seductive. Some girls just like it rough, I guess. Unlike me, of course.

"Taneena told me to call you about Lotus," I said.

"Lotus," he repeated flatly, not helping me along.

"Yeah, I saw a picture of her and I'd like to talk to her," I explained. What a lame story. What street corner girl has a portfolio in circulation?

"Three hundred is a lot for a conversation," he said. Of course, Taneena would have called him about the weirdo who was snooping around.

"Yes," I said. "It is. But I understand the lady is indisposed."

He abruptly told me an address and hung up. I wasn't sure why he had decided to let me make this unorthodox appointment, since I had not identified myself as Smitty's go-between, but I committed the digits to memory and got out my *Thomas's Guide.*

"Knox?" I asked when a gentleman answered the door. He looked like he went with the voice on the phone.

I got a look of pity and disgust. Bodyguard, then.

Of course Knox would not open his own door. A pimp with as many women as Taneena had jumping would be top drawer, and he'd be able to afford hired muscle. He'd need it too. The Ten Commandments tell us not to covet our neighbor's wife, but they don't say anything about his cash. Or his cocaine.

Not sure who I expected to meet, I shouldered past the bodyguard and went down a short hallway to yet another door. I noticed that there were compartments cut in the wood paneling of the hallway. Guns or other weapons ready to drop if war was declared and battle came down? The place was also monitored by a security camera. Somebody had invested money in setting up his headquarters.

"Harris," a voice inside the main room said, and I almost threw the door shut and ran back down that hall. It was a voice from my past that filled me with fear and shame. We all have some dirty secret that we desperately hope will never be exposed to anyone else's view. This was mine.

But I had a client. I'd taken his money and promised to do a job.

And, may all the gods of pagan Greece assist me, I was horny. My barely repressed curiosity about what the transsexual prostitutes' panties contained had me itching for something larger and more familiar.

"Mojo," I replied heavily, and went to confront my disgrace.

He didn't weigh an ounce more than he had in high school. But he'd added a grown man's muscle. That football uniform wouldn't fit anymore, but the tailored Armani suit he wore fit goooood. It looked as natural and fine as a fox coat does on a fox. He was a color that reminded you why they called his people black. He was Zulu black. Yoruba black. Africa's child and yet as American as the Scotch-Irish mutt I was.

"Knox," he corrected. "Everybody knows me as Knox now, Harris."

"What are you doing here?"

"I could ask you the same question." He held out his left hand, and a woman I had not noticed before poured something that smelled like very old Scotch into a glass, and put the glass in his hand. I spared a glance for her, reluctant to drag my eyes away from my long-lost scapegoat and lover. She was Lotus. And someone had beaten her up with professional care. Recently too.

Mojo drank a sip of expensive amber Scotch, smiled at the liquor's aroma, and gestured me into a chair. "Go on out now, honey," he told her. *Honey*. I felt a pain in my chest that reminded me I'd never started taking the once-daily baby aspirin I'd bought a month ago. She left walking proudly despite the livid marks on her face, without a pout or a backward glance, obviously confident in his ability to handle her business. The memory of her small, high breasts barely covered by her spaghetti-strap violet dress disturbed me.

"Cocksucker," he said evenly as soon as the door was closed.

It had been ten years. I still wanted him. Would this sad story never end? I bowed my head, acknowledging his authority as I never would a preacher. Mojo got to his feet, came around the desk, grabbed me by the front of my shirt and my tie, and slapped me. Like Lotus, I let him do whatever he was going to do. Did she love him as much as I once had loved him? Did I love him now, or was I just so guilty I was willing to let him do whatever he wanted to me?

"Does your family know you're a pimp now?" I asked, surprised by my sudden desire to hurt him.

"What did you expect me to do? Getting caught in the shower with you ruined any chance I had of a football scholarship. Unlike you, my family wasn't prepared to pay cash up front for a crack at the Ivy League. But I heard you were stupid enough to throw your admission to Yale away."

"Yeah," I said, and he slapped me again, harder this time. "If this doesn't stop pretty soon, people will think Lotus really is my sister," I jibed. My attempt at a wry chuckle didn't quite work because I had a fat lip. The inside of my mouth had gotten cut on my own teeth. The taste of my own blood was sickening.

"You God *damned* fool," he said, pronouncing each word with heartfelt care. Then he grabbed me in a rib-cracking embrace, and kissed me. My body responded instantly to his tongue slipping between my teeth. I returned his kiss with all the care that my wounded mouth allowed. Then I remembered that he was tasting my blood along with my spit and tried to wrench my mouth away. He wouldn't let me escape. My struggles subsided and I had to just stand there and let him rape my mouth. As if you can rape the willing. All he had to do is stick his hand in my pants, and he'd know instantly how much I wanted him. Just the way he had always known.

He loosened my tie and took it off over my head, then unbuttoned my shirt. "You going to keep my secret?" he asked, brushing his lips over my nipples. His hands clasped my waist lightly but with so much erotic authority I wanted to faint.

"You kept mine," I choked. "Why did you do it, Mojo? Why did you tell them it was you who was the queer and not me?"

"Secrets," he mused, baring my torso and unbuckling my belt. "We all got 'em, don't we, Detective Harris? All the cops are criminals, and all the thieves are saints. Here you are guilty as sin, trying to catch bad guys, while I just pander to their worst tendencies. But we're done with secrets now, aren't we, Harris?"

When he pushed me toward the desk, I struggled again, and this time he got me in a headlock and took me down, bent forward over its cool surface, as glossy and smooth as a mahogany-colored glacier. He kept one hand on the back of my neck while he used the other one to tug my trousers down. I wore a jockstrap underneath it because that kind of underwear works better for my purposes. Normally it helps me to hide. But this afternoon it was exposing me.

"I didn't tell them," he said, parting the cheeks of my ass, "because I could let them think I was queer, but they'd still think I was a man, Harris. Remember the first time we fucked? You'd come into the locker room to photograph me for the yearbook, and I teased you into taking some nude shots. But I wanted you to undress too. And you said you wouldn't because you were afraid that if you took your clothes off I would think you weren't a man. I promised you that I didn't

59

care what you looked like naked, that to me you would always be a man."

The length of him slid into me, so thick I thought I could not bear it, and then so long that his girth was wiped out of my mind. The world's most perfect cock was inside of me. I couldn't allow myself to enjoy him; I didn't deserve it. And I was angry with him for wrestling me onto the desk. My body tried to escape, but there was no place to go. "I always loved the way you would wiggle," Mojo said. "Do you know how good you look with my dick in you? It feels so fine when you struggle on my cock. I could just stand here for an hour and make you do all the work. 'Specially if I slapped your big white ass."

"All day? Slapped my ass? Oh! Please!"

"I never break my word, Harris. And I never keep any of my bitches waiting."

Then he fucked me good and proper. I no longer cared if I was betraying myself by crying out. Let the bodyguard know he was screwing me. Let Lotus hear my guttural cries for rescue from peril that fed my very soul. No more hiding. No more bogus medical excuses from taking gang showers with the other boys in my gym class. No more visits to the doctor in Baltimore who photographed the shame between my legs. I am that photograph in medical textbooks of the rare and horrible creature, the perfect hermaphrodite—except that my cock is too small to penetrate anyone. Out of concern for their reputation in polite society, my parents would not bow to his pressure to castrate me and raise me as a girl. No more tucking a prosthetic in my jockstrap every day before I went out into the world. No more avoiding public bathrooms and carefully calculating just how high Bambi and his latest call girls were before I joined in the fun with an artificial prick that would never knock anybody up or give them the clap.

"You're one in a million, Harris," Mojo said, and it was literally true. "Do you know why I collected this little family of he-shes, brother? Once you've had a boy with a pussy, and you can't find another one like him, it's not that big a reach to chicks with dicks. Is it? *IS IT?*" And there came the blows from his huge hands that finally set me free. I came from the pain, crying with joy and shame because he was finally giving me the punishment that I deserved. Only someone who has tortured himself very nearly to death can appreciate the bliss of finally being hurt by the person who has the right to injure or kill him. I almost wished he would kill me. Except that he'd made me feel so good, I realized I could no longer be insouciant about my own life expectancy.

"Let me up," I demanded. He had one arm bent behind my back. He let go of it and lay forward on me, toying with my tits.

He paused. "Naw," he said, as if he had seriously thought it over. "I gotta get what's coming to me." The fuck that he threw me then was purely selfish. I couldn't get my breath, he slammed into me so hard and fast. My hips were taking a beating on the wooden edge of the desk. I'd have bruises tomorrow. The tweaking at my nipples was another fiery challenge to assimilate. He was deliberately making me sore inside. "You don't have to walk tomorrow, do you?" he asked once. I could hear the sneer on his face, imagine the way he twisted up his eyebrows when he asked me that question.

"I don't have to walk tonight," I affirmed. What is it about getting fucked that makes you get off on your stud's pleasure? The thought of him coming inside of me was so exciting that I couldn't keep track of my own needs anymore. I would happily have postponed any climax of my own to intensify his. Instead, he squeezed my throat and ordered me to close my muscles down on his dick, to milk it for him as it clawed its way in and out of me. My cunt is smaller than a woman's, and having a small penis as well was no compensation. I couldn't penetrate anyone else, and it was difficult to allow them to penetrate me. But Mojo was ignoring the limits of physiology, and when I clamped down on his cock, he hurt me in a whole new way before he finally came, and thrust so hard at me that it felt as if his cock had broken through to my guts.

"Bastard," I said, feeling sweat cool between us. His arms around me felt like coming home.

"Get up," he said, and dragged at one of my arms. But he wouldn't let me stand up. Instead, I was shoved onto my knees. "Suck it," he said, swiveling his hips. I could see the sheen of sweat on his curly black public hair. "Clean my dick off. If you can get it up, I'll let you have it again. But this time I'll fuck you like a real boy, Peter Pan."

I swallowed his cock a half-inch at a time, partly to tease him and partly to help myself remember how it was done. Oh, right—you just stopped caring if you could breathe or not. Simple. My throat was just one more hole that he could use, but wouldn't it be nice if every asshole or cunt had a tongue in it? He couldn't seem to decide if he should be sweet to me or cruel. Sometimes he stroked my hair lovingly and sometimes he fucked my skull with deliberate brutality, his hands clamping my face to his groin until I saw a black mist and knew I was about to pass out. I didn't fight him, and for a second, I did wink out. I think that scared him because he was marginally nicer after that, allowing me one breath per ten thrusts. It was enough to sustain life, but barely. Soon his cock was hard again and leaking salty trails wherever it went. The extra lubrication was welcome.

"Get on the couch," he whispered, and herded me there with his foot. I crab-walked, not daring to rise all the way to my feet. He stripped off his shoes and slacks, stretched out on the black leather on his right side, and motioned for me to put my backside up against him. He lifted my left leg and slid his slobbering cock up my ass. "How'd you get so tight?" he asked. I didn't bother to reply. "Jack yourself off while I fuck you," he said tersely, and I put my hand on the cock that he had protected with his lie.

"Do it nice for Daddy," he whispered, nuzzling my neck. My leg up in the air allowed him to get into me as deep as a bucket hitting the bottom of a well. Only it felt like this bucket was a hell of a lot bigger than the shaft it plumbed. "Let me see how much you like getting pumped," he encouraged, looking down at my hand. "Red little boy cock," he whispered. "Jerk it for me, sweetheart. Is Daddy fucking the come out of you? Tell the truth. I'll know if you lie to me. Don't you ever lie to me."

"No, Daddy, I'll never lie to you," I gasped, my hands a blur. My dick might be small, but it felt so good to manipulate it while he filled my ass that it brought tears to the corners of my eyes. "Oh, Daddy, you are fucking the come out of me. Yes, you are. Oh, please don't stop."

His cock was a reassuring presence, in and out, in and out, unfailing in its steady rhythm. "Daddy will always be here for you," he said in his deep, honeyed voice. "You can come on Daddy's big cock as often as you need to, honey. But you better not come unless I tell you that you can."

"Please! Let me, please!"

"Now?"

"God, yes, now."

"It's awful soon."

"No, Daddy, it's not soon, it's been a really long time. I've had your dick up my ass for a really long time and I need to come now, Daddy, I really do, oh please, I'll do anything you want."

"I've heard that before," he chuckled. But his thrusts in my ass sharpened, speeded up. "If I let you come are you going to make it a good big one?"

"Yes!"

"Do it for me, Harris. Let me see you shoot. Else I'll have to take this big thick dick away from you and slip it into some other boy. You wouldn't like that, would you?"

"Oh, Daddy—oh, you can put your cock wherever you want. But I need it now. I do. I'll come like you say. I'm going to shoot. Only let me now—now? Now?"

"Of course you can," he said, like it had never been in doubt. And my wrongass body did indeed ejaculate at his command. The thick liquid spurting out of my hole made me dizzy with its smell of warm honey and sex. The sight of my orgasm made Knox lose control as well. He turned me onto my belly and fucked me up the ass while I begged for mercy and begged for more cock with no pride or copyediting for inconsistencies. He got a big thick load up me: I could tell by the number of shudders that accompanied his orgasm, and the fact that the upper reaches of my ass felt heavy and hot even after his cock softened and slipped out.

Lotus came in the door with a pile of warm, wet towels on a tray. She went to Knox first and bathed the lower part of his body, receiving a loving kiss as her reward. Blushing, she came to me next and shyly put me to rights. She'd also brought a couple of cotton men's kimonos with her, and after she belted them, Knox drew both of us into the circle of his ebony arms.

Then we went into another part of the house, where there was a living room that opened out into a dining room area and kitchen. Lotus brought us food and sat close to Knox. He fed her from his own plate, and I was too happy to be jealous. I let her sit nestled close to him and took our dirty dishes into the kitchen myself, rinsed them and loaded them into the dishwasher. There was more Scotch on the counter, and I poured some for all of us. Three cut-crystal tumblers on a tray. I worried for a bit that Lotus would want a pastel drink with an umbrella and some fruit in it, but she tossed back her Scotch quicker than I could.

"Are you going to help us?" she asked me as the fumes from the Scotch made me suddenly very tired.

"Help you what? Lotus, I'm supposed to buy back the videotape and run you all out of town."

Knox shook his head. "You aren't buying any tape from me, man. That's evidence. See, if we go to the police and tell them that prick of a politician beat up my girl, he's going to claim that he didn't know she was pre-op, and the jury will let him walk. But what we got on that tape is him quizzing me about her, saying he won't take her into the bedroom if she isn't 'fully functional.' Plus a little something to prove that he wasn't talking about wanting a pussy. All a these rooms got cameras in them because I'm sick of my girls getting hurt. Sick fucker thought he could suck dick and get fucked and then fuck her up. No way that plays in Fort Knox, baby."

"Do you know how dangerous it is to go up against a councilman?" I asked. "Smitty's family has got more money than my family ten times over, Knox. He'll crucify you."

"Well, that's where you come in," he said, and toasted me with a half-empty glass. "You know where all of those pricks have the skeletons in their closets. You can walk us through the system. Once we've made our point, I don't mind leaving town."

"There's no place in America where you can hide from the Martingale clan," I said.

"Yeah, but I doubt they got connections in Thailand. We're going to bag us a crooked politician's

66

ass, then we're gonna get enough money out of him to take my entire family to Southeast Asia and buy all a these girls a box. Except Taneena. She's a top."

"What about me?" I asked. He was asking me to break faith with a client. I had taken Smitty's money and given Sheldon my word that I would do a job. My life had been such a series of fuckups. Disappointing my family by being born somewhere between male and female. Betraying my lover. Dropping out of college without even trying to make a go of it. Humiliating my family more by becoming a cop. Fucking up being a cop. Becoming a P.I. Now was I going to mess that up too? Where was my honor? Where was my honesty? And what kind of a man could I be without those two things?

In ones and twos, girls began to come home. Each of them handed Mojo a roll of cash and got a kiss, a grope, and a few endearments in her ear. One of them claimed Lotus, greeting her with romantic intensity, and the two of them went into the kitchen to neck and pet. The bodyguard also came in, and he was greeted by two of the girls, who ordered Chinese food and turned on the television. Some of the women regarded me with speculation, and Knox had me slide over to sit where Lotus had been. When he began to fondle me, one of them pointed it out to the others, who shrugged and went to pay for the food delivery.

"Hollywood nights," Knox said, and his stubble brushed my face as he kissed me. "Right now you're thinking what your choice is going to be. And I'm telling you that you got no choice. Now that I have my hands on you I am not letting you leave again. This is your home." He took my hand and put it on his bulging crotch. "All you got to do is give me the money you brought to pay for a chat with Lotus. Tomorrow we'll go back to your office and you can give me the rest of Shelly's money."

The idea of letting Knox manage my life the same way he managed his stable was too appealing. I reached for the inside pocket of my jacket, which I'd retrieved from his office on our way to the living room. It would be humiliating to give up that cash, partly because every female eye in the room was riveted on me, to see if I really was one of them. A moneymaker for the Pimps Up/Hos Down Bank and Trust.

I brought out cash, all right, and the very tiny gun that was hidden behind the bills. While Knox's attention was distracted by the cash I brought it up to the base of his skull. "Get up," I said in his ear. "Don't make me embarrass you in front of your ladies."

He muttered something about putting the cash away in his safe. We rose to our feet and went back toward his office. There I had him sit down with his hands behind his back, and I used my necktie to firmly secure his hands to the slats of the chair back. The bodyguard was still in the living room, stoking up a hookah with a couple of Knox's working girls. He wouldn't be able to stop me before I was out the door and gone. While Knox watched me in fury, I stepped over to the control console for the security system and removed the tape that had captured our encounter. It went in my coat pocket as silently as sorrow too great to allow for noisy tears.

"Don't you want the tape of Lotus too?" he asked,

eyeing me with hate but with admiration too.

"There's nothing on that tape," I said. But I picked it up anyway, curious to see what was really on it. Maybe some decent porn from one of the girls' bedrooms. "There never was. Bambi just got tired of me holding his father's death over his head. This was all a setup to get you to take me out of circulation. The only person who was going to be blackmailed is me. You're probably the one who beat up your girl, and she let you because you promised her something she's always wanted. That operation in Thailand, probably. Shelly figured I wouldn't be able to resist a reunion with you. But you know what, Knox? You never really asked me if I wanted you to fuck me. From the beginning, you just assumed that you could. And I won't say I didn't like it. Because you know that I did. But there was never any love between us. You didn't give it up to protect me. The school administration blamed it all on you because they were glad to get rid of a troublemaking black man who was screwing too many white girls and making their paleskin boys look bad on the ball court."

"Shelly did come to me," Knox confessed. "But I was going to double-cross him. Don't do this, Harris. Don't walk out on your second chance for happiness. Stay with me. We can still do all the things I promised you."

I couldn't afford to listen to him. "There was never any love between us," I insisted, and walked out with that lie ringing in my ears.

The corrupt people who run this playground are alive enough to reach for what they want. They still believe that life has something sweet enough to offer them that it's worth any betrayal or robbery to grab. You couldn't accuse me of being corrupt, could you? Because I'd do the job my client had told me to do even though he was crooked as San Francisco's Lombard Street. But you couldn't exactly accuse me of being alive, either, could you?

There is no statute of limitations of murder. It was time to hold Sheldon Fawn responsible for what he and Mrs. Bambi had done. I could probably wangle a deal that would let me walk without serving time, despite withholding evidence. Either way, it was time to get off this merry-go-rund. And I'd always liked Thai food. Maybe Mojo had the right idea.

Date Rape

She woke up with his dick inside of her. The impersonal, tunneling thrust of a hard cock that was close to coming made her gasp. It was alien. Anonymous. Unwanted! But unstoppable. The fact that she had fantasized so often about being taken this way just made what was happening now even more frightening.

She tried to move her hands to cover her pussy, which felt sore, as if this had been going on for a while. They were tied to the bed. Her ankles as well, held so far apart that her thighs screamed every time he pushed into her. The man was nothing but an atavistic stink and a shoulder, lurching over her face, brushing her cheek, but too far away to bite. She heaved her torso up as far as the ropes would allow. Her back protested, her shoulders screamed, and she couldn't get him off. She thought: *You never know how much bigger they are than us until they stop being nice. Men hold themselves up when they make love, but when they have no reason to be careful, they lay down heavy as a sack full of wet sand.* She couldn't even see him! There was a hood over her face, a hood made of a thick, black, stretchy cloth that blocked out the light and muted sound. She could breathe through the fabric but had to will herself to slow down, tell herself each time her lungs gasped that she was getting enough air. Hoping it was true.

The attack slowed. "I know you're awake now," he grunted, then his hips sped up, and she couldn't help but echo his animalistic "uh—uh—uh." Wait a minute. Was he close to coming, or was she? She barely noticed the hood being removed.

Lost in a struggle against her own inevitable orgasm, Bessy had trouble remembering the man buying her a drink at Glasnost, the vodka bar. Luke. He was a tall, skinny boy who had to be some kind of über-geek, because he still had a job as a network administrator. His company had moved him to Chicago, so he only got to visit San Francisco, where he used to live, to fix high-level problems for their branch in the Bay Area. He wore big black smartypants glasses and spoke in a soft accent that marked him as a man from Tennessee. The little stem of the vodka glass had looked ridiculously small in his oversized hands. He had gotten her attention by mentioning that they were both swallowing the same kind of oysters. "You like that Rooskie moonshine with black pepper, too?" he had said, offering her a shot. "That's my favorite. Bites like a bad girl."

When the bar closed, it was raining, as it had three

weekends in a row. He drove her home, but talked her into getting into the backseat to chat with him for a minute before she went into the house. He had a bottle of some kind of liquor in an inside coat pocket, but she refused to take a pull off of it, afraid she might get sick. She was really liking this boy, and things were getting kind of vague, all she could really see was his gangly face, the small neat beard on his chin, and those big eyes behind the math professor glasses. Then he started to touch her, and she really lost contact with reality. His hands seemed to know her body as well as her own hands did, but because those hands belonged to another person, they had the advantage of being able to surprise her.

Quicker than she would have thought humanly possible, he had her sweater pushed up and the front of her bra unhooked, her breasts bare and cold in the chilly air of the silent car. His hands covered them, folded over them, made her feel as if her breasts were enormous balloons she could hide behind. They were full of hot need, ready to follow that man and his big hands anywhere in the wide wicked world. Never mind what the rest of her thought. Her nipples had made their minds up for sure.

Luke's daddy would have whistled at Bessy and called her a looker. She was a short, sweetly round modern missy with a Bettie Page hairdo that had a streak of red in it to warn you that the timid and tentative 1950s melted away like five-cent popsicles. This girl was not wearing two pairs of panties to hide her pubic hair from the photographer. Her piano-sturdy and elegant, short legs were plump, with black spiders tattooed on the back of each of her chunky biteable calves. When Luke saw her with the rough, black-and-white-streaked oyster shell in her hand, throwing ocean-flavored meat and liquid down her throat, his cock wanted to follow that track, see her smile stretched wide; her eyes fill with slow tears. He would have wanted her based on her bratty, sultry looks alone. To find out that the dot-com bust had shredded her job as a data administrator but left her with enough of a golden parachute to start her own phone sex company simply warmed his nuts another notch. She was so scrappy, clever, and perverse that she stood out even in a city full of brainy, dangerous women.

"You look pretty this way," he said, his breath and tongue warm against her ear, his hands hungry upon her breasts. "Slutty, but pretty. Do you wonder why you've let me expose you this way, so that any guy who passes by can see that I'm about to get lucky with you?"

She tried to say something, but he kissed away her plan to speak; his tongue obliterated her faltering language.

"Never take a drink from a man you don't know," he said. "I've drugged you. In a few short minutes you're going to pass out, and you won't be able to move. I'm going to take you to my hotel, carry you out of my car, and take you up to my room. Then I'm going to strip you naked, tie you to my bed, and fuck you until I can't get it up anymore. If I think you still need to be fucked after that, I'll get some help."

One of his hands stopped kneading and plucking at her breast, went between her legs and up the skirt that she had almost not put on. But *to hell with it,* she had thought, *it's Saturday night, and even if I'm going out alone, I don't want to wear jeans.* "This is where I'm going to be," he said, fingering and pumping an opening that her amoral nipples had persuaded to get slick. "Hope you're not too tight, honey, because the tighter you are, the more this is going to hurt." He exaggerated his accent a little. "We're gonna have us a monster truck fuck, Sweet Lips." When he used that nickname, he tugged gently on the ring in her left labia, then the ring in her right. He somehow knew just the right angle to make her clitoral hood slide back and forth, and her clit woke up and got ready for company.

His honeyed voice was persuasive, almost hypnotic. Bessy wondered if it was wise to let herself go down, give in, let him do what he wanted to do. But the fingers inside of her felt amazing, as if she'd never been fucked before. He was just rough enough. "No," he said, pulling out, "I'm not going to let you come before you go night-night. That's it, girl, sleep tight."

Luke left her curled up in the backseat with his jacket over her face. He knew she wouldn't move it until he got her where he planned to stake her out and enjoy her completely. Once he drove over to his hotel, he couldn't really hoist her into his arms and carry her to the elevator. Twelve-hour days and a red-eye flight had left him with no time for the gym and a weary body. But she followed his instructions to keep her eyes closed, lean on him, and stagger. The parking lot attendants and staff at the front desk were used to seeing their guests come in on party legs, and didn't raise a single bleached and pierced eyebrow. Once upstairs, he carefully stripped his complaisant, loopy love doll, marveling at the depth of her navel and the viola curve of her hips. The rope and leather cuffs were on top of his suitcase; he had made sure he rented a room with a bed that sat on a frame with legs, rather than one of those stupid plywood platforms that stymied bondage. Such a classic figure inspired him to trot out an equally classic bondage position, the spread eagle. He stretched her out with her arms above her head and her legs spread wide

Luke had long ago stopped trying to talk himself out of having sex with girls who were helpless. The more he admired and wanted them, the more real their imprisonment had to be. Capturing beauty, plundering it, was a sport to him, but it was also more than that, it was the zeal and scorching bliss that kept him from walking to Japan. Bessy's body welcomed him even if her psyche was still ambivalent or reluctant to admit defeat. She was something special. He enjoyed using her, keeping hard and holding his own orgasm at bay, knowing she was far away. But when he called to her, it was even more exciting to see her try to summon her hands to her defense, and fail. He had cinched rope around her knees and hoisted them toward the head of the bed, as well as pinioning her ankles, so the only thing that happened when she tried to clap her thighs together was that her pussy got unbearably snug. The sudden constriction made his Adam's apple bob.

But his cock responded by getting harder, his woody turning into a bar of steel. "Baby, if you fight me, I'm going to come real good, right now," he promised. They were eye to eye. His brown eyes, her hazel eyes that had gone a hard gray. Adversaries in a fight that had been rigged. "Honey," he said compassionately, "you can't help yourself. I'm making you do this. So show me how it feels, is this what it feels like to be raped? Show me. It's not your fault. You got that submissive thing wired into both of your X chromosomes." (Oh, Lordy, would that ever piss her off good!) "You can't help feeling all these things, I'm making you feel them. Give me what I want and maybe I'll let you go. Maybe I'll pull out and put on a condom."

She kept on fighting, growling like a tiger, her eyes rolling. Sweat slaps resounded as their bodies met, separated, and met again. As he came, he slapped her face, calling her name, and Bessy shuddered underneath him, hips dancing to a tune that she swore she hated. Luke recognized her sex sounds, the injured crooning of a woman who's given up her slit to pleasure. His cock stayed hard enough for a split second to allow him to stir her crock just a bit, so she could hear the sloppy sound it made. "I've left my cum in you," he said. "It's going to be running down your inner thighs, bitch. That's what I've got you here for, to dump my load into. Before the night is over you'll have my cum in all of your salty-sweet holes, lovergirl. As long as it takes. Because that's what I want. To mark you. Make you mine. Leave a part of myself inside of you, where you can never wash it out or piss it out or shit it out. I've stained you with my cock."

As his hands tightened on her forearms, she came again, hard, came around the limp slug of his slippery and satisfied cock, climaxed to his jeering chant of, "Whore, whore, whore." This orgasm gently shoved him out, like a wave of the ocean leaving a shell on the beach. Luke nuzzled her neck, told her she was beautiful, then heaved himself off her body and gave her some water out of a squirt bottle. "Aren't you going to say thank you?" he asked.

She spat at him. "You should be thanking me," she replied. "If I'm a whore, where's my money, punk?"

He laughed the way men do when a joke challenges their honor. He wasn't amused. He went to his suitcase and returned with something she couldn't see until he stuck it in her mouth. "Here's your payday, bitch." The punishment for spitting was a gag, shaped like the first third of a penis. It went into her mouth after he'd given her another squirt of moisture—spit from his own mouth. Then he blindfolded her and caned her on the inside of her thighs. He used a thin plastic rod that was short and flexible enough to fit, bent slightly, in his suitcase. He did it hard and fast, no warm-up, and her frustration at not being able to scream out loud made her try again and again, until her vocal cords were as sore as the welts on her legs. The pain of a cane was like having lightning strike twice in the same place. She hated canes, but after she had passed through the terror and fury, her body automatically manufactured a great deal of lubrication. "You'll be glad you can't rub them together now," he said with great satisfaction, slapping her inner thigh.

Then he massaged her cunt, expecting it to be extra-wet. He put his fingers wherever he pleased, let his other hand savor her breasts. He stroked nipples and clit at the same speed, breaking her in with peaks of pleasure while he smiled like a pimp at her lack of self-control. Bessy had a big clit, and most guys didn't like it, but Luke jerked her off with the confidence of a farmboy milking his one-thousand-five-hundredth cow. Under his spell, Bessy felt groggy again, as if she really had been drugged. Then things changed. He quickly untied her, flipped her over, dragged her legs into a new position, and shackled her once more. She was up on all fours, ass in the air, and she did indeed want to keep her legs apart because the welts on her inner thighs were begging to be left untouched.

The penis gag had a tube in the center of it so that she could breathe through her mouth, but it kept her from making any coherent sound. The blindfold was big enough to completely cover her eye sockets; there was no way to sneak a peek out of the bottom of it. But she could hear him. And he was talking about what a shame it was to have all this fine pussy spread in glory for all the world to see, and him all fucked out and unable to victimize her anus. "Fortunately, I have some help," he said, and Bessy smelled a strange man's cologne. The bed shifted between her legs, as if weight had come down on the mattress, and something slick and oozing boy slime touched her asshole.

She mewed a refusal, a question, panic, bargaining. But nothing came out, and even if she had been able to form a sensible sentence, he wasn't listening. "Open wide for Daddy's best friend," he said, and the slight pressure on her butthole increased. There was a dribble of cold lube, which ran down on either side of the cock and left unpleasant sticky streaks on her legs.

She'd been butt-fucked before, but it wasn't exactly a frequent occurrence, more like an annual "oh God I'll never drink Tequila again" mishap. But the man who was claiming her ass wasn't going to detour and slide his poker into her pussy instead, no matter how she plunged around.

If it had hurt, if it had been the kind of sex that left you feeling ripped up and angry, that might have been better for her self-esteem. She might have felt cleaner. Because you really weren't supposed to cream when a stranger ravished you, much less when he was poking your rear end. The stranger's technique was slow and steady. She couldn't refuse him, but each time he moved forward, she found that her body had mysteriously agreed to accommodate him. This kind of penetration burned a bit more, generated a little more queasiness and doubt than vaginal engagement, but when she thought of herself as doomed and relaxed, head down on the bed, it wasn't that bad.

Then he reached around and started fiddling with her clit. "I'm afraid Daddy had a talk with the bell-hop about your clit," Luke said, sounding honestly apologetic. "You know you have such a big clit, so it's perfectly clear when you're in the mood, darlin', and a girl who has a big clit like that is just begging for somebody to come along and tweak it and use it to get her to do all kinds of dirty things. Does he know how to move you, honey? Is that man in the boat going to get you to cooperate with us? Looks like stormy seas ahead, child, oh, watch him rock. Rock and roll. Roll that big ass of yours, Bessy. I'm handing the reins over now. Let's see how you buck."

There did indeed seem to be reins attached to her gag, because the stranger was moving her head, using the leather straps to drag her back onto his cock. She would struggle to move off it and he would bring her back, from time to time renewing his attack on her clit, which left her bowlegged and limp with lust. Eventually he put the reins in one hand and used the other hand to spank her.

"If you don't want him to keep on spanking you, you better fuck yourself," Luke advised her. She could smell him at the head of the bed, and guessed that he was getting a second cock stand. Bessy took the spanking for as long as she could, but the pain of impact and the sweet ecstasy of clit-diddling combined to melt her resolve. Soon she was sawing back and forth like a mare in heat, her anus as open as a mother's arms. Then everything screeched to a halt. There were two hands clapped on her butt, which loudly announced its freshly spanked status. Her hips were frozen in place while the man behind her punch-fucked her ass, selfishly intent on giving her a cum enema. Luke, that fallen angel, reached back between her legs and took her size XL clit between thumb and forefinger and jerked it off like a little cock. It was weird, weird, weird to come with something big in her ass, to come when she couldn't move, when she couldn't make a sound. Like something trapped between two panes of glass or a frozen frame of film from a movie. But the orgasm was real enough, as were a wave of miniature comes that followed it, like faint double, triple, and quadruple rainbows.

The bed squeaked, the mattress was level, and

nobody was touching her. She heard Luke say, "This is a cash-only business," and then the door open and shut. He was unbuckling her cuffs, taking out the gag, and she slid off the bed as soon as she was free, angry at the thought of having to lay on top of the sweat and other secretions of her ravishers.

He caught her between his knees and brought her attention to his upright and duplicitous cock. "You're a monster," she said, but he trapped her wobbly limbs and got her down onto her knees. The position was so familiar that she didn't really want to leave it once she entered its safety. Only good things happened to Bessy when she was on her knees. "Look at that big plump hotdog," he said, bouncing his dick on the palm of his hand. "Fresh out of the steamer. If you suck me really good, maybe I'll let you go."

"You'd better not, you fucker," Bessy said, and let her tongue swoop across the slightly raw head of his cock. He moaned and laced his fingers into her hair.

"Don't tease me, girl," he warned her.

"Shut up, Luke. You don't have a safe word either," she snapped, and proceeded to give him a cop-car chase of a blowjob that would have driven a normal man into a lamppost. It was a razor's edge she walked, with tongue and teeth, lips and palate and throat. Everything she did felt so good that he couldn't summon the willpower to take his dick out of her mouth, but none of it was going to make him come.

"Baby, don't make me break my promise to you," he panted. "Cum in every hole. I said it. It has to be. A man of my word, I am."

She pulled back enough to make a retort. "That's not your cum in my asshole," she pointed out.

"Have the DNA results come back so soon?" he quipped. "Are we going to take this to Maury Povich? Find out who the father of your next batch of brownies is?"

"You gross motherfucking hillbilly," she said, shaking her head and laughing.

"Besides, my punk-rock fiancée-to-be, there might not be any cum in your back door at all. Could be that was nothin' but a dildo."

"That was no dildo!" she insisted. "Somebody was back there fucking me."

"Oh? Would you rather it was the bellhop instead of me with a plumber's helper?"

"I think I hate you."

"If this is hate, I can do without the love," he said. "But not the lovin'. Suck it."

"I'll blow you," she grudgingly admitted. "But I'm not marrying a crazy man. Not ever! No way."

She was sweet to him then, partly because she was tired and knew they couldn't go to sleep until he had come again. But she couldn't bring him to climax until Luke persuaded her to masturbate while she was swallowing as much of him as her face could take in. It was the urgent sounds of her coming that made him come too, and it seemed to her that his dick was still shooting as he dragged her up into his arms and kissed her like she'd just won the lottery.

"You're gonna wake up in a hotel room with a very strange man," he said, throwing a sheet over her. "Your white-trash Modesto ass just might wake up in Las Vegas some night with Elvis handing me your wedding ring."

"Luke, you cocksucker," she said, "shut up. And the next time you come back from Chicago, it better be because you plan to stay." A veteran bottom, Bessy had only a few twinges of guilt before she fell asleep. Was it hot to pretend things like this with Luke because she knew it was a fantasy, or was it hot because Luke was so serious and accomplished at turning her fantasies into reality that she often forgot, mid-play, that they had negotiated all the things he was doing to her? Her resistance was real, she knew that, and she knew that she had never been able to respond sexually to a man who couldn't meet her resistance with an evil grin and a firm hand. Her need to be taken was so strong that she wasn't even sure it qualified as safe, sane, consensual sadomasochism. Luke was safe because he could scare her, make it real, then comfort her and help her to come down from the intense and dangerous place they had visited.

Luke didn't reply to her parting shot. There were no jobs in San Francisco. He had tried to find one, and repeatedly failed. The next day, in the airport, he blinked away tears so he could see his cell phone well enough to dial for his messages. She had refused to see him off in person. He told himself he would call her when he got home, told himself that he would somehow manage, with emails and instant messages and Fed Ex packages, to keep her attention until he could swing another business trip to the West Coast. Did she think that it was easy for him, that he could just fuck her and leave and not feel anything? Bessy frequently teased him about not being able to keep his dick in his pants; but he never screwed around on her. She had made sex with other people as boring as a laptop with no video games, as unappetizing as eating pizza off of someone else's dirty paper plate. Did she understand that there was no discarding her? She lived all around him, every minute of the day. He was always aware of the women he saw who didn't look like her, the stupid conversations that never would have happened with her, the things he saw or thought that he couldn't instantly tell her. He survived their separations by coming up with elaborate scenarios for games he could spring on her the next time they met. Saved up his spunk and witty remarks and appetite for danger like they were money in the bank.

"The pussy juice on my dick is harder to wash out than sperm on hotel sheets," he whispered ruefully, getting in line to board his flight back to the Windy City, where he had never seen a girl with spiderwebs tattooed on the backs of her knees. "You got me, girl, you ravished me, and you ain't going to leave my system quick as a dose of GHB."

Boy in the Middle

The whole world of fetishists and sadomasochists comes to the Folsom Street Fair in San Francisco, and this year, I felt like this kinky cross-pollination was for my personal benefit. I was going to party with two friends from Kansas, Jonathan and Kitty, an FTM Daddy and his British girl; their friend Winston from London; and my long-term friend and new flame Gaby from New York City. Gaby and I got dolled up in leather for the fair, but Jonathan as a Scoutmaster shepherding a Brownie and a Cub Scout got all the attention. The third time they got stopped with a request for a photo, the chrome-and-latex, boots-and-jockstraps crowd swept Gaby and me away. Knowing this was likely to happen, we'd agreed to meet later at a party in a huge and gorgeously equipped dungeon in the South Bay.

I'd met Jonathan at a leather gathering in Denver, where he went out of his way to gather other FTMs together so we could have our own mini-conference. I was immediately attracted to his tall body, masculine face, and gentle manner. He was like a full-bodied cup of coffee, and Kitty was like the donut with sprinkles that you just had to have with your java. She was petite, saucy, and cheerful, and combined shrewd observations with a bubbleheaded manner that charmed my fist right into a rubber glove and then into her. But it was pretty clear that if I was going to play with them, Jonathan and I would be focusing our attention on Kitty, and there would be a minimum of interaction between him and me. I wasn't sure why—perhaps Jonathan was heterosexual; maybe Kitty had had bad experiences with bisexual guys. It didn't matter. It was fun to terrorize Kitty as "Elder Hartmann, one of Daddy's good friends from church." I knew they loved me. Respecting their boundaries was just part of becoming a family.

When I'd last visited them in Kansas, they'd told me about their friend Winston, a devoted leatherboy whose lover and master had suddenly died of a stroke. His tragedy touched my heart, so it was wonderful to finally meet him. He was a lanky, pale British guy who was as irreverent as Kitty. Like most Americans, I was a chump for their cute accents and caustic humor. The sight of his knobby little knees in the Cub Scout uniform made me want to grab him in a big bear hug and gnaw on him. These citizens of the British Isles who never see the sun are ideal vampire bait. But I was careful to be a little distant with Winston, not wanting to be taken for a pushy American top who thought he could have anybody he wanted.

Gaby couldn't possibly have been more different from the butch women, FTMs, bears, and leathermen who were usually my lovers. I'd known her for decades. She was bohemian Big Apple Jewish royalty, with legs as long as RuPaul's, a model's small, pert breasts, and curvy hips that drove the Puerto Rican boys crazy. Her hair was cut short with a long wave in front and streaked blonde, and she wore makeup with gold dust in it, so she always had a vague shimmer about her, as if she was a visitor from another realm, next door to where the Victoria's Secret angels hung their wings. She'd been an AIDS activist before most fags realized there was anything to get political about. Her knowledge of lesbian literature and sex radicalism was encyclopedic. Talking to her was like making out with a PhD candidate in queer studies, dressed up like an expensive hooker. In addition to facial hair and a transman dick, this was one of the things testosterone had done to me: sent me chasing after femmes, eager to get their skirts up and their legs apart. I wanted lipstick on my dick and silk panties on her pussy and stiletto heels in the stirrups of my sling. I was a fag who apparently sometimes liked to have sex with pretty girls.

Winston had been afraid to come to the play party, not wanting to be the odd man out. But I told him he could be the boy in the middle. My friends were punctual, and we drove to the club together. After arriving at the dungeon space, the five of us picked out a corner where it looked like both Kitty and Gaby could be comfortably restrained for the travail that Jonathan and I had planned for them. Winston had been happy to obey an order to guard one potential play station while Jonathan and I scouted out others, and he carried my bags without being told to do so. (Gaby is not exactly the kind of girl that you use like a pack mule.) So after Gaby had knelt to be collared and was resting her head against my right thigh, I offered Winston a pair of handcuffs. "I'd like you to wear these while you help me," I said.

He stepped back and looked even more pale. For a minute, I was afraid he might throw up. Then I realized it was just the fluorescent lights giving him that faint green tinge. "Oh, no," he whispered, "I'm afraid I couldn't, sir. Please forgive me."

"That's all right," I reassured him. "But don't stray, keep close to me, I'll need you to keep my gear sorted."

I took Gaby's hand and carefully hoisted her to her feet. She is taller than me, which makes my dick hard. I love walking around with her gorgeous self, a short guy, having other guys look at me and wonder what the hell it is that I do to her that keeps her holding my hand instead of theirs. Jonathan was trussing Kitty to a leather horse, then he got out his strap. He hunkered down to say something private in her ear, and it looked to me like they were going to be too far into one another to need any help or company. So I turned Gaby around and walked her into a rope spiderweb, and began to truss her into it, so that she would have to lean forward into the ropes. I wanted her to be able to feel rope all around her, squeezing her body, when I flogged her.

Just as she left my hands and went into the web,

Winston tugged on my keys and bent down. "Sir," he said, "I'd like to wear them, please." Surprised and tickled, I unscrewed the rolled-steel, English handcuffs and ratcheted them down to the lowest setting so they fit snugly on his thin wrists. He seemed to change when the cuffs went on. He was more himself, somehow; stronger and more grounded. I wondered how long it had been since he had played. Had Jonathan told me he'd given up S/M since his lover passed away?

Winston had little, deft hands, so I sent him around to the other side of the spiderweb to pull cords through and keep the rope untangled. He picked up on what I was doing as quickly as a real Boy Scout, and while I created rope diamonds and Japanese arm and leg ties on Gaby, he was always at my elbow to repeat the work on her other side or hand me what I needed. We were very polite with one another, establishing just the bare minimum of a hierarchy. But I loved being able to watch his cute-as-jailbait ass, which jeans under chaps showed off to perfection. Despite his shaved head, I could see that his hairline was receding. This is one of my oldest fetishes: what could be more masculine than male pattern baldness?

Gaby is one of the heaviest masochists I've ever met. It had been a long time since I had been able to do a complete whipping, running the gamut from soft and teasing whips that tickled and soothed, through heavier floggers, on to braided cats, and finally to the whistling slice of a cane. She hadn't been whipped for quite a while either, so her bruises came up fast, like a novice's, and the smell of her sweat, the knowledge that her blood was so close, pulsing just beneath the thin surface of her swollen, marked skin, drove me into a prolonged state of sadistic bliss. You could have cut my arm off at the shoulder and it would have kept on going till every item in my whip case had been gainfully employed.

In between whips or paddles, I stood close to Gaby, pressing my leather against her bare skin, fondling her, sometimes fucking her just a little bit. Behind me, I could hear a heavy slap as Jonathan's strap descended, and his firm admonition, "That's what you get for moving." Kitty was crying and struggling, saying, "I hate you, Daddy." I could only imagine what a hard-on that gave him. Both of our scenes attracted the attention of dungeon monitors who were either perving on us or genuinely concerned. It was a little odd to see Gaby wink and smile at a dungeon monitor who was wringing her hands over my girl's bruises and involuntary, heartfelt screams.

While I kept most of my attention on Gaby's backside, Winston carried out my instructions for what to do with the rest of her. When he gently massaged her breasts, he had a goofy half-smile that told me he really liked touching her. Sharing Gaby's body with him made me feel closer to her, as if it had confirmed my possession of her. And Winston's lusty appreciation affected my own sex, made me hard and harder. Eventually I couldn't stand it anymore, I had to fuck my girl. Once more, we would be breaking form at this party, because I hadn't seen anybody else engage in penetration. Nothing more sexual than fondling had taken place at the other bondage stations.

But Gaby was too tall for me to fuck her in standing

bondage. Winston was adept at helping me to let her loose. When I had her in my arms, and she was crying on my shoulder, saying, "You've never hit me that hard before," he spontaneously went to his knees and pressed up against me. His body against my leg sent a shock through me. Daddy wanted some more of that. I took one hand away from comforting Gaby so that I could muss up his stubble and tell him he was a good lad.

A table nearby had been vacated, and we fell onto it. I feel like a multi-armed Hindu god at such moments, somehow pulling out lube, condoms, and gloves while rearranging my dildo harness so that my raunch rocket is ready to launch, getting the bottom into position, locating paper towels, and seeking out an orifice. Gaby's Pilates program paid off; she was limber and ready to dance the night away. We fit together so perfectly, it made me groan. I love watching her move back and forth on my shaft, knowing what it's doing inside of her, feeling so grateful to her for wanting me, my hips hunching to a mean rhythm, fucking the come out of her and me. She talked to me the whole time, saying all the dirty things I love, an articulate, detailed, and incorrigible slut. Her perfume was mixed up with the smell of our sex, a signature for the potent memory it would become. Her lust made me a big shot with a desirable commodity. But the real treasure was her, the generosity with which she loved me and took pain from me, the way her body was thrown open to me.

Winston knelt by the side of the table, keeping one of his hands on me or on Gaby, watching what we were doing with a hungry stare. When I simply could not fuck her anymore, and I'd come three times, we huffed and puffed our way apart and he brought us water and towels.

Maybe it was something about the angle of his eyebrows as he offered me a warm, wet washcloth. Maybe it was the sight of his denim-clad ass, resting on his boot heels. But I didn't even put my cock away before I grabbed him and somehow heaved him onto my lap. The normal rules of gravity are sometimes suspended when desire is especially keen. He landed across my thighs just as Jonathan and Kitty came sauntering over. Jonathan looked quite satisfied with himself; she was rubbing her bottom and looking a little confused, hair askew.

"Do you want it over jeans or on your bare ass?" I demanded. I wanted to see Winston's buttocks tense and relax as I beat him, but some of my transgendered brothers don't like public nudity.

Jonathan beat me to it. "I vote for bare ass," he said in his flat, butch Midwestern voice, and down the drawers came. How had Winston undone the buttons on his jeans that quickly? And how did I come to have Jonathan's strap in my hand?

If you'd asked me if I had another scene in me, I would have laughed in your face. But Winston's body was calling out to me. I knew he was very, very sad. I wanted to make him cry. I wanted him to feel the masochistic hunger in his body again, and know that he was still alive. I wanted to call him back to the land of the living. Not out of disrespect for his dead lover, but to keep Winston from following him too soon. If I could. So a power beyond me lent strength to my arm, and I walloped that boy like a Victorian housekeeper cleaning the drawing room rug. He couldn't help but throw himself around a little, but I had one arm around him, clamping him against me, and he wasn't honestly trying to get away. Since I was hurting him a lot, I could forgive him for reacting to the pain.

When hissing and howling turned into tears, I laid on a few more strokes, then stopped and just held on to him. I petted his swollen, red behind and told him he was the best boy in the world. Oh, how I longed to lube up his asshole and feed him my cock, a half inch at a time, preferably while he was still crying. I wanted to fuck him while he mourned for his lost master, and fuck him through those tears and into a new place where he could respond to someone else. Then he said, "Why did I think I could ever give this up?" and climbed down from my lap.

I had just met him, and we hadn't even talked about playing, much less fucking. So I regretfully let him go, and while he knelt between my legs, I took his handcuffs off, staring at his mouth and wondering what it would look like stretched wide around my fat cock. I would have turned down a platoon of horny Marines to introduce myself to Winston's tonsils. But these are the kind of deals that nobody ever offers you, just like you never win the lottery.

The five of us decided we'd had enough of the party. We piled into my car, drove to a late-night diner to get food, and flirted sleepily with one another while we ate whatever strange thing our two A.M. zombie impulses dictated. After I took my three friends home,

Gaby came back with me, to my own four-poster bed, where I arranged her on all fours and used her again, idiotically happy to have this much sexual need. I knew I'd feel like hell the next day, but it was worth it to misbehave in such style.

She wanted me to fuck her in the ass, but I couldn't. The image of Winston's schoolboy buns was too strong. If I was going to sodomize my first, perfect femme bottom, I wanted it to be about her; not a proxy for someone I'd just met.

I got around to it before she had to go home. But that's another story.

Flannel Nightgowns and White Cotton Panties

For Tim Woodward

My master has told me that we must start all over, from the very beginning. I will be spending my vacation at his house, taking nothing of my own with me but the clothes on my back. We will be together for every hour of every day. I will eat what he gives me, wear what he has for me, sleep when he allows it. If there is a deity that looks after slave girls, I pray to that deity for grace. Let me fit myself to him as easily as water curves around a stone in its path. Perhaps even more than grace, I need courage. Since I received his written orders, the time when I am to present myself and the place, fear has opened a vast cold cavern in the center of my being. Even when I am holding perfectly still, I am vibrating to the secret rhythm of this terror.

Perhaps he would be infuriated to hear me call him my master, even though I have taken that liberty with his face and form only in the silence of my own heart. It is easy to displease the powerful. He is so far above me that he has probably lost all sense of how much power he has. Some gesture or word that means no more to him than clearing his throat could crush all my hopes and dreams, drain my life of meaning. I lived in a state of frustration before, gnawed at by a conviction that I was not like other women, afraid to look too hard at that difference lest it prove to be tainted with madness. It is bad enough to live in the blinders of ignorance, but if those blinders have been removed, how could you go on if you knew no rider would ever appear to take your reins and spur you toward his stable?

This time that we will spend together is a test. It will determine whether he will accept me as his own, and train me to become the living image of that ownership.

I met this man through the good graces of my sister-slave, the friend who gently helped me to untangle the snarl of doubt and prudishness that choked my sexuality. She already had a master of her own, and out of love for her, he showed me enough to be taken out with the two of them, in the realm where it was safe for her to openly wear the tokens of her slavery. I know when and how to kneel, a few appropriate positions in which to display myself, the respectful forms of speech, the rudiments of service in the drawing room and bedside. But she is the slave of his heart. I would not want to be his second girl, even if that position had been offered to me.

Once I knew enough not to embarrass them in public, my friend and her master took me to a party. I was distracted by equal parts of arousal and intimidation. So the fantasies that I had really could become a reality—for women as beautiful as these! He encountered a colleague who expressed an interest in me. I went through my paces with a pounding heart and a dry mouth, painfully aroused by the screams of girls in duress and far happier than I. How does one contrive to be artless when so much is at stake? This new man was less than ten years older than myself, soft spoken but authoritative, with what seemed to be a well-built body. He was wearing leather pants, a turtleneck shirt, and a professorial jacket. His graying hair was close-cropped, and there were laugh lines around his blue eyes. His two front teeth were slightly crooked. Not that I had more than a split second to assess him out of the corner of my eye.

My sister-slave's owner had taught me a simple routine. As my body bent and twisted, extended and retreated in submissive choreography, I felt a surprising amount of gratitude toward him, this master who would not collar me. He had created an opportunity for me to be examined. And he displayed me well, using hand signals rather than verbal commands. After my dance, I was sent away with my friend to do some little task for him, and when we came back, the stranger was gone.

Now it was dark, and I was outside his house, ringing the bell. He came to the door and brought me inside, taking one of my hands between his own. "You're here," was all he said, but his voice was a deep, subtle instrument that conveyed welcome and perhaps a little relief. The possibility that he had feared I would not obey his summons—that he actually needed me to be here—settled my stomach and stiffened my resolve. This was a master of good repute and great experience, a man who had been recommended to me by people I trusted, and I thought every molecule of him was handsome. *Please*, some part of me was crying, hammering at the clear but immovable walls that held my slave-self back, *please rescue me, set me free*.

I realized that he had placed something in my hands. "Put this on," he said, showing me down the hall and into a bedroom. "Then come back into the living room. Whenever you feel ready."

He closed the door, leaving me in a room that was a little girl's fairy princess dream. The bed was sized for two adult bodies, but it had frothy, girlish white lace curtains and linens to match. The flocked, white velvet wallpaper was flecked with rhinestones, and the moldings were painted birthday-cake-frosting pink. There was a shelf full of character dolls, expensive collectors' items, and some first editions of two fiction series for young adults. One featured a girl detective; the other, a nurse. I sternly suppressed the impulse to go to these books, pick them up, look at the illustrations, and lose myself in fiction. The double doors of the closet were sliding mirrors. Avoiding their judgment, I turned my back and stripped off everything I wore and folded it up, then stashed the small stack (shoes on the bottom) in the last drawer of a dresser decorated with stenciled golden crowns. Curiosity led me to open a door, and it led to a bathroom with art deco fixtures of nude women posing in sprays of flowers, and black-and-white tile. Since he had not told me to get my ass into the living room as quickly as possible, I took the liberty of a quick shower.

Walking back into the bedroom, which I assumed was to be mine, I thought again about his statement: we must go back to the beginning. My hands shook a little as I approached the bundle of fabric that he had given me. It had not had the sleazy feel of nylon stockings, a spandex dress, or silk lingerie. Nevertheless, the garment that shook out from the folds could not have surprised me more. It was a simple flannel nightgown, red hearts on a white background. I pulled it over my head, and as it fell around my shoulders, I felt something land against my right foot. A pair of white cotton panties had been folded up with the nightgown. I slid them up over my legs and hips, a little embarrassed by their snug fit and full, 1950s cut. I was completely covered in the most modest outfit possible. The contrast between it and the desire that simmered in my belly was indecent. There was a pair of fuzzy slippers by the bedroom door, and since my feet were cold, I put them on. No one had handed me a script, but I was in costume, and I knew where the stage was. So I went toward the living room, frosty stage fright nipping at my heels, herding me forward.

My master was sitting on a large, comfortable leather sofa, wearing red silk pajamas and a heavy paisley brocade dressing gown. A cigarette smoldered in an ashtray on the end table, a bit of bad-boy insolence in politically correct northern California. There was also a glass full of red wine. The lights in the room had been lowered, and the dimness leached some of the tension out of my shoulders. He did not turn to acknowledge me. It was as if he didn't realize I was there. The wide sofa faced a large-screen television, and as I watched him, hungry for more knowledge of him, he lifted his right hand and pressed a button on the remote control.

The screen was suddenly occupied with the life-sized bodies of beautiful, young men and women copulating in front of us with what looked like genuine enthusiasm. From time to time one of them would turn to stare at us, as if they knew we were there, privy to their revels. I was shocked, first by the pornography, and then by the fact that it had shocked me. I was rooted to the spot, short-circuited.

"What are you doing up so late at night?" he asked with patient tenderness.

It was enough of a hint for me to guess what was required of me, and I fell naturally into the role that was consistent with the flannel nightgown and the juvenile bedroom. "I couldn't sleep, Daddy," I whispered.

One corner of his mouth quirked up. He was pleased with me, then. But this amusement at my quick wit was not part of the fantasy, and he quickly assumed a more neutral expression. He patted the sofa. "Do you want to sit down?" he asked.

When you are a slave, there is no "want" about it. You must go where the hand of your owner beckons. And so I went, albeit awkwardly. The ultrasoft flannel caressed my naked breasts. I parked my hopefully cute little butt in the middle of the end cushion. He turned to regard me thoughtfully, taking a drag on his cigarette, a sip of wine. "I don't know if you should see this," he said, and lifted the controls.

"Why not, Daddy?" I asked, staring at the screen with my mouth slightly open. I had come into the room in a state of arousal, and all of this sex, even though it was relentlessly equal and cheerful, made me uncomfortably aware of my panties and what was inside of them.

"I guess you're old enough to be able to watch an X-rated movie," he said, carefully flattering my imaginary adolescence. "If there's anything going on up there that you haven't seen already."

If I left that coarse comment alone, the evening would take a different turn, I sensed. But I did not feel like a promiscuous teenage wildcat in the presence of this strong and quiet man. I was a novice, and a beginner, just as he had dictated. "I never saw anything like this before, Daddy," I said breathlessly.

I could not take my eyes off the screen. A man was undressing a woman, running his hands across her breasts, his fingers dragging at her nipples. Then things got more interesting, less bubblegum-happy. He turned her so that her back was to the camera as he tore her dress down the back, exposing the curves of her ass. Then she was facing the camera again, hands behind her back (held there by him?). Only one of his hands was visible, and it roamed across her breasts, pawing at them, squeezing crudely, leaving red marks behind. The woman twisted in his grasp and moaned, her legs separating as if against her will.

My imagination was not powerful enough to reproduce the feeling of those hands upon my own skin, but I was leaning forward, trying to find that touch. The rising emotions in my body were entrancing, but there was another reason to keep my eyes forward. My skin on the right side of my body tingled, sensing my master's approaching warmth. He was coming toward me, settling his greater weight on the cushion next to mine.

"Never?" he asked, and I had trouble remembering our earlier exchange.

"No, never," I exhaled.

Was he touching me? I thought that he was, but what control he must have, to put hands on me so lightly that I could wonder if contact had been made. I looked down and saw that he was simply holding his hands near my shoulders and my arms. What I felt was the energy between us. I was being stroked by the mere probability of his skin meeting mine.

The couple on the screen were kissing, deeply, ferociously, her head twisted back to meet his mouth. Strands of her long black hair flew through the air, partially hiding the things his fingers were doing to her nipples. I was breathing more quickly, panting, and when the tips of my master's fingers touched my lips, I gasped, frightened by the sudden incandescence. The porn actress slid down her man's body, pivoted, and seemed to put her head into his hand. His fingers twisted in her hair, and the camera focused on the hard cock that he bounced in his other hand. He slowly brought it forward while she halfheartedly struggled, not seeming to realize that when she opened her mouth to protest, it only made her more available for the lesson he was determined to teach.

As his cock head slid between those beautiful, swollen lips, my own parted. My master was looking at me with pure hunger in his eyes, and he had slipped his thumb into my mouth. My groan was silent, blocked. A callus rubbed the roof of my mouth. He didn't move his thumb much, just barely rocked it to and fro, but I had let him into my mouth, and I sucked on what he gave me. Suckled, rather, and titillated with supple strokes of my tongue. Kissing and sucking upon the dream of someday being fed his cock. Intoxicated by the presage of that initiation.

I dared swivel my eyes to look at him. My knowing mate grinned back at me from his cruel, appraising blue eyes. What a relief it was to see no sympathy there, no hesitation, no possibility of reprieve or mercy. *He's real,* I thought, and my heart speeded up, throwing itself against the cage of my ribs. *This is really going to happen. He will make it happen. He will use me for his pleasure, and at last I will know what it is like to have real pleasure of my own.*

He took his thumb out of my mouth, settled deeper into the sofa, and took a gulp of wine. It must have been the reflected shadow of the thick red liquid that made his face seem flushed. I kept my eyes front and center, trying to look nonchalant, but I knew my body was flinching slightly every time a woman on the screen was caressed, bitten, or penetrated. When his hands settled on my shoulders, I willed myself to ignore him. "Your shoulders are so tight," he murmured, and his fingers dug into my muscles, massaging me. "Let me see if I can loosen you up. Then maybe you can go back to bed and sleep." I adjusted my body slightly to give him access as his hands wandered further down my back, fingers grazing the top of my buttocks. Then he was focusing on my upper arms, and as I continued to watch the orgy on screen, a light tickling pressure melted across my breasts. He was sneaking up on my nipples, touching the flannel that lay upon my skin rather than the skin itself. But I still felt him, and his intentions, and my breasts seemed to swell to an uncomfortable size. I could feel my nipples crinkling painfully, and between my legs a sharp sensation made me want to excuse myself and run back to the bathroom.

Since I permitted this much, he grew bolder, until there was no denying that he was fondling my breasts. I could not help it, my legs parted slightly. The tight crotch of the white panties was digging into me. "You're getting to be such a big girl now," he crooned. "Do you like it when I massage you?" As he spoke, he was unbuttoning the yoke of the flannel nightgown and sticking his hand inside it, rubbing my collarbones.

"Oh, yes, Daddy," I whispered as a nameless blonde was made to suck one man's cock while another man entered her from behind. The man who was fucking her struck her on the ass. Lucky bitch.

"Massage is really good for you. It helps your body to develop properly. And you know I want you to grow up to be a beautiful young lady. Would you like a breast massage?"

Before I could reply, he skillfully peeled the front of my unbuttoned nightie over my arms, effectively pinning them at my sides. My breasts were exposed.

He put one hand around my throat while the other explored me freely. My body surprised even me with its hunger.

"What beautiful big titties you have," he said, escalating. "I'd love to kiss them." It wasn't a request for permission, just a warning. When his mouth closed over my nipple, I thought at first I could not stand the intensity of the sensation. Then it took me over, and I yielded to his mouth, even when he sucked roughly at the hard nubs and bit them. He came up for air and smiled at me. "Daddy sometimes gets a little rough, doesn't he?" he said. "But you don't mind, do you?"

"No, Daddy, I don't," I stuttered.

"Of course not," he sneered. "I think it would be a good idea for me to see how the rest of your development is coming along, don't you?"

I thought a shadow of resistance might prevent my surrender from becoming tedious. "What do you mean, Daddy?"

He kissed me then, still squeezing and twisting my breasts, then took his mouth away and said in my ear, "Spread your legs, you little bitch."

I tried to comply, but in my haste, forgot how long the nightgown was. So my knees were stuck only a foot and a half apart. He wound his fingers in my hair, grown long in lonely hope that it might someday be used in just this fashion, and he pulled just enough to create a delicious pressure on my scalp. "Pull your nightie up for Daddy," he suggested, licking my ear and my neck like a big lascivious dog. With numb fingers, I complied, inching it up a little at a time. As soon as it cleared my knees, he gently edged his hand along the inside of my nearest thigh, as if he was warming it.

"Do you ever massage yourself?" he asked, sharply tweaking my left nipple.

"I don't know what you mean, Daddy," I gasped, struggling to stay put despite the pain.

"Really. Well, then you should spread your legs a little further, baby, because Daddy is going to masturbate you."

I acted as if I had never heard the word. "*What* are you going to do, Daddy?"

"This," he said, coming close to kiss me again. Then his finger went under the edge of my panties, between my inner lips, scooped up a little of the moisture that was running freely there, and took it up to my clit, where he gently rubbed it into the top and sides of the hood. I could hardly kiss him back, I was moaning so much. How could a man know this much about a woman's body? Within minutes he had taken me to the very edge of an orgasm, and he kept me there for an insufferably long time. "What's going to happen if I keep on doing this?" he asked, taunting me.

"I—I don't know—I don't know—" I lied, so deep in character that I almost believed it.

"Do you want to find out?" The finger was tracing figure eights within my labia, outlining clitoris and opening, over and over again. He sucked on my nipples, hard, then told me, "Say it. Ask me."

My tongue was twice the size of my mouth. So he slapped me on the inside of one thigh, then the other. I could not catch my breath. The reality of the pain was not anything like what I had imagined, but I was prepared to adapt to what my body told me, and fall in love with it. He kept slapping me until he was tired of it, then he gently stroked the burning skin, giving me a chance to find my voice.

"Please—Daddy—please masturbate me," I whimpered.

It took only a slight increase in pressure and speed for his fingers to reduce me to a babbling orgasmic mess. "Sweet baby," he groaned, taking me in his arms. He lifted his fingers to my mouth, made me suck them again, then put his hand between my legs and forced them back into an open position.

"Do you see what's happening to that lady in the movie?" he asked me. We were currently being shown a close-up of a huge torpedo of a cock, housed inside a shaved pussy, pummeling it. How the actor came all the way out and then accurately found her hole again without the guidance of his hands was a marvel to me.

"Ye—es," I replied, reaching for him. He pinned my hand down.

"Would you like to know how that feels?" he asked, and went into me without waiting for me to reply. I didn't know how many fingers he had put into me, but it was as if no one had ever finger-fucked me before. I suddenly had feeling where there had been little or no sensation before. And I understood, in my flesh, why the woman on the screen might not be feigning her insatiability.

"Oh!" was the only response I could make. One word that could not begin to contain all that I was discovering at his behest.

"Say it again," he told me, tongue once more against my ear, a sultry insult. "Say the words. The words that Daddy taught you."

I repeated the phrases he had used already, and he introduced more of them, key groups of dirty words that we both found enormously exciting. I was such a spoiled girl, receiving all of this physical attention. None of the men who had wanted to fuck me had touched me this much before getting down to what they saw as the main event. With his thumb on my clit and the rest of his fingers engaged within me, my master showed me again and again that I was the very opposite of what I had often been called—cold, frigid, withholding. Through much of this, we were eye to eye, and I could feel him learning me, appreciating my responsiveness, but seeing much more of me than my shudders and gasps. Sometimes my reactions were so pronounced that I was afraid he would think I was overacting, but his expression told me that he knew I was truthful, and he was excited by my openness.

"You like looking at the men's things, don't you?" he asked, pulling his hand away, leaving me shockingly empty. This time he would not proceed until I agreed. "Don't you want to know what a real one looks like?" he asked me, taking one of my hands in his own. I nodded, and he guided me to the lap of his silky dressing gown. There beneath the heavy fabric lurked an equally heavy shaft. But before I could touch it directly or heft his ballsack, he made me circle it with my hand on top of the brocade, and slowly jack him off while he made me repeat all the names he could think of for his parts. Baby talk, adult slang, and medical terms were all deliciously sacrilegious as they went back and forth between us in stage whispers. Any guilt I might have felt about enacting a fantasy like this one, which would have been so offensive if it were real, was absolved during this exchange. We were so clearly playacting, two adults turning each other on in what might have seemed a farce if we were not so engrossed in it. We even giggled together, a time or two, but I think he sensed that if he allowed too much levity, I might become hysterical.

When he finally showed his swollen penis to me, I bent toward him of my own accord, and he allowed my approach. I stared at the stalk and crown of his sex, wondering if I had ever really looked at a cock before. How many billions of heterosexual women are there on this battered planet of ours? And how few of them have ever really studied a rigid prick—or one in repose, for that matter? Much as I desired him, I realized I was afraid of his erection. Some of this was the shame that had been drummed into me from childhood, but some of it was based on a long experience of disappointment, and perhaps I had also picked up on my lovers' ambivalence about their own genitals. But this man had his cock screwed on nice and tight; he knew exactly what it could do, and he preened beneath my gaze.

"I'm going to teach you some important things about growing up," my master told me, taking his tool in hand and pointing it toward my lips. "This is what you're here for, to worship my cock. To worship the thing that gives you pleasure and rules your heart. Do you love me, baby? You love me, don't you, my favorite little girl? So kiss it, just do that for me, kiss it. Kiss it the way that I kiss you."

It was a salty kiss, because the head of his cock was drooling pre-come, and he deliberately smeared the stuff across my mouth, then told me to lick my lips and swallow it with a smile, and come back for more. The kiss led of course to other things, and soon he was riding back and forth within my throat, coaxing me to do what the women in the movie were doing. "They like it," he said. "You've seen how much they like it. And once you get good at doing it, you'll like it too. But even if you didn't like it, you would still have to do it, and do you know why? Because I am your daddy, that's why, and little girls always do what their daddies tell them to do. I made you, so I own you."

Soon my eyes were running with tears and the back of my throat was sore. The thick, sour taste of his secretions lined my mouth. "I know what you're thinking about," he said, rocking his hips. "You're thinking about what it feels like to have this inside of you someplace else. Are you making Daddy's cock get hard so he can fuck you with it?"

I took the risk of letting his cock slide out of my mouth so that I could stare at him wide-eyed. "What does *fuck* mean?" I asked. I was no virgin, true, but it was also true that I had no idea what it would mean to be fucked by this man. His power over me was so complete and welcome, I didn't think there could be such a thing as vanilla sex with him.

He chuckled and rubbed his gray crew cut. "It's better if I show you rather than tell you," he decided. "Slide off the couch and kneel by the foot of the coffee table. Take off your nightgown. Bend forward. That's right. Now, I want to make sure that we're not interrupted. This is a very important lesson. So I want to make sure you can hold still."

"I'll hold still for you, Daddy," I vowed, my breasts pressed uncomfortably flat by the cold slick wood of the coffee table's surface. Black leather bumpers ran around all of its edges, padding my hips. He ignored me, walked to the head of the table, and buckled straps around my wrists, chaining them to the legs of the table. I pulled once (of course), but I was well-tied. The cuffs were snug and the chains sunk deep into the wood. I could not free myself. He was behind me, taking off his dressing gown, and peeling my panties down. Cold air humiliated me with goose bumps all over my bum. The tight panties were made out of fabric that was thick enough to keep my legs together. But I felt as if my pussy peeked out anyway, she was so swollen, the sweet slick mouth of a siren.

When he rubbed the head of his cock against my tender slit, I began to cry. Sob, actually. I struggled with my bonds. I really did try to escape. He had been wise to tie me. But even as I thrashed around, I knew it would have upset me to break free. The frenzied motions I made were somehow a part of giving way to him. I could not go to him quietly, I suppose, as if it were no little matter. Perhaps it was *my* way of testing *him*, to see if he really was the lighthouse and harbor that I needed.

"Shush," he soothed me, stroking my flanks. "Daddy's here. I'll take care of you. Don't cry. Are you afraid it's going to hurt? Don't worry. If it hurts

I'll stop. But you've been wet for so long, and you know what it means when you get wet. It means you're ready to be fucked. It means you need it. And I want you to have everything you need, honey. That's what daddies are for."

There was an introductory thrust, a shallow one, and then a slow, steady push that seemed to fill me to my heart. I cried out, and the sound of it was so poignant that it made me cry afresh. Yes, I cried out with no small amount of grief for the freedom I was about to lose, my autonomy, the illusion that I did not need anybody else in order to be happy. But I also mourned for the years that I had lived without this glory, the weight of his body upon me, his steady and sinister intentions, the goodness of his erotic selfishness.

"Does it hurt?" he asked, moving a little.

"Oh, yes," I said, quick to take up my cue. "It hurts, Daddy. Oh, please stop! Please stop, Daddy. You said you would if it hurt." He really did feel bigger than any other man who had taken me, perhaps because he was plowing me from behind, perhaps because of the way my legs had been pinioned.

"Shush," he exhaled. "Shush, now, my little slut. Daddy's little sex slave. Daddy knows what's best for you. You're just a little hole for me to use. My tight little whore in training. And it doesn't hurt that much. You need to be stretched wide. It's about to feel better—much, much better. Oh, yes. It is. Better and better."

Well, I could tell that it felt better for *him*. And I almost lost myself in the old habit of withdrawing from my body, watching the man who was fucking me, allowing him to get off without participating. There was something oddly maternal about loaning a man my body that way, and some enjoyment or warmth resulted from knowing I had pleased him. But my master was not going to be taken in that way, or should I say, patronized? He put one hand under me and reminded me that he knew how the little button down there worked. Before long it was pretty clear that I would come before he did, and he rode me skillfully all the way through that climax, down into the valley, and up the hill into another. It wasn't until I had collapsed on the table, resting all of my weight limply upon it, that he put both hands on the cheeks of my ass, spread them so that he could watch what he was doing to me, and gave it to me at a tempo and depth calculated to please no one but himself. Still, at the end, when he told me to beg for his come, I meant every word.

He left me restrained while he cleaned himself and tied his robe. Then he unbuckled the straps, lifted me onto my feet, and took me into the bedroom. There, he peeled back the covers and put me on the clean lace-edged sheet. But I was to get more than a kiss goodnight. He said, "From now on, you can't come unless you have something inside of you. Do you understand? It isn't good for little girls to do without that. You need to be opened up, and you need to be kept filled up. That way you'll always be aware of your sex, and always ready to be used by your master. And I don't want you touching yourself either. When you need to come you have to ask me. And I'll decide if I want you to get off or not."

So he tied my hands above my head, to the rails of the canopied bed, and spread my ankles and tied those apart as well. Before he covered me up, he said, "I have a surprise for you," and showed me a small dildo. "Tonight I used your mouth and your cunt," he said. "But you have to learn how to make all of your holes available to me." I gasped as a doubled length of rope was cinched tight around my waist. He greased up the imitation cock and pushed it carefully up my unhappy ass, where startled muscles did all they could to push it out. Then the rope came between my legs, holding the plug in place. The harness was finished with a large, intricate knot that rested on my clit. He slapped lightly at my pussy to show me how accurately it was placed.

He leaned forward to give me a good-night kiss on the cheek (oh! his star-blue eyes), and left my side without covering me up. He paused by the door, but he did not turn off the light. "I'm turning on the security camera now," he said. "I'll review the tape in the morning, so I'll know if you made yourself come or not. Sweet dreams, little slave. You played your part to perfection. It takes an intelligent girl to assume a persona of such simplicity. Tomorrow, you will have your reward: a sound spanking, before breakfast. Then you will get to meet some of Daddy's friends."

I wanted him to spank me. But I didn't think I could say thank you, any more than I had been able to just spread my legs for him and placidly accept that first firestorm of a fuck. "Sleep well, master," I said, trying not to make it sound like a curse as I writhed, unable to silence the prong within my bowels.

Despite the bright light and the insistent pressure within me, I fell asleep at once, as soon as his eyes no longer provoked me. Without thinking about it or being told, I had learned one of the slave's most valuable skills: to rest whenever an opportunity to do so is given. I would need every hour of slumber I could scavenge from his schedule, for the next day was to be a demanding one. He had already hung another outfit on the back of the bathroom door: a hooker's leather micro-miniskirt and a fishnet halter top. I was so tired, I didn't even twist my head up to see if I could catch a glimpse of my shoes.

Gender Queer

Carleton was still trying to get his strawberry-blond cowlick to lie down when the doorbell rang. He gave his too-thin, five-foot-eight body a critical glance in the full-length mirror, threw the tube of styling gel back on top of his dresser, sighed, and went to get the door. At least he had a suntan and his calves were showing some muscle from all that bike riding. He had eaten both breakfast and lunch, and planned to eat dinner as well. He was no longer the anorexic teenage girl who'd had to be hospitalized twice. Testosterone and the free weights in his bedroom were sculpting his arms and torso into a body he could accept, maybe even love.

The local FTM group had almost a hundred people on its mailing list, but the typical meeting was less than a dozen guys. Tonight, by the time he'd admitted the last arrival, there were only six other than himself, so everyone fit comfortably in Carleton's living room. The red recliner he usually claimed for his own had been occupied by a new person, someone he thought he recognized from the audience at one of his more horrendous speaking engagements. She looked ready to bolt, so he didn't ask her to move. The regular guys already had places on the three-seater sofa and the room's other two chairs. A tower of large paisley pillows resided in one corner of the room, so he dragged two of them into the circle, wedged one of them up against the bookshelf for whatever it was worth as back support, and sat down, legs crossed, to see who would start the meeting.

"I guess I'll go first," Bear said, in a voice that had only recently stopped cracking like a teenage boy's. Bear was the biggest guy there, a wide and tall Latino who had his own gardening business. He had good news: a letter from his psychiatrist and an appointment with a doctor who would do the chest surgery he had been saving to afford. Everyone was excited for him except Greg, who had spent a summer in San Francisco, avoided any gendered pronouns, and called himself "no-ho, no-op." Carleton had engaged in some behind-the-scenes diplomacy to keep the other guys from asking Greg to leave the group. "He doesn't even call himself an FTM!" Lou (who still tended bar at the local lesbian dive) had objected. "What is all this 'gender queer' shit? Either he wants to transition or he doesn't."

"Come on," Carleton had retorted, "how long did it take you to make up your mind? Let him take his own path. We get enough judgment from the outside. If he can be happy in his own skin without taking testosterone or getting any surgery, who are we to make that decision for him? Our website says we are for anybody who: (a) wasn't born male, and (b) has questions about their gender."

After everybody had high-fived Bear, Lou wanted to bitch about his lesbian girlfriend and fantasize about the perfect straight girl he would never be able to date until he got his phalloplasty. Carleton wondered, not for the last time, what he was doing providing a haven for a bunch of straight men. He was the only self-proclaimed bisexual in the group, and there wasn't much empathy for the problems he had getting up the nerve to go to a gay men's sex club downtown.

The others kept glancing over to the short-haired woman in Carleton's recliner, waiting for her to introduce herself or add some comment that would help them to understand why she was there. When they weren't giving her pointed looks, they were glaring at Carleton. As the unacknowledged leader of the group, he was supposed to facilitate such awkward things for them. Tonight he refused to do so, because the only time he had looked directly at the rosy-cheeked butch, he had seen the silver sheen of silent tears coursing down her face. Partly because he was in no mood to entertain, the guys left fairly early, planning to continue their conversations at a diner owned by two retired gay men. "I'll catch up with you later," Carleton said to their suggestion that he join them.

When he shut the door, the new group attendee was right behind him. "You're not going anywhere," he said firmly, and led her into the kitchen. Her. What a fucked-up language English was. What the hell did he know about this visitor in his home? Nothing.

Well—she had been pretty nasty to him when he gave his talk at the community college's Human Sexuality 101 class. "Aren't FTMs just butch dykes who gave up because it got too hard to be queer?" she had demanded. "Why do you think there's anything radical about claiming male privilege?"

"Tea?" he asked, pulling out a chair and moving a plate of cookies closer to her. The kitchen had big windows, and he'd painted it a soft yellow, then painted his kitchen furniture white and made delft blue cushions and place mats. "You've got a choice between Earl Grey and peppermint."

"I think I could use some caffeine," she said shakily, and picked up a peanut butter cookie.

"Baked those myself, I did," Carleton said in his best Eliza Doolittle Cockney accent. "I'll make someone a luverly wife someday."

She smiled. "I didn't know we were going camping," she quipped.

Carleton laughed a little more than the shy joke deserved. The electric kettle had the water boiling quickly, and he was soon able to bring a tray to the table with mugs of black tea, a creamer shaped like a black-and-white cow, and a beehive sugar bowl. The spoons were not alike. He collected antique silver at garage sales. It was a poor substitute for sucking dick, he reflected, but one claimed one's fag identity however one could in the Midwest.

Before picking up the tea, she faced him bravely. "I owe you an apology."

"No," he interrupted, wanting to put his guest at ease. "It's okay."

122

"No, it's not, and I can't accept your hospitality until I tell you I'm sorry for heckling you when you came to our class. I appreciated the fact that you didn't blow up at me. You spoke with a lot of dignity and courage, and after you left, I went and got every single book on that reading list you handed out. I've been so messed up, it's like I can't think my way out of all of the memories and fears that keep coming up for me. I'm really scared. I think that's why I wanted to tear into you. Looking at you, I felt—I wanted..."

Her voice trailed off into a whisper. The tears were back, and her shoulders were shaking. "What?" Carleton asked gently. He put his hand on top of her own, stroked it lightly.

"You looked so fucking happy and I wondered what it would be like to be you, to stand there without these sandbags strapped to my chest, and feel my body straight and strong and free. I wanted to know how it felt to shave my face and walk out my front door whistling. To have the guy at the gas station call me sir and not have anybody give me a second look. But how can I do that, how can I even think that?"

Carleton had a sip of his own tea to calm the pounding of his heart. How well he remembered his own version of this woman's angst. His ex-lover had not spoken to him for eight long years. Nor had he seen the twins that he'd helped her to conceive. A mutual friend sent him photos of the children and news about them. If Deborah ever found out that the woman who had broken her heart by becoming a man had even that much contact with the kids, Carleton didn't like to think about what she would do.

"There's nothing wrong with how you feel," he said. "You can't help it. You've probably always felt this way." His guest nodded, and he handed her a tissue. "What's your name, buddy?" he asked.

She hesitated. Carleton thought he knew why. "No, don't tell me your girl name," he said, just a shade impatiently.

"It's the only name I've got," she confessed in a wobbly voice. "But I hate it. I hate it so much I don't even want to say it out loud."

Carleton fortified himself with a large bite of cookie washed down with tea that was still too hot to gulp. "Well, we can fix that," he mused. "I was an only child, and I always wished I had a little brother I could climb trees with and take camping. I even had a name all picked out for him. Moss. Isn't that a funny name?"

"I like it," she whispered.

"It goes with your green eyes," he commented, then blushed. What was he doing looking so closely at her olive-skinned face and the soft shine of her black hair? "So, Moss," he said, suddenly all business. "You don't exactly like being a woman, but you're not sure you want to be a man. And there's no safe place to talk about these things. You have trouble even thinking about them in the privacy of your own mind." She nodded. "I wish I could give you a desert island where you could change into a boy and see if you liked it, and then change back if it didn't make you happier." He smiled. "But we just don't get any holidays from gender, do we?"

Moss shook his head. Carleton appraised his guest.

"Your chest isn't that big," he said. "I can show you how to tape yourself down. I think I've got my old binder around here somewhere. Want me to dress you up, little brother?"

"Sure," Moss said, throat dry. She decided to let this slight, bossy-but-kind stranger proceed. If she went home now, she might lose herself looking for the bottom of a bottle. There had been too many nights of drinking and not enough honesty. She had promised herself to stay clear-headed long enough to think this frightening conundrum through.

Carleton led him to the bedroom, stopping in the bathroom to get some tape and bandage scissors. "Off with your shirt," he said, turning his back to rummage through a plastic storage bin in the bottom of his closet. The binder was, of course, the last thing in there, all the way at the bottom. He resisted the impulse to tidy everything up and shut the closet door. He would show Moss how to do the things that he had only been able to read about in Lou Sullivan's book about how to pass as a man. Making things easier for new guys was one of the ways Carleton exorcised the pain of his own coming out process.

Moss was standing straight, arms at his side. What a cute boy he would make. "Is it okay if I call you 'he'?" Carleton asked, pulling off a strip of tape, then tearing it with his teeth. Moss's only response was a tight nod. Then Carleton set to work taping down his little brother's chest, hoping that his touch didn't intensify his new friend's shame about his body.

As if he could read Carleton's mind, Moss said, "I like the way you touch me."

"And normally you don't like being touched?" Carleton asked softly.

"That's right," Moss affirmed. The tape was unpleasantly sticky, but it was good to have those breasts removed from view. "I love breasts," he said thoughtfully, "but only on other people."

"I'm right there with you, buddy," Carleton said, and smoothed down the last strip of tape. "Is that too tight?"

"I wouldn't care if it was," Moss replied. Carleton held up a length of putty-colored elastic cloth that looked kind of like a girdle, except for the two shoulder straps. "Put this on," he instructed, sliding it up Moss's arms, "then I'll fasten the hooks and eyes up the front. You can do this yourself if you've got a mirror. But wait, I don't want you to look yet." Over the binder went a black T-shirt. Then Carleton turned Moss around to see his new silhouette.

The difference was shocking. "But nobody would think I was a boy," Moss said. "I couldn't pass. Could I?"

"Please, Mary, I can make anybody look like anything," Carleton lisped, and ran back to the bathroom. He returned with makeup sponges and a few pots of color. By carefully dabbing at Moss's cheeks and upper lip, then dotting his skin here and there, he created the impression of a five o'clock shadow. "My man, you been working out!" Carleton exclaimed, circling Moss's upper arms with his hands. "But that haircut has gotta go. No self-respecting gay boy has a mullet." Moss did not protest, so Carleton got out his electric clippers and proceeded to give his little brother a proper fag buzz cut. "Now look at you!" Carleton exclaimed, proud of his handiwork.

"Do I really look like a gay guy?"

"Yes. We could go barhopping right now."

"But what if somebody gropes me?"

"Hmmm. Do I have a spare packer?" Carleton opened the drawer of his nightstand. "It's chocolate brown," he said. "The only color they had the first time I went to the sex toy shop. I'm not a racist, but I kind of thought a white boy should have a peach-colored packer."

"I don't care," Moss said, laughing. Carleton dropped the spongy little cock with its two small balls into a women's nylon kneesock and tied a knot in it, then clipped off the excess stocking. He approached Moss, undid his jeans, and noted with approval the Y-fronts he found underneath them. "Been cross-dressing long?" he asked, tucking the small cock into the fly.

"Ever since I could buy my own underwear," Moss said seriously. He had expected to be repulsed by the dick. But it felt right having a bulge to fill out his pants. There was something else that felt even better. Carleton was close enough for Moss to smell his aftershave. A muscular, tanned arm was thrust down his shorts, and Carleton's flat chest pressed against Moss's artificially tamed torso. Moss said, "Can you move that a little to the right?" then took Carleton's face in his hands and kissed him.

Carleton almost swooned. How long had it been since a man had explored his mouth with his tongue? Moss was a good kisser, thorough without being sloppy or pushy. He wasn't sure what to do with his hand and almost withdrew it, but Moss clamped his legs together, trapping it there.

They moved toward the bed, but Moss's courage gave out when they reached the edge of the mattress, so Carleton helped his brother up and onto its surface. "Relax," he said, laying at his side, one arm across his chest. "We don't have to do anything that you don't want to do."

"Can I see your chest?" Moss asked.

Carleton hesitated, then unbuttoned his Oxford shirt and pulled it out of his pants. He doffed the T-shirt underneath it. Moss explored his scars with gentle fingers, then sucked his nipples sweetly, kissing them alive. Before Carleton could become uncomfortable with that much attention, Moss began rubbing his back, encouraging him to come close for another kiss.

They embraced with growing passion. "I love how strong you are," Moss gasped. "And I love it that I can use all my strength with you. What can we do? Can I touch you? Will you touch me?"

"Anything you want," Carleton promised. "But if I take off my pants, I better get at least a hand job. My dick is so hard it hurts."

"Sure," Moss said bravely. "Let's see your equipment."

Unzipping his khaki pants, Carleton said, "You just have to promise me that you're not going to think I'm a girl once you see me naked."

"No," Moss said, appalled at the very idea, then quietly freaked out at the idea that she—no, he—she?

he?—was affirming someone's manhood. "Carleton. You're my big brother. I know you're a man. You're the best man I've ever met. The cutest one too."

Carleton said, "Aw, shucks," and tossed what remained of his clothes off the bed. It felt weird to be the only one who was naked, but he hoped to remedy that situation soon. In the meantime, he hadn't been lying about his hard-on, which desperately wanted some of Moss's attention. The younger guy was quick to kneel at his side, then lie down between his legs to get a better view.

"Wow!" Moss said. "Hormones did all that to you?" Carleton's clit had become a ruddy appendage that looked like a small cock head. Moss experimentally put his fingers on either side of it and moved the hood/foreskin up and down. Carleton gasped. Without thinking, Moss reached down for some moisture to ease the jack-off. Carleton stiffened, then rolled over and retrieved a bottle of lubricant from the nightstand. "Use this," he directed, and Moss silently cursed himself for an insensitive fool. Of course Carleton didn't want anyone to touch his vagina.

"Oh! God!" Carleton gasped as lubricated fingers circled his sensitive dicklet. "That feels great."

"What does this lube taste like?" Moss wondered, then answered his own question by putting his mouth over Carleton's cock. The very shape and size of it warned him that he should not lick it the same way that he would lick a girl's clit. Instead, he sucked, moving his head up and down, and put one of Carleton's hands on the back of his head.

Carleton was reeling from the hot, wet, teasing

mouth. "Oh, little brother!" he exclaimed. "Where'd you learn to do that?"

"So you like the way I suck your dick?"

"I'll give you about five years to stop."

The next time Moss stroked Carleton below his dick, there was no negative response. It seemed to be okay to stroke the sensitive tissue as long as there was no penetration. "Stick your fingers up my ass," Carleton gasped. "Fuck me in the ass while you suck my fuckin' dick, man. I'm so close to coming. Please, I need it really bad."

In a trice, Moss's left hand was lubed up and working its way home. Index and middle finger found ample room for their invasion. How hard would Carleton want it? Moss settled for a slow, steady in-and-out beat that was not likely to make Carleton's ass push him out. He was rewarded with an even bigger package in his mouth and two hands on his head, holding his tongue on its rigid and yearning target.

"Oh, yeah!" Carleton yelled, and bucked into Moss's mouth, his ass contracting around his little brother's probing digits. It was a good orgasm that left Carleton feeling sleepy and drained. Moss withdrew, and they cuddled on the bed together. Carleton pillowed Moss's head on his shoulder. "You're a treasure," he said fondly. "Wish I could feel your dick up my ass."

"Next time?" Moss asked.

Carleton answered him with a kiss. When a tongue went into Moss's mouth, he decided to allow it. Normally this was where sex would end, and he would pull away to allow his overheated body to settle down. But Carleton seemed determined to keep him turned on. The kiss was so exceptional that he barely noticed Carleton unbuttoning his jeans and sliding them down over his hips.

"Lie on your belly," Carleton ordered. "I want to take you from behind."

"Say what?" Moss protested.

"Come on, little brother, let me get some of my own back. I want you. There's no stone butches in this bed, just hot dudes who need to get done." His hand slid between Moss's legs and his fingers played with the moisture and the inflamed flesh that they found there. "If you tell me you want to stop I'll know you're lying, man. Don't you want to be my pussy boy?"

Moss giggled into his folded arms. His bare ass felt cool, and Carleton's hands were practiced and delicious. His body wanted more. And for some weird reason, sucking Carleton off had not been like making love to a femme. "Just make me the same promise that I made you," he told his tutor.

"I will," Carleton said, and meant it. "I won't think you're a girl if you let me fuck you, Moss. But this is the only body you have, and it doesn't deserve to be ignored. Sex can mean whatever you want it to mean."

He was rubbing Moss's clit and using his thumb to separate the folds that guarded the entrance to his wet hole. There was plenty of hip motion to urge him forward, and Moss uttered small cries of pleasure. "Get your hands down here," Carleton urged him. "Stick your hands in your pants and jack off for your big brother. Jack off to show me how much you love to get fucked."

There was something very sexy about rubbing his clit with his hand behind the packer. Moss could lose himself, if only for a few minutes, in the fantasy of jacking off his own cock. Then Carleton was inside of him, filling him up, and it felt absolutely right. "Give me more," Moss snarled, and fucked himself on Carleton's sure and steady hand. "Oh, God, you're so good, it's so hot, please don't stop. Don't stop! Don't stop!"

Carleton was happy to oblige. He fucked Moss until "little brother" came with his own frantic finger agitating his slit. "You're doing good," he encouraged, and kept on going. "Do it for me again. I know you've got more than one shot in you. Come again for your big brother. Let me see how much you want me inside of you. Oh, God, Moss, I love fucking you. I don't think I'm ever going to be able to stop."

But eventually he had to, because Moss begged for a break. By then Carleton's cock was up again, and he quickly got Moss busy at his crotch. "See what you do to me?" Carleton hissed. "I'm going to come in your mouth, boy. Fill that sweet sexy mouth of yours up with my come. Do you want it? Do you want my come?"

When Moss made a garbled noise of assent, Carleton grabbed him by the ears and fucked his face. "Suck harder," he ordered, and Moss's obedient mouth gave him just the right amount of pressure to tip Carleton over the edge and into a hot rush of very satisfying pleasure.

Finished, they spooned one another, both needing to pee and reluctant to get up to do so. Carleton experienced the usual quiet melancholy he felt after sex. It was good to come, good to be touched by someone who understood that you could be a guy and still have girl parts, but this intimate act reminded him again that his body was not perfectly and entirely male.

"Are you okay?" he asked, and kissed the top of Moss's head.

"Mmmm. Dreamy," Moss replied. "I feel so amazing. I don't want to stop."

"You don't have to," Carleton told him. "You're not a bad person. It's okay to be a tranny."

"Is that what I am?" Moss wondered. "Or am I just a butch dyke who likes to dress up and pretend to be a boy?"

"What's the difference?" Carleton asked. "You could sum both of those identities up as forms of atypical gender expression. Oh, hell, why am I lecturing you, of all people?"

"I don't think I want to take testosterone," Moss said, and withdrew from him. He padded off to the bathroom.

Not yet, anyway, Carleton thought, putting on pajama pants and a light cotton robe. As he passed the bathroom, he heard the sound of Moss pulling off the tape, returning his chest to its usual configuration. Carleton put a TV dinner in the microwave and punched in the numbers to heat it up.

When Moss came into the kitchen, he was fully dressed. He had washed the faux-beard off his face. But he came up to Carleton and gave him a loving hug, a grin, and a smooch. "Thank you for going out on a limb for me," Moss said.

"Are you hungry? I can nuke you another TV dinner," Carleton offered.

"No. I have to get home."

They said their good-byes as the microwave beeped for Carleton's Hungry Man fried chicken, and he let Moss out the front door. Before he carried his food out to the TV tray so he could watch his favorite home decorating show, he checked out the bedroom.

Moss had tidied up, putting Carleton's used clothing on the bedroom armchair. But the binder was gone.

"Good for you," Carleton said to his vanished friend, and went back to his meal.

Learning the Alphabet

Like many stories about the lust of one man for another, this one begins with a predatory older man in leather stalking a younger man who is ignorant of his destiny. But the two men this story concerns were not in a leather bar, nor were they headed for a bondage fête. These were streets that most natives of New York City did not brave. It was 1971 in Alphabet City, the Lower East Side of Manhattan.

From the sidewalk, it wasn't always easy to tell that this was a place where pizza deliveries and house calls from the cops didn't happen. The streets were silent, no children playing and very few cars. The occasional corner store had large bald patches on its shelves. From time to time, there was a more dramatic reminder of the area's evil reputation—an entire row of elegant brownstones with panels of plywood nailed over the broken windows and doors; a single house that had literally exploded, and then simply been left in that condition, with blocks of stone and plaster shrapnel scattered in the street.

Who was more dangerous here? Ulric wondered. The brown-skinned people, the drug dealers, the other criminals, the punks, the young and angry queers, the artists, the junkies, or the junkies who were also artists? It was, he thought, the kind of neighborhood where housing projects looked well kept. He ought to know: he was looking at one right now. Some architect on the city's payroll had indulged in a Spanish Civil War–era Cubist fantasy. The brightly-colored assortment of severe, square and rectangular shapes had no relationship to the older, more ornate 1890s buildings around them.

This housing project was surrounded by several feet of what could have been a lawn if grass had not been permanently discouraged by garbage, children running wild, and the occasional junked car. A tall wrought iron fence topped with razor wire surrounded the compound. But the residents had broken bars off to make a gap wide enough for two men to walk side by side. There was already an official gate, of course, but this was something the inhabitants had made: a rebellion against the fence, which might have been erected for their protection, but looked and felt like something built to keep them penned. What would it be like to be a young boy here, to grow up behind bars and know that you had a ninety-percent chance of being put in an even worse cage when you became a man?

Ulric's people had been tall and muscular. He was less heavyset than his mother's brother and most of his peers. He had been changed when he had barely attained manhood, his body not yet thickened with the muscle of middle age. But on these streets, he had nothing to fear. In hand-to-hand combat, he was strong and fast enough to take on a group of fighters, and a knife or a bullet would not kill him. He had demonstrated all of these facts when various desperate men and one crazed woman had tried to rob him, rape him, or just chase him out of the neighborhood.

Now he was a part of it, as unwelcome as arson or a methamphetamine lab; like them, as unchangeable as bad weather. There was even a bodega where the resident santero sold a charm against him: a miniature of Ochosi the Hunter's bow and arrow, fashioned in pewter. But the arrow had two points, like the fangs of a snake. The charm appeared to work because only the Spanish-speaking people knew about it, and Ulric did not like to take victims who were already being fucked over. Good Catholics and devotees of Santeria alike could frequently be found with the amulet around their necks.

The black men who strolled these streets with feral grace were unbearably handsome, and Ulric would have lived in this neighborhood just to watch them, even if he had to hunt elsewhere. He loved to linger in the shadows and listen to the cadence of Cuban or Puerto Rican Spanish. Perhaps he could have fed elsewhere and then used his erection with a man whose features showed the Native American contributions to his bloodline. But his self-control usually vanished in the presence of an open vein; Ulric fucked the same men that he killed.

When night fell, winter or summer, Ulric hit the

streets dressed in black leather, wearing his unfashion-ably long hair in loose curls around his shoulders. He had big gold earrings and daggers in his jacket and boots and mouth, and he was driven by a hunger as inescapable as Alphabet City's poverty and madness. On this particular evening, he had followed someone to the housing project. Someone who was as white as he was. A young man who had listened to Lou Reed and the Velvet Underground with a little too much high school fervency. Cannon was trying to score. He had his short black hair up in spikes and wore black eyeliner. His T-shirt and jeans were black, and he wore boots much like Ulric's own. But he had no leather jacket. The jacket had been traded for the cash that he hoped to trade for heroin. A lot of heroin. This young man intended to kill himself tonight, and he wanted to go out banging.

Ulric had seen Cannon before. He kept idle track of the young white people who scrabbled for drug money and squatted in various abandoned buildings. He had even sampled some of the drugs that they prized so highly, hoping that one of them might quiet the fire in his veins that forced him to hunt and feed each night. Alas, the same body that made him virtu-ally immortal also identified and nullified the drugs, just as it would ruthlessly and completely eliminate a viral infection or heal a cut that had gone to his bone. He knew that Cannon had a girlfriend. She had died yesterday, doing too much of a score that Cannon had warned her was way stronger than the usual stuff. Cannon must have loved her very much to give up his leather jacket, let alone his life, for her.

But if that was so, why did Cannon make so much money in Times Square? It was an odd job for a heterosexual. Jackie and Cannon were there almost every day, looking like twins. The girlfriend was a pickpocket, and she occasionally persuaded a motherly tourist to give her "bus money" home to New Jersey or Kansas. (The more gullible the tourist, the more distant her fictional destination.) But Cannon was a hustler. He went into porn shops, bars, hotel rooms, and cars and came out with enough cash to keep living fast and loose. Was he fast and loose? That was what Ulric wanted to know. Because he preferred it slow and tight.

Cannon's grief had fucked up his usual street smarts. He was about to let himself be led into one of the buildings. There, Ulric knew, he would be relieved of his cash and given a beating that would only make him wish he was dead. Like a sinister night watchman, Ulric came along, gently touching the minds of those who saw him, bidding them forget and go elsewhere. No sentinel gave the alarm when he slid behind Cannon and the three men who were conning him. Ulric didn't judge them for trying to get paid without handing over the merchandise. Selling the same stuff twice meant twice the profits. But he had a prior claim on their patsy. Like the wolf that he became when using a human form was not to his advantage, Ulric's territorial instincts were strong.

The five of them went up the stairs. Ulric stepped ahead and held the apartment door open for everyone. As he quietly shut the door—a polite and literally invisible butler—one of the dealers grabbed Cannon from behind and pinned his arms. A second man began to go through his pockets. Ulric sent the third member of the conspiracy into the bedroom to retrieve all of their stash.

It was more than enough heroin to keep an entire squat of gutter punks high for a week. "I'll be taking that," Ulric said, slinging the strap of the camera bag over his shoulder. "And this," he said, taking Cannon away from his assailants.

The young man barely had time to register his anger at the assault or his surprise at being rescued before the two of them were back on the street and walking briskly away from the housing project. The three burly black men who had tried to jack him up were sound asleep on the floor of the apartment. Ulric was irritable from the effort it had taken to remove the incident from their minds. He hated the greasy feel of other people's personalities and memories. So he was in no mood to play nice when Cannon slipped out of his embrace and bolted.

COME HERE.

Ulric usually would have retrieved his victim physically, but he was still in the mode of exerting mental control. The thought he threw at Cannon stopped the grief-stricken punk in his tracks. But he fought against its compulsion, his invisible being thrashing like a hooked shark, and Ulric was impressed by his strength. NOW! he insisted. Cannon came toward him as if he were swimming through newly poured, wet and sludgy concrete. Ulric took a firm grip on his hair and towed him along to the punk's most recent lair.

"I'm going to do you where you live, man," he told

Cannon, shaking his head, deliberately hurting and provoking him. "I'm going to fuck you on the same bed where your chick bought it."

"No, you're not," Cannon blustered, ego-wounded by the awkward, bent-over posture Ulric had imposed on him as much as by the pain in his scalp. "I'll shiv you. You'll be the one who buys it." He tried to punch Ulric and failed, his fists flailing. "Let me go!" he cried, and was humiliated by the childish and querulous sound of his own voice.

"Okay," Ulric said, and released him. Cannon shot off to his left, crossing the street diagonally. Luckily there was little traffic; Cannon had not looked both ways before leaping off the curb.

CRAWL TO MY HAND AND KISS IT.

This time, Ulric threw more of his strength into the call. When Cannon struggled to him on filthy, bruised knees and put his lips to his hand, Ulric felt all of his victim's outrage and astonishment. And something else. Arousal. Unlike Jackie, Ulric knew that Cannon did a lot more for his tricks than let them suck his dick. That arrogant rock star mouth was almost as sweet as his dimpled bum promised to be.

"Shall I make you crawl the rest of the way?" Ulric asked.

"No," Cannon said. He stood up cautiously and brushed off his black jeans. "I'll come with you on my own two feet."

"Then run," Ulric said, and shoved him in the direction of his squat. "Run! If you can beat me there, I will let you go."

Cannon wanted to run away, but he didn't want

to play this game with Ulric. He didn't want to make any move that could be mistaken for a desire to go on living. If Ulric was his executioner, he would accept that, he told himself, stubbornly clenching his jaw and planting his feet. It was what he had gone looking for after he sold his jacket: a death that would carry him to the place where Jackie waited. So let this crazy man kill him here, without any demeaning games.

Then Ulric spun him around and forced his chosen prey to stare at his naked hunger. He hissed at Cannon, and there was nothing human in that sound, or in the red-eyed and fanged visage that seemed lit from within by a green, unhealthy phosphorescence. Ulric was all teeth and claws, a hunter as primitive and vigorous as a bear or an eagle. Nothing as clean and quick as a bullet was waiting for Cannon. "What the fuck are you, man?" the junkie sputtered. Then he was cutting pavement with his booted feet, running so fast it looked like he expected to launch himself into the air and fly.

Ulric strolled after him, speeding up only enough to keep him in sight. When Cannon was close to the appropriate alley, he wrapped himself in ebony magic and slid by him, worming his way between a Dumpster and a wall of uncollected garbage bags to reach the piece of plywood the punks had wiggled loose from the back door of a brownstone. He waited until Cannon could see him, then ripped the plywood off the building and threw it over the young man's head. It went over the fence, over the yard next door, and was still flying with enough force to break windows when it hit the third building down.

"You lose," he told Cannon and dragged him into the fetid darkness. The floor at their feet came to life, rustled over their boots as a mob of squealing rats fled the derelict building. Anyone watching from the street would have seen a storm cloud of pigeons ascend from the roof. Only the insects remained, their patience in inverse proportion to their short lives.

Cannon and Jackie had dragged their salvaged mattress up a flight of stairs and shoved it under the windows that faced the street. The stairs were littered with the empty wine bottles that Cannon normally arranged behind them, booby-trapping the stairs so he and his lover would know if anyone tried to sneak up on them. The bed was relatively clean and covered with layers of rich-colored fabric, the red, brown, and orange paisley Indian prints that Jackie loved. There were two sofa pillows to prop them up when they wanted to sit up to fix, and a bunch of other large pillows strewn across the room to make extra seating for a party. Jackie had done some artwork on the walls, murals of women in bondage and men with guns, overlaid by unsettling mosaics made of eyes and teeth cut out of magazines. She had even set up a small kitchen with milk crates, a Coleman stove and metal picnic plates and cups.

But the hunger in Ulric left him with little sympathy for this shattered domesticity. He picked the young man up and threw him onto the bed. "Stay put," he warned him, and took a cigarette lighter out of his pocket. Guided by his night vision, he moved around the makeshift loft, lighting candles. When he turned back to the bed, Cannon was sitting there cross-legged, watching him warily. The candle flames were repeated in miniature upon the punk's enlarged pupils. Before Ulric took his place beside him, he found the breakfast tray where Cannon and Jackie stashed their spoons, an alcohol lamp, a box of cotton balls, vials of sterile water, strips of rubber tubing, and syringes.

"What are you doing?" Cannon asked stupidly as Ulric lit the lamp, unfolded one of the paper packets of dope, and dumped a generous amount of it into a spoon along with a squirt of sterile water.

"Cooking your first shot," Ulric said, gently agitating the spoon so the powder would dissolve in the bubbling water. "Pull off a cotton," he ordered, handing him a new marshmallow-shaped wad of the stuff. Behind him, Cannon silently twirled off a tight bit of cotton. When he leaned forward to drop it in the spoon, Ulric caught his scent, hauntingly masculine and tragically mortal. Cannon was so full of grief and blood and lost chances.

"Are you going to get high before you kill me?" Cannon asked quietly.

"I can't get high," Ulric said shortly, annoyed with him. "Pump your arm up and tie off."

The hustler moved with alacrity. Suicide could wait until the rush was over, apparently. In less than a minute he was prepped, swabbing above and below the crook of his elbow with an alcohol wipe. He and Jackie had done this right; they often made contemptuous comments about the stupid junkies who gave themselves tracks and abscesses. The only people they shared needles with were each other. Ulric thought briefly about adding a little of his own blood to Cannon's hit, but there was no reason to prolong his suffering. Cannon had doomed himself. Sooner or later, the meat grinder of the street would turn him into hamburger. No sense in wasting the salty liquor that surged through his veins and made his heart plump.

Still, he would show Cannon this brief mercy, his favorite anodyne. Taking the young man's arm across his knee, he deftly tapped into a vein and pushed the junk home. Cannon gasped as the warm joyous surge of smack went up the back of his neck and out the top of his head. "That's good shit," he said inanely, and didn't fight Ulric when the vampire slid his arm around him and helped him to lie back.

While Cannon's muscles went slack with bliss, Ulric began to kiss him. He also unbuttoned his shirt. Cannon's skin was as pale as Hollywood's version of a vampire. *China White,* Ulric thought, and brushed his nipples. Cannon's body responded to Ulric's hands and to the mental suggestions he sent him. The rush lasted longer than he had any right to expect, and was tinged with eroticism that quickly became urgent. This was different than getting done by a furtive married salesman or a slumming executive who was committed to the corporate closet. Ulric wanted him with a pagan strength that had never been contaminated with homophobia. Chicks didn't touch Cannon this way either. Ulric wanted his whole body, and he wanted to fuck him, not be fucked.

Gutting Cannon's inhibitions, Ulric soon had his delicious victim completely undressed. Cannon was well named. His cock was unusually thick, and his sac was heavy, bulging with two big balls. Getting a hard-on when he was high was normally hit or miss for Cannon, but Ulric used his own hand and mouth to good effect, and soon the punk's cock was jutting into the air, bold and stiff as a foot-high mohawk. The vampire detected in Cannon a tendril of fear about having his cock bitten and made it dissolve and fade away. Then Cannon simply doted on having Ulric suck his dick. The immortal savored the taste of Cannon's first gift of pre-come, one more sign of his surrender to Ulric's spell of erotic ecstasy. He came off Cannon's cock and forced the boy to kiss him, let him taste his own dick drool on Ulric's tongue. He also let Cannon's tongue probe his fangs, and he allowed the young man to keep some of the fear and adrenaline that flooded him. Fear would subtly change the flavor of his blood, make it zing in Ulric's mouth and body.

"Now it's my turn," Ulric said, and undid the snaps at the crotch of his leather pants. His own cock was limp, and would stay that way until he tapped the boy.

"I don't suck dick," Cannon said, laying back with his arms over his head. The tufts of black hair in his armpits were an invitation to chew on him. He put one hand around his hard cock and pointed it at Ulric. "Do me some more, man. Come on. You know you like it."

Ulric shook his head. "Don't give yourself airs," he said, and slapped Cannon hard. If his head had not already been cushioned by a pillow, his neck would have snapped back. When Cannon opened his mouth to curse at him, Ulric slapped him again. The punk's lower lip bled, and Ulric gathered him up and licked it avidly. Cannon struggled, but could not escape, and once more he was reminded that Ulric's strength exceeded his own. "You taste better than apple brandy or mead," Ulric hissed, and threw Cannon back down on the bed.

Once more he went to the alcohol lamp and spoon. Cannon was soon at his elbow, fascinated by the process of preparing a shot. Ulric laughed at him. "Do you want this?" he asked, showing Cannon the loaded needle.

"Yes," Cannon said. "You know I do."

"Then suck my dick," Ulric replied.

As Cannon quickly bent, thinking to service him, Ulric caught him by the throat, drew him into a crushing embrace, and bit his throat. The hunt had been maddening, hours of foreplay, invisible cock-and-ball torture. As Cannon's blood fled down his throat, Ulric's cock began to fill out and come to the party. "I wouldn't want to stuff a piece of limp meat into your mouth," Ulric said, and put Cannon down on his dick, hand on the back of his neck.

Dizzy from being bitten, seduced by Ulric's psychic power, Cannon found an odd desire in himself to give this stranger a hell of a blowjob. Cocky fucker. Let him see what it felt like to be driven out of your mind. If he could make Ulric lose control, or make Ulric want him or like him, might he be able to escape? Ulric smelled so good and his cock felt so right in Cannon's mouth that he didn't even think about the irony of his strategy. What was he going to escape to—death by his own hand? Hadn't that been the plan just a few hours ago?

The lanky, long-haired stranger's cock was a forbidden savory. Ulric hovered in Cannon's mind, observing him without altering his response. The other man was a good cocksucker. His attitude toward Ulric's hard dick was worshipful. His mouth melted over it, bathing it in hot saliva. He sucked slowly, built pressure bit by bit, coaxing every possible type of sensation out of Ulric's cock head and shaft. With one hand, he guided the cock down his throat, where there was no perceptible resistance, and with the other he fondled Ulric's ballsac, stretching his nuts just enough to make Ulric gasp and thrust more deeply into his mouth. *Why would someone who loved dick this much pretend to be a piece of straight trade?* Ulric mused, then said out loud, "You love doing this, don't you, Cannon?"

The punk shook his head, laughing at himself, rolling his eyes in protest. Ulric got the mental image of a girl in the backseat of a car, holding her panties in one hand and covering her pussy with the other. "Please don't fuck me," she said. Ulric smiled involuntarily then came back to the business at hand. He shifted his position so that he could reach Cannon's cock. He grasped it just below the head and ran his thumb over it, smearing pre-come all over the sensitive, spongy mushroom. Cannon tried to fuck his hand, but Ulric only tightened his grip and moved his thumb to the junction of nerves below the cock head, on the bottom side of Cannon's cock. The suction on Ulric's dick became more intense and sustained, and Cannon moved his head back and forth, giving Ulric permission to fuck his face. That required Ulric to stop teasing the bright red tip of Cannon's sex and grab him by the ears instead. The rougher Ulric got with the kid, the harder both of their cocks became.

But if he was going to come, he needed more of Cannon's blood. Ulric was floating in the midst of a familiar dilemma. Bloodlust and the keen desire to put Cannon on his back and pierce his butthole were at war. Most gay men tortured themselves by prolonging sex as long as possible without coming, and ran the risk of not being able to get off at all if they delayed orgasm too frequently. Ulric was resisting the need to drain every drop of Cannon's blood, absorb every bit of the vital energy that animated him, and feel the explosion of satiation that would only come when Cannon's heart stopped drumming. Could he stave off the need to kill long enough to come? Fucking dead boys didn't usually work. He needed to see their faces reacting to the gut punch of his big dick.

Ulric pushed Cannon off his cock and sat him up, wrapped the tourniquet around his arm and told him to yank it snug. "Now for your reward," he said, sending Cannon pacifying and soothing thoughts. The heroin went home once more, and Cannon slumped, eyes rolling wildly. For a moment, Ulric was afraid he had overdosed the kid, but no. Cannon was just getting into the intense feelings of liberation and fear-lessness. The rules that governed proper conversation, sober sex, no longer applied. He had no inhibitions now, and grabbed Ulric's face to kiss him. "I think I fucking love you, man," he said, licking Ulric's sharp left fang. "Good smack, a big mean dick, what else do I need? I want you. I do. I want you so much, I...can't tell you."

"Shut up," Ulric said fondly, and flattened Cannon on the squalid bed. He loosened and removed his own clothing, wanting to feel Cannon's hands on his naked back and buttocks. He stretched out on top of him and returned his kisses with fervor. Their hard cocks nudged one another like blunt spears, but only Cannon's leaked. Ulric's body was stingy with its fluids. He would come without ejaculating just as he could not shed tears when he wept after a poignant kill.

"I wish you could get high with me," Cannon whispered. "Do you know this is the first time I've ever done this? Had a man in my bed with no money on the nightstand. No agenda. Free to do whatever I wanted with him." He had apparently forgotten who was the boss. But Ulric didn't need to remind him just yet.

Mouth-to-mouth kissing turned to nuzzling one another's necks and chests. Ulric opened the other side of Cannon's throat. Cannon's hair gel crackled against the palm of his hand as he manipulated the position of his head. "I am high," he confessed, and opened his mind to the boy beneath him. Cannon's eyes widened as he was hit with wave after wave of pleasure that made the best sex and the best dope he had ever taken seem as bland as banana pudding. "This is my drug," Ulric said, and lifted his head, showed his victim his bloody muzzle. He kissed Cannon without licking his teeth clean, made the boy taste his own blood.

Cannon began to shake and his heels beat out a rapid tattoo on the mattress. Ulric went into his mind and body, trying to return everything to equilibrium. But Cannon hung on to the link between them, fought against its closing with more raw power than he had shown when he tried to physically resist being kidnapped, raped, and killed. "Don't take it away," he sobbed. "Please, man, don't take it away. I'm a junkie and I can't live without this. I can't. Don't you understand? It makes everything okay. No fear, no doubt, no anger, no shame, just…scarlet redemption."

"Don't worry, you won't have to live without it," Ulric said. He licked Cannon's nipples while he groped along the side of the mattress for the tube of lubricant they used when Cannon screwed Jackie in the ass. He found a battery-operated vibrator before he got the tube of K-Y and wondered who it had fucked last, the boy or the girl of this strung-out couple. Cannon's mind still clawed at him, demanding admission. He begrudgingly sent him a trickle of his own need and gratification. The boy calmed down, but he began to chant, "Fuck me, fuck me, fuck me" in a low, dirty voice that Ulric was pretty sure no client had ever heard.

"If you want to be fucked, lift those legs and spread 'em," Ulric ordered. "Come on. Let me see that fuzzy dimpled butt of yours open. Oh, yes. Make that asshole wink at me, Cannon."

His cock was as hard as a living partner could make it. Why not just fuck Cannon dry? Why was it okay to kill him, but not okay to hurt him unnecessarily? Ulric smiled at himself and briskly lubricated his cock. The feel of lubricant sliding around inside of Cannon would mimic ejaculation. He would miss the feeling of shooting just a little bit less.

It wasn't exactly easy to get into Cannon, but the coppery smell of his blood and the boy's glazed and happy eyes made the slow insertion worthwhile. Ulric's hunting instinct was clamoring at him to strike and take everything now, now, now! But he teased himself and the boy beneath him by gradually working the fat head of his cock past a sphincter that wanted to be violated and did not have quite enough experience to gape open at will. The vampire amped up their rapport, and all of Cannon's resistance fled. Ulric slid into him and gasped at the sensation of being surrounded by smooth, swollen, and vulnerable flesh. Cannon's hands dug into his shoulders and the punk threw his feet around Ulric's waist, drawing him in even deeper. "If I could I'd get your fuckin' balls in me," Cannon said, eye to eye with his killer. "You got me, dude, you got me where I live. Oh, God, fuck me blind and stupid."

Ulric would have been doing exactly that even if Cannon had not requested it. He brought one of Cannon's hands down to his crotch and encouraged him to stroke his own cock in time to Ulric's hips. Together they drove Cannon to a place where everything that was sweetest and happiest about him was distilled. Ulric drank in his existence, then tilted Cannon's head back and raped his carotid artery. The other bites had struck only veins. This strike was different. The blood spurted as if Cannon could not give it up to Ulric fast enough. It was too much to swallow, yet he took it all in. Ulric felt as if the tissues in his mouth and throat were sponges, absorbing blood at a rapid rate, just as his soul was being assailed and enriched by Cannon's unraveling aura.

In exchange for this bounty, he drove his cock into Cannon with a calculated savagery that kept him on the edge of coming for so long that the spike-haired boy bit his tongue. Ulric told him he was a cunt, slapped him, and ordered him to shoot. He got what he wanted, and a wealth of tasty sobs as well. The white blood was thick between them, and the smell of Cannon's come was so enticing that Ulric came without warning, shaking and shouting as the weird sensation of an orgasm without ejaculation possessed him.

"Never been this good before, never, never," Cannon raved. "Kill me now. I'm ready to go. Please. Please. Kill me now."

Ulric's psychic connection to Cannon slammed shut. He was suddenly imprisoned in his own body, no longer awash in shared sensations, the mingled thrill of being fucked and screwing Cannon's near-virginal ass. It was harsh to feel his loneliness restored so suddenly. It pissed him off so much that he very nearly administered the killing blow to Cannon's heart. But his own heart wasn't in it, and he quickly realized that something very strange had happened. He was replete, full to the brim, and the drive to hunt no longer raved in every cell of his body. He could seek a new hiding place, allow dawn to send him to sleep, and stay quiet till night fell again and the drama must begin once more.

"No," he said, rolling off of Cannon. "I don't

believe I will." He reached for his leather pants and hoisted them on, shrugged on the T-shirt. He was trying to stuff his feet into boots without bothering with his socks when Cannon came after him, clawing at him like an angry girl who wanted to scratch his face and pull his hair. Ulric stopped him with the palm of his hand against his face and shoved him down to the bed. "Stop it," he said sharply, and got his boots on.

"You're going to leave me like this?" Cannon demanded. "You promised to *kill* me, man!"

"So you've got a reprieve!" Ulric shouted.

"But now that I know—now that I've seen it, felt it—if you won't kill me, make me like you! Let me be that way, have those feelings, I *have* to be like you."

"Not in a million years," Ulric said. "This is my hunting ground. I can't share it, and I won't give it up to a novice. I never wanted to be this way, Cannon, and I won't spawn any miserable descendants."

"What have I got to live for if you won't help me?"

"I picked you out because you wanted to die! If you were going to be dead by morning anyway, where was the harm in me taking what I need from you? At least I could offer you a happy death. But you were just too good, Cannon. So blame that tight little butt of yours. I got what I needed from you without killing you. If you want to die you will have to do it yourself." He picked up the plastic bag full of smack and tossed it onto Cannon's naked stomach. "Here. It's all yours."

"And it's shit!" Cannon stood up, taking care to keep beyond Ulric's reach. "I can't do that garbage anymore. It's nothing compared to what you've got."

When Ulric got to the top of the stairs, Cannon was also there on his knees, grabbing at his hand. Who knew a mortal could move so fast? "Please," Cannon said. "I am begging you. I'll go someplace else. You'll never see me again."

Ulric stopped and extricated his fingers from Cannon's grasp. Dawn was uncomfortably close, and he had to force himself to be patient. "Are you really prepared to feel everything that I do, Cannon?" The punk rocker recoiled from his bleak face, but Ulric held him fast in the talons of his mind and opened his heart. It was a cruel thing to do to a being who would not be able to contain vampiric emotions. Because what Ulric felt once his bloodlust was slaked was utter stark loneliness. Living forever meant that his only companion was an avalanche of boredom that buried him alive.

Cannon screamed and clawed at his own face. Ulric grabbed both of his wrists before he could blind himself and slammed him into the nearest wall. "We all *suffer*," he said through clenched teeth, making a mockery of his own and Cannon's pain. "But you got a second chance. You can choose to be grateful or you can let yourself get trampled to death by horse. I don't care which."

Then he was gone, and Cannon could not have said how he left.

Was he lucky? He felt like the unluckiest man in Man-hattan. Dizzy and sick to his stomach, Cannon curled up in the dark around the baggie of dope and cried himself to sleep. He woke up after a few hours of fevered sleep and realized it wasn't possible to heal on his own from losing that much blood. So he put his clothes on, went down the stairs for the last time, and began a long, slow walk to the hospital. Street by street. A, B, C. First, Second, Third. Relearning the alphabet, how to count; taken back to the barren basics.

The Only One Who Can Save Her

"I am the only one who can save her!" That single insistent phrase kept repeating itself in his mind until he thought he would weep. It urged him to act, to take up arms if necessary, to do something, *anything*. But there was nothing he could do. Not yet. Not yet. He had to watch, he had to be alert, be observant, continue the surveillance, gather more information, be sure, make a plan, make absolutely certain of every detail. Because when the time came to dig deep within himself and release the hero who would take her to safety or die trying, the operation would have to go like clockwork. One event would have to follow another with military precision. His head hurt, and the corner of his lip was bleeding again. His hands were chapped and cracked with the cold. Every part of him was numb except his scalp, which itched beneath the oily weight of his hair. He made an impatient move to push the hair out of his eyes, but kept his fingers from making contact at the last moment. Touching himself was a sickening experience.

But there it was again, like a fire alarm or an air raid siren. "I am the only one who can save her!" And this time he must have spoken it out loud, because a passerby gave him a judicious look and crossed the street.

The watcher yanked his head away from the cowardly pedestrian—*just one of the milling herd of gentile sheep, his kind wouldn't be any use at all when the battle of Gog and Magog began in earnest, when the thousand years of peace rolled up like a treaty with the Indians*—and focused his hungry, eager gaze on the lit squares of window, three stories above the street, where she was held, caught, trapped like a fly in a hideous and evil web.

He stamped his feet, and not to keep them warm. No, he was dancing impatiently to his one-line tune. The rain had pasted his simple blue suit and white shirt to his torso and thighs. Hoping for shelter, he had tucked himself under a big crepe myrtle whose roots had buckled the sidewalk and crumbled the edge of the curb. *Thick, relentless, blind roots. Crawling through the darkness, penetrating the soil, like worms moving in grotesquely slow motion.* But the rain seemed determined to dodge through the whispering leaves and find his aching flesh. Did he have a fever? The knot in his red-and-blue-striped tie had gotten tighter since it got wet, and now it felt like a noose around his neck. But he could not bear to take his attention away from the yellow glass, which seemed as remote as an angel or the smell of his mother's Sunday pot roast. He might miss something. Some vital piece of information, some signal—oh, how wondrous that would be—from her.

"I am the only one who can save her!" *Yes, me, the failure, the faithless one. But haven't I kept my vigil here, Lord, haven't I kept it without a murmur for six long weeks? Empty, sterile, hard, and hopeless weeks. And never a word from you, Heavenly Father, never a ray of hope or a glimmer of insight about how I am going to overpower him and release her from bondage to his satanic will.*

But that should be no surprise. Those long months spent knocking on doors here in the devil's headquarters, knocking and knocking, always being polite and soft-spoken no matter how many times he was laughed at or cursed or people just pretended they weren't home. And never a word from the great *I Am* to comfort a homesick boy who really should have been sent to South America or someplace else where the vineyards of the Lord were ripe for the harvest. Not this salted plain of a city where nobody wanted to hear about Joseph Smith or the golden plates that were a new testament of Jesus Christ in the Americas.

Perhaps he should have been more patient and simply waited until he could go home, like his mission companion, Elder Swenson. Curtis Swenson, the wiseass. Didn't even have the decency to get angry when people set their dogs on them or came to the door blowing marijuana smoke in their faces. Life was just a series of jokes to that buffoon. At the end of nine months, they had not baptized one single convert. When they took their woes to the mission president, he warned them that the Big Easy was a tough nut to crack. The next day, Swenson had shown up with a handful of peanuts in his suit coat. All day long, he kept cracking one after another open and offering them to his surly companion, Lehi Farmington. "I'm telling you, we gotta practice," he quipped. That beatific farmboy smile underneath Swenson's thick, black glasses put Lehi in a rage.

Funny. He had not thought of his real name, his family name, for weeks. He was just "the watcher" now. He moved to a spot under the tree that looked a little drier, but a branch overhead suddenly dipped, and half a cup of cold water went down his back. Taken unawares, he swore like a jack Mormon, someone born to a Latterday Saint family who didn't practice the religion. The profane words rapidly led him back to the past again, when he had nearly lost his faith. He had decided he was going to ask to be released from his mission calling and sent home. It would be a permanent disgrace. His family would be hurt and appalled. Perhaps this was why Elder Swenson had been able to successfully persuade him to stick it out just one more day. They had gone without dinner and knelt by their beds all night long, praying. They had continued to fast into the morning. As if food was the thing that Lehi had to give up in order to deserve a blessing from the Holy Spirit. And, of course, that was the day he had seen her.

The two missionaries had tried canvassing a poor, black Creole neighborhood, where Swenson's bad high school French might get them past a front door or two. But it didn't work. Lehi had let Curtis steer him limply from one debacle to another. He couldn't even be angry anymore. He was just bored and indifferent to it all. Too tired of being hurt to give a shit about the lack of enthusiasm for their arrival on yet another staunchly Catholic family's front steps. The sun was going down, but Swenson wanted to keep on going.

"The Lord will show us a sign today, I'm sure of it," Swenson said earnestly, looking at Lehi with so much sympathy and pity that he couldn't stand it. He just walked away. Curtis began to follow him, calling his name, so he hailed a cab and got in. Cabs were all over this city like roaches. "Where to?" the driver said. Lehi gave the driver their home address even though he had no desire to return to the cramped studio apartment he and Curtis shared that was even more uncomfortable than most bachelors' digs. Then it occurred to him that Curtis would find him there sooner or later. He didn't want to talk about this one more time, or get down on his knees for yet another prayer that left him feeling lonely and afraid. Whether his eyes were shut or open, he kept seeing Curtis's naked body in the shower. Fasting was not going to make that go away. So he asked to be taken to the French Quarter instead. The driver let him out in the middle of a crowd of people who were going to a popular jazz club.

She had stepped out of the backseat of a long, sleek, expensive-looking car. A man with a white-blond crew cut, wearing a white linen suit and a broad Panama hat, was carefully handing a woman with long, bright auburn hair out of the limousine. He had a walking stick tucked under his left arm. It appeared as if he thought the woman was the only thing that mattered in the whole world. It had seemed like love, but Lehi knew now that it was simply the proprietary attitude a lion will display when it falls asleep on the carcass of an antelope. When the woman came out into the streetlamp's light, Lehi couldn't help but stare. She was wearing a skimpy, full-skirted white dress that looked like a petticoat. The lace was practically transparent. The dress was so low cut, he could see her breasts, as round and white as those of a broken Greek statue of Aphrodite's nude torso.

Lehi was suddenly exhausted and dizzy from hunger. To his dismay, he found himself slipping, stumbling as if he might faint. Instantly, the woman's escort was between them, and the ferrule of the walking stick was in the hollow of the missionary's throat. The man—the thing that appeared to be a man—had opened his mouth and snarled at him. The teeth he displayed were inhuman, those long, sharp fangs not shaped for a human jaw. The disheartened missionary had the impression of a wolf's golden eyes, the fur of its muzzle in little points, stiff with dried blood. Thinking about it, even tonight, gave the watcher a new set of goose bumps that had nothing to do with the foul weather. Frightened by his defensive display, the beautiful prisoner had grabbed her escort's arm, and a bold evening wind had lifted a lock of her red-gold hair. Lehi saw what those viper's teeth had done to the white column of her frail throat. A voice had roared inside his head, DO NOT TOUCH HER.

It was the voice of a fallen angel. One of the lieutenants of the army of the damned. As he slipped and fell into the gutter, Lehi knew it. He knew that this was why God had sent him to New Orleans, to find that thing, track it to its lair, and slay it. And save her, if she had not already yielded to temptation and joined him in evil. The flesh was so terribly weak. Lehi felt a pang of grief for this. Of course, free agency, the capacity to do evil as well as good, was a vital part of God's plan for us. Without the possibility of sin, there can be no such thing as virtue. But surely the odds were stacked unreasonably against virtue. God (or somebody even more powerful) was tossing human lives like a ball bearing into a rigged roulette wheel.

Perhaps tonight was the moment when she would lose heart and give in to the monster. The watcher bit at his nonexistent nails and deliberately pressed his foot down upon a sharp node of the tree root that erupted out of the sidewalk, so that if she was in pain, he could share it. Perhaps help her to bear it. If only she could know that she was not alone, that help was on the way. Then she could hold out for one more night, until the light came and salvation was possible.

Yes. Just one more night. The watcher suddenly knew that this was the last chapter of his vigil. When opportunity came, he would be swift and relentless, like Joshua before the walls of Jericho. God would strengthen his arm. He would be like Daniel in the lion's den, Nephi chastising his elder brothers, Joseph rejecting Potiphar's wife, Moses who slew the Egyptian overseer for beating a Hebrew slave. After all, he was the only one who could save her.

"Darling," Diana murmured, twitching back a corner of the heavy drapes and taking a peek at the street, "it's raining so very hard outside." The gold brocade of the curtains scratched her fingertips. They were probably made out of plastic. Ordinary fabric didn't last very long in this climate. She sighed at the dark night sky. Silver streaks of rain could barely be discerned, pattering upon the ground. But she could smell the rain and hear it, even through the double-paned glass, and from its increasingly emphatic rhythm she thought the storm might grow quite a bit worse. "Must I really go out in this?" she protested, smoothing back her cropped white hair, imagining it soaking wet and dripping down the back of her neck.

"Diana," her red-haired beloved said, "you know perfectly well that the rain bothers you not one whit." That was the way she talked, this Victorian Englishwoman who had chosen to love an ancient revenant. Diana turned to look at Clarissa because the sight of her was still the greatest pleasure in her life. She was arranged in a high-backed rattan chair. She slipped a bookmark into her novel and placed it on the battered mahogany side table. They had rented this three-story apartment already furnished, and Diana personally thought the crackle-backed mirrors, faux antiques, and "plantation-style" furnishings were corny.

The ceiling fan swept patterns of shadow and light across Clarissa's face. After all of the years they had been together, she still gave the vampire her full attention whenever she spoke to her. And she never read the newspaper at breakfast. In fact, Diana wondered if

Clarissa bothered to keep track of events in the outside world at all. She must, the vampire decided. It would be one of the ways she would think she was taking care of her "undead" lover. They had already shared more than a century together, and they'd been able to unearth precious little information about donors, but they shared an unspoken intuition that giving blood to a vampire probably did not result in quite as long a life span as stealing human life bequeathed. Limited time is precious time.

Clarissa was wearing a purple silk dress with a fitted bodice made with princess seams, and a full, long skirt that made a lovely noise when she walked. The color of the fabric had been picked out carefully to accentuate her red hair. It took several petticoats, trimmed with expensive lace, to animate that skirt. Beneath her dress she wore the matching corset Diana had laced her into when they woke, and underneath that was a white cotton chemise and nearly transparent drawers, which fastened at her knees with ribbons. Both garments were frothy with additional lace. Despite the modest length of the drawers, the crotch was nothing but a slit—a Victorian notion of both convenience and propriety. How had women managed in all those layers of fabric before central air-conditioning?

Clarissa's face was full of love and amusement. Her large brown eyes sparkled, lively and quick. Her long auburn hair was put up in a radiant crown. Diana had done that as well. It was her pleasure to tend Clarissa's body, to wash her, perhaps shave her here and there; dry and brush her hair, groom it; select her clothing; dress her; do her makeup and brush perfume behind her ears, in the crooks of her elbows and knees, and right at the juncture of her thighs. She knew every inch of her property, and yet her amorous captive would always be a mysterious country, waiting to be explored.

It was also Diana's pleasure to undress her lovely submissive. The need to do so, then attend to other even more basic needs, was one of the things that warred with her desire to slip into the night and hunt to kill. Clarissa was able to satisfy her appetite for blood alone, but Diana had acquired more lethal habits in the years before she had encountered someone bred to be her donor. She could handle Clarissa quite roughly, but never with completely uninhibited joy in her own strength. What would it be tonight? Murder or fucking?

Clarissa blushed a deep carmine color, as if she could tell exactly what Diana was thinking. Diana realized she was staring at the other woman's half-exposed bosom and licking her teeth.

"Clarissa," she said, putting all she felt for her into a simple puff of air that spelled her name. The redhead smiled and gave Diana one of her hands. The slender, bleached-white-haired butch bent to kiss it like the gentleman she had longed to be in her long-ago mortal childhood. Goose bumps ran up Clarissa's arm, raising the sprinkle of fine gold hairs on her forearm and upper arm. She would have been appalled to hear that she had hair on her arms, but she was a mammal, after all, and Diana's keen eyes noted details that a mortal—or a donor—could not help but miss.

In fact, when Clarissa looked at Diana, she missed very little. She was wearing dark slacks and a black, button-down shirt, to blend in better with the darkness. Clarissa once more noted Diana's height, a little greater than that of the average modern man; the unnatural, olive-toned radiance of her Roman skin; the long fingers that gave her lover so much probing pleasure; and the air of predatory strength that came off her body like a bracing cologne of female masculinity. Diana was her clever, dangerous, doting darling. Clarissa would love her until her last breath—and beyond, if there was any mercy in Jesus.

As they stared at one another, a bolt of lightning that had struck nearby lit up the room, and a large thunderclap made them both jump. Perhaps disturbed by the vibrations, the large python in the glass case that occupied the whole of one wall of the drawing room lifted its arrow-shaped head and the first three feet of its body. It flowed across the floor of the tank to the *T*-shaped tree at one end. Clarissa turned to watch the muscles of its back and belly at work, moving it up and around the tree one vertebrae at a time, flexible as the spine of a cat, nearly as strong as Diana. The alien beauty of the pattern of its brown, black, and white scales comforted her, as did the vertical pupils in its golden eyes. She loved it for being so different from herself. Eventually all ten feet of the serpent were knotted about the tree, and it was quiet again, perhaps enjoying the mystical dreamtime that Diana believed all snakes shared when they were well fed and quiescent. Perhaps because it had fed more recently than its mate and sister, the python stayed in its glass home, close to the heat lamps. There was no lid on the cage, so it was free to come and go as it liked. Clarissa did not mind occasionally waking up to find a large reptile curled up at her feet, enjoying the warmth in the bed.

"Will you be all right?" Diana asked, drawing her lover's face back to her with a gentle hand on her cheek. "Do you want me to feed you supper before I go? Do you have enough entertainment for the evening?"

Clarissa was awake during most of the day. That was her habit during the winter, so she could take care of business that the vampire could not. "I won't be awake for more than another hour or so," she said fondly, reminding Diana of facts she already knew. "My reading will keep me occupied, and I'll sleep well, anticipating your return. Don't stop to play the chef for me. I think of the two of us, your hunger is the sharper."

Diana laughed ruefully to acknowledge this truth. "Then I'm off," she said breezily, but she left the room reluctantly, and came back once she had put on her hat and overcoat, to kiss Clarissa's hand and face and run her fingers along the sensitive skin at the neckline of her dress. She could tell the other woman was flexing her thighs as she stroked her. It made Diana happy to know that she had given this woman so much pleasure, and done it so reliably, that she was very quickly ready to be bent over the arm of the chair and entered. It made postponing the moment of conquest so much more delightful. She would tease Clarissa well tonight when she returned to their bed.

"Deep sleep," Diana whispered. "I'll pine for you till I can return."

Clarissa could not hear Diana once she left the room. The threadbare carpets still soaked up quite a bit of noise, and the vestibule by the front door was large enough to also absorb sound as well. Clarissa pictured her outside, striding purposefully, ignoring the rain, hands deep in the pockets of her black wool coat, already absorbed in her plan for the night. She really ought to take an umbrella, it would make her less conspicuous. But perhaps she'd thought of that on her own. Clarissa also knew Diana would check the house's security system before she left, because she always did that when she was leaving Clarissa alone.

Diana had indeed taken an umbrella, the green-and-red tartan. Once she was on the front steps of their home, she smartly unfurled it, enjoying the sharp crack it made as the nickel steel ribs stretched out the canvas cover. It was an expensive umbrella with an old-fashioned thornwood handle. Diana could afford beautiful and well-made things, and she saw no reason to deny herself the pleasure of their company. Clarissa was the only luxury in her life that she might someday find she was unable to afford.

Where was Diana likely to find a scoundrel? She was tired of hunting in the park. Homeless people were so depressing, and few of them were evil enough to put up a good struggle. She headed for a red-light district more disreputable than the French Quarter. The police showed up too often there, to keep the tourists safe. She was thinking of a certain bar that catered to mixed-race, transsexual women and their gangster boyfriends. Diana appreciated the style with which these ladies of the evening, women-on-purpose, handled their outlaw status. She also recognized herself as being akin to them. For much of her life, she had passed as male, finding it easier to conduct her affairs without the barriers placed in a woman's way. Surely there would be a drug dealer there with tainted wares, or a queerbasher lurking outside. Perhaps a john who raped or beat his date, or always refused to use protection. Diana especially liked to hear about victory over that sort of villain. The tall, spare, platinum-blonde woman saw a cab and hailed it, and it came to her like an obedient golden retriever.

"I am the only one who can save her!" There it was again, echoing in his head like an unwelcome commercial jingle, repeating itself over and over until he thought he would go mad. His teeth ached from clenching his jaw, it made him sweat and tremble. But he could not stop, he could not turn aside, because it was true. It was true! He was the only one who could save her.

The watcher had finally gotten lucky. The monster had left its lair. Lehi hoped that God would forgive him for not being able to save the poor unfortunate he was about to slay. But at least, after tonight, there would be no more killing. It had taken Lehi a month and a half to plan this assault, and though he had mentally rehearsed it a hundred times, his hands were still shaking with fear. Still, he would go forward. He must rescue her. It was for her sake that he had abandoned his sworn duty to preach the restored gospel in this modern Gomorrah. For her sake, because of the terrible danger she was in, he had endured the contempt and ridicule of his mission partner, who now thought of him as an apostate.

By now, Elder Curtis Swenson was probably back in Utah, sleeping in the same bedroom he'd grown up in, safe in his parents' ranchhouse, on a quiet tree-lined street in Heber. The missionary did not like to think about what his own parents must be going though, their humiliation and public disgrace because their only son had abandoned his sacred purpose here. Their anxiety about what had become of him. Their lurid assumptions about the vice which perhaps they thought had lured him away from his calling. It was a bitter picture—he, who was willing to risk so much to obey his Heavenly Father, falsely libeled as an apostate.

Enough. A time would come when he would go home. He would comfort them. He would tell his parents, his four grandparents, his three sisters and four brothers, his thirteen aunts and uncles, his twenty-five cousins, and the rest of his family the truth, or as much of it as they could handle without thinking him insane. They would understand why he had done this, they would be proud of him. It had taken two weeks of prayer and fasting for Lehi to confirm that this *was* what God had called him to do. The last days must be close indeed for such a creature of Satan to have been loosed upon the earth to trouble the righteous. Who knew how many murders it had done, what perversions occupied its leisure hours?

The wrought iron fence was not wired into the

house's security system, which was state of the art. But he went around the block and came up the alley behind the house, to avoid being seen by a passerby. When he lifted the heavy catch on the back gate and went into the courtyard, he startled a small flock of enormous crows that had been nesting in an oak tree. They departed cursing his name. He didn't like these large, black birds, which always seemed too smart and malevolent. So he was glad to see them fly away. But he felt as if there was still a presence in that tree, lurking, wishing him evil. He also felt guilty to be creeping around like a thief, uninvited, on someone else's property. But there was a higher law, and he was obedient to the promptings of the Holy Spirit. Clutching his gym bag full of tools and weapons, the missionary turned his back on the tangle of Southern jungle and moved closer to the house.

Lehi had been upset when his parents told him he had to get a job, the summer he turned sixteen. He had other plans, plans that involved cars and girls and drive-in movies. But he could recognize the sense in what they said, that it was time for him to start saving money for his mission and Brigham Young University. There would still be time for recreation in the evenings and on weekends. And he wanted to do the right thing—show that he was going to grow up to be a good man, make his parents proud of him.

He got the first job he interviewed for, working for a hardware store. Eventually he was promoted to the department that installed security systems for businesses and well-to-do homeowners. It was pretty easy to get the hang of the basics. No more difficult, really, than making your own radio, which he'd done in fourth grade. And now all that knowledge was going to come in very handy. There are no accidents. God had guided him to that job, knowing that he would need that specialized knowledge. He said a little prayer of thanks to his Father in Heaven and groped in the bag for his wire cutters.

Despite being soaked to the skin and freezing cold (this city was permeated with a wet chill in winter that troubled Lehi more than three feet of good clean Rocky Mountain snow), he took his time. The system was complex and well-designed. There was a backup system in case the power went out, and at least one backup to that one. The monster knew he deserved to be ferreted out and destroyed, so he was paranoid, and threw up these redundant barriers. Lehi had to be meticulous to dismantle it without summoning the security company's guards. He thought he had succeeded in setting up dummy circuits. The power had been diverted away from the window he intended to go through, but the rest of the system did not realize this. Even if he had made a mistake, he doubted she was staring at the control panel at this very moment. She would not see it go dark. If there was a company monitoring the system, it would take a while for the rent-a-cops they dispatched to get here. By then he would have rescued her, and they would be far, far away.

Lehi used a glass cutter to score the window. He applied masking tape to the compromised section and broke it with the heavy butt of a screwdriver. The pieces hung together so he could remove them without making a sound. He carefully stashed the broken glass behind a rosebush that grew close to the house, so he would not step on it if he had to leave via the same window. Then he grabbed for the window frame and pulled himself up. There was a protruding ornamental stripe of stone in the house's foundation that provided a toehold.

Behind him, four feet of a twelve-foot python let itself hang down from a branch, and a wedge-shaped head regarded him through merciless eyes. It had smelled an intruder. Furthermore, this stranger had interrupted a hunt for a tasty dinner dressed in black feathers. This called for investigation.

All those pushups he and Curtis had done together while praying to be kept safe from the temptations of the flesh were paying a dividend now. Everybody knew how hard it was for healthy young men to deny themselves any kind of physical release. Sometimes you woke up and found yourself losing your virtue in your sleep. How could that be a sin? It wasn't like you were spilling your seed on purpose, as Onan had done, and incurred the fatal wrath of Yahweh. It didn't mean anything, it certainly didn't mean you were queer. Still, he wished Curtis had believed him. It would be good to have some help, just one other person who knew the truth. He himself had hardly believed it, but our God is a living God, and revelation is alive in this age. It had sickened him to follow the creature at a safe distance and document its crimes, but he knew he could not forsake this calling. He knew beyond a shadow of a doubt that he was about to incur the wrath of one of Satan's especially powerful minions.

If Lehi had seen the huge serpent that uncoiled itself

from the oak tree and followed him toward the house, he probably would have lost his courage, despite the Psalms of David he was muttering under his breath. He had grown up in rattlesnake country, and his fear of that poisonous desert warrior had been reinforced by the Biblical tale of Eve's fall from grace.

The house was completely dark. He took a penlight from his bag, clicked it briefly to check the layout of the room, then turned it off and cautiously felt his way forward, willing each step to be silent. It was a big house. But he knew from observing the pattern of light in its windows that she usually stayed in the drawing room until midnight, then went upstairs to her bedroom.

He did not see the small dog door open, or spy the long, thick body that oozed in through it. The snake moved with deliberate slowness so that the door closed without making a loud slap.

Lehi went more quickly, afraid of running out of time. He must not fail. There would be no second chance, and if he was caught, the penalty would be a jail sentence or worse—a soul-tainting death at the hands of that thing, her loathsome captor. Was it possible that she was still pure? The vampire had feasted upon her, wrapped her in his foul arms and sunk his evil teeth into her helpless throat. Lehi almost wept imagining the beautiful woman being corrupted, ravished. Did he force her to partake in debauched and sinful sex acts? Had he done it in her mouth? Did he take her from behind, perhaps entering the wrong place, in defiance of God's injunction that we be fruitful and multiply upon the face of the earth?

No, no, the watcher had come in time, she was still safe. No one that beautiful could have been marred by his rot, his foulness. Lehi had known since that moment when he glimpsed her being handed out of the limousine by the monster that she was his hapless prey, a morsel he intended to taunt and torture before he destroyed her. Such cruelty, Lehi could not imagine. The monster must have to restrain her in some way, or surely she would have escaped on her own, while he was out hunting. Perhaps the missionary would find her stretched out upon her own bed, naked, locked in chains, and he would have to search for the key while she struggled to reach out to him and pleaded for him to hurry, hurry.

Lehi stumbled and went forward even more quickly, desperate to complete his holy search-and-rescue mission.

Alas, there had been no one lurking outside of The Jester with secret ill intentions. The rain was a nuisance. Occasional gusts of wind swept the falling water sideways, underneath her umbrella, and Diana hated having her clothes get wet. Surely there was no harm in going inside. Perhaps she would pick up the mental signature of a villain there. But once inside, Diana had found only two genetic men, both of them potential tricks who were secretly envious of the femininity all around them. Neither of them would harm a woman who went home with him; all they wanted was to get closer to their own need to become female.

But she had found a woman who was already dying. Chiquita was a Tex-Mex transplant, a brown-skinned, Spanish-speaking girl who wasn't doing well in a town where the other brown beauties spoke supercilious French or Creole and shut her out of their conversations, parties, and homes. She stayed because she had been told to go as far from home as possible to die, so that she would not disgrace her family with her transsexuality or her "faggot's disease," in the words of her own father. By tasting her saliva, Diana knew she had a strain of HIV that was multiple-drug resistant. While the virus could not harm Diana, it was about to steal Chiquita's beauty and leave her in pain, wasting away until she died.

Diana had bought the woman a drink. She was already rather drunk, and having a handsome man pay attention to her in front of the *culos* who had snubbed her was quite a trophy. At one point, she even dared lean forward and grope Diana's crotch, where she found a soft, rubberized toy called a "packer" that Diana had ordered from Good Vibrations in San Francisco. Now there was a city the vampire intended to visit, as soon as Clarissa was out of her Anne Rice phase. But she had heard that there was another vampire there, a man who had a nasty habit of eliminating the competition. At any rate, it wasn't long before Chiquita was calling her "Papi," and eventually Diana was able to pry her off the bar and take her home.

The dying woman had rented a small flat not far from the bar. The bed and a dresser were the only furniture in the room. But that was enough. Chiquita giggled when Diana picked her up and arranged her on her own bed. Along with the physical touching and flirting they had been doing all evening, Diana had been carefully infiltrating Chiquita's mind, soothing her, making her feel loved and excited.

Diana swept the hair off the brown girl's shoulders and adjusted her in her arms, fitting her more closely to her body. The transwoman's hips were more narrow than a genetic female's, but her little butt felt good in Diana's hands. She smelled like saffron and cinnamon. Her estrogen-enhanced breasts were small, vulnerable. She had wrapped her long legs around "him" (Diana had insisted that she keep her high heels on), and she cried out in Spanish for Papi to do it now, do it hard and quickly. But that was not for her. Diana had no erection for her, just as the transgendered sex worker had no vagina to receive it. But that didn't really matter, since the vision of romantic, wildly pleasurable sex that Diana sent her was better than anything the sex worker had actually experienced in her bitter, hard-partying life.

Making sure she had Chiquita's arms pinned, Diana bit into her tender throat. A mortal's lifesaving instincts sometimes overrode a distracting hallucination, and she was in no mood to fight for this kill. She only wanted to be gentle with Chiquita, to send her off with a lovely memory of inhabiting the flesh. The jet of blood was quick and furious. The taste of it was as compelling as it had been the first time she drank the life out of someone. The need for it was stronger than any instinct that had driven her in her mortal life. She needed it more than sex or air, hungered with a pain greater than the agony of a starving child. And the voluptuous experience of having it, being filled, oh, that was grand. Better than coming. So good that you almost could forget how lonely this desire made you once you became its ungrateful, immortal slave.

The Latina had a comic book notion of romance, ideas of good sex that came straight out of the worst pornographic paperback novels. Or perhaps it just seemed that way because Diana was a cynic and a lesbian who had little empathy with heterosexual ties. Nevertheless, she knew how to fake being the kind of man that such a woman wanted. So she supplied Chiquita with the right amount of force, the right size of cock, a gentle pressure against her genitals that felt good, but no awkward handling that would make their nature too clear, and a long rolling wave of an orgasm that felt so wonderful, she wouldn't worry too much about coming with a trick.

Like any person who had lived on the edge, Chiquita was strong. Diana drew deeper upon her body and soul, wanting her own orgasm, the rush of energy she experienced when the life force of a living human being was diverted to feed her own. She braced herself to lose control. She would jerk around like a spastic thing, spasming with delight on the cooling body of her victim. This was something she never wanted another to witness.

Suddenly, Diana's head exploded in a blinding bolt of pain. She could barely think or stay upright. Then the pain moved down, to her heart, and she thought she would quit breathing. It was as if someone had flung an ax into her chest. "Clarissa!" she cried. "I hear you, I'm coming!"

Diana flung herself out of the apartment, hoping the door had a spring lock that would engage on its own, and sprint-ed for the stairs. There was no time to heal the wounds on Chiquita's body. She would have to come back to deal with her later. Once she got the front door of the building open, she ran down a car, yanked the door open, and tipped the driver onto the street. She sent a mental siren ahead of herself, willing traffic to stop at intersections and move over to let her by. It served her right for going out in the rain!

Lehi looked up at Clarissa reproachfully, wishing he could lift his hand to rub the throbbing wound on his cheek. Just as he stepped into the living room, he had been struck by a huge snake. It had bitten him in the face, then twined its body around his neck and arms, cutting off his air and pinning his limbs. He screamed in terror, and wet himself. Clarissa had been screaming too, which only made the snake tighten its fat coils.

It had released his body when she called it and held out her arms, but the two of them had backed him into a massive oak business chair. The snake had woven back and forth in front of him, threatening to strike again if he moved an inch. Clarissa had fetched rope from the utility closet. She would not sully the beautiful red rope in her own bedroom on the body of this intruder. Plain white nylon was good enough for him.

Now he was tied hand and foot. The uncanny, outsized snake had actually inspected his bondage, and gone to coil itself around Clarissa's body only when it understood that he really was immobilized. He did not understand how such a tiny woman had made him, a man, so helpless. She stared back at him, her lip curling as if he was a bit of something disgusting on the bottom of her shoe. Even worse was the thing that she carried in her arms. She looked like an unrepentant Eve who was about to run off with the only being who had tipped her off about what was really growing on those damned trees God was so finicky about.

"Thank you, Orpheus," she said, scratching the thing's head. "You can have a rat as soon as Diana comes home. As many as you like, my brave watcher. And a gross of gold, baby chicks besides."

Lehi was quaking from a sickening rush of adrenaline. The news of Diana's return had sent more terror rampaging through his bloodstream. The fear was almost strong enough to erase his humiliation. He dimly realized he had been mistaken about the vampire's gender, but that was too much to process just yet. He still had the prisoner's best interests at heart. He must not be turned aside by the fact that she had been seduced and deceived. There is redemption from every sin. "You don't understand," he whispered. "I wasn't going to hurt you. I came to save you. Please, there's still time, won't you let me take you away from all this?"

Clarissa pounced on his duffel bag, unzipped it, dug around inside, and produced a long, sharp stake. "You weren't going to hurt anybody with this?" she asked ironically, twirling it like a drum majorette's baton. The snake uttered a piercing hiss that made Lehi jump, despite his bonds. His mouth was painfully dry, his tongue stuck to the roof of his mouth.

"Only him. Has he hypnotized you? Her. What has she done to you? Put you under some sort of demonic spell? If you come away with me we can go to the bishop's house. I'll call the elders together, we'll lay our hands upon your head and cast out the demons that plague you. But you must escape from this place of despair and sin. It's a hell on earth."

Clarissa looked around at her comfortable, albeit eclectically furnished home and wondered at this religious zealot's wrongheaded confidence. Hell? Where was hell? All she could see was Diana's paintings, her pythons, and the rattan living room furniture. This was the place where they loved one another. It was her sanctuary, a place she kept safe for her love, and all she needed of heaven.

The front door was thrown open, and Diana rushed in, bringing cold air and spatters of water with her. She practically flung off her coat. The vampire embraced her mortal lover, searched her body for injuries, hurt her in the urgency to be sure she was unharmed. Only when she was sure that Clarissa had not been touched did she turn her attention to the intruder. Lehi had the oddest feeling that Diana was looking at the ropes, not at him. "Well, well," the vampire chuckled, "somebody has been taking notes when she should have had her eyes closed in ecstasy."

Clarissa swatted at her lover like an aggravated wife who's heard her husband tell the same joke every day for twenty-five years. This simple gesture of domestic familiarity hurt Lehi, smashed his heroic dreams. He began to understand that the story of his life had entered its last chapter.

"What shall I do with him?" Diana asked her lady, circling her waist with one arm. The stays of her corset made her torso very firm and springy. "He is quite mad, I can see that without going very deep. He won't give up. If I let him go, he'll come straight back again. And he seems obsessed with you, the dirty little pup. I wonder how he spotted me."

"The same way I did," Clarissa guessed. "If he is mad, he's mad for the truth."

Diana dipped into Lehi's memories and saw the two of them stepping out of a limousine. They had dallied on their way to the club, and made love in the backseat. Clarissa had refused to allow Diana to heal the love-bite on her neck, saying she wished to feel it burning there while she listened to the music. She had promised to keep it hidden beneath her hair, since Diana had taken it down in the darkness anyway. But as she took her lover's elbow, a stray bit of wind blew her auburn tresses aside. It also carried the scent of fresh blood to Diana, whose fangs emerged by reflex. Lehi had been out for a walk to wrestle with his own dark angels, and in his simple world of good and evil, it had not been difficult for the missionary to believe the literal truth of what he had seen: that a vampire existed, and escorted a mortal woman, who must therefore be in peril.

"So," Diana agreed, blowing out a gust of warm air. Then she indicated her prisoner once more. "What's to be done?" she asked, saddened by the swim through Lehi's unrequited longing for Clarissa, his sexual confusion, his despair and hatred. Little minds always contained the most poison.

Clarissa took the stake from behind her back and showed it to Diana. Her hand shook. "He was going to—he brought this thing into our home—he would have violated you! Murdered you. My love, my only love. We would have been parted *forever*."

Lehi's vague hope that the mortal in this weird duo might feel some kinship with him, might find a way to preserve his life, popped out of existence like a soap bubble.

"Kill him," Clarissa said to the floor. Then she looked at Diana and stared Lehi straight in the face. "I want her to kill you," she said. "You deserve it. You were going to kill her. And I don't want to think about what you were really intending to do with me."

The missionary's mouth fell open, and drool dried on his lower lip. Her. The creature in that suit was a woman. Lord help us, the sins that had been committed in this house exceeded his imagination.

"So convenient," said Diana, shedding her coat and loosening her tie. "I had just an appetizer, really. Death interruptus." She sauntered over to Lehi and touched his neck, stroked his shoulders. Lehi was horrified to find himself aroused by the creature's handsome and virile presence.

"Take your hands off me," he blustered. "If you're going to kill me, just get it over with. Don't dally."

"I think...not," Diana purred. She continued to touch the bound man, deliberately putting him in a lather of physical excitement. Death was quite an aphrodisiac, after all. "So much pleasure," she hissed in the missionary's ear. "Life offers us such rich possibilities for connection, for sensation. And all this wealth was wasted on you, wasn't it? Wasted on your narrow mind. You were ruled by fear, by shame, by other people's opinions of your worth. But what is all of that, I ask you, to the delirium that sweeps through your flesh as I play my hands across it?"

"I have kept myself clean so that I can return to my Father in Heaven and dwell with him forever," Lehi wept. "I have kept the commandments. I am one of the faithful."

"Yes, I know, a latter-day saint," Diana sighed impatiently. She gradually moved her face closer and closer to Lehi's throat. "I'll honor your request to remain pure, Elder Farmington. Even though it's a kindness you don't deserve. Since you are so very righteous, I am sure you won't mind if I—" She bit down into the vulnerable tissue that housed her nourishment, and this time she drank with no need for self-control. The river of blood went on and on, as if Lehi's body were an eternally brimming cask of heartwine. Diana barely heard a shrill, pathetic chant of "Please! Please! Please!" As the peak of the feeding frenzy took her, Diana actually lifted the missionary and the chair off the floor, to force more of the intruder's substance into her own mouth.

Then Diana dropped that burden, having gotten all from it that it had to give. She wiped her mouth, feeling stained by her intimate contact with the lunatic. The boy was gay, she had discovered. Sometimes it was not possible to fend off a victim's deepest secrets. They came into you along with their blood. Lehi had known that he could not succeed in this mad quest. He had deliberately put himself in the way of destruction because he could not tolerate the growing feelings of love he had for his mission companion. He had judged himself unworthy and sentenced himself to death. So much shame, so much ignorance about what it meant for men to hold one another. It was hard for Diana to raise her eyes to Clarissa's, but she was regarding her steadily, with no distaste or judgment in her face.

"Why don't you hate me?" she cried, taken by a rare moment of remorse.

"Because you are good to me," Clarissa replied.

"But I've taken you away from everything normal and good, I've made you the object of hatred like the stupid violence of this ass. And the only thing I could give you that might compensate for this isolation, this break with humanity, you refuse. You won't let me—"

"I won't let you change me," Clarissa answered back, as calm as Diana was agitated. "Because no vampire can bear the presence of another, unless compelled to remain in a state of pain by the other's stronger will. I cannot be separated from you, my love. That is the only death I truly fear. And we do not know if a donor can be changed. The attempt might kill me."

Diana covered her face with her hands and tried to regain her composure. This assault on her home had been a nasty shock. Like any Roman aristocrat, she had deep-seated notions about the inviolability of her estate. She would have to take stock of their security and make some radical improvements. Perhaps she should take Clarissa to another state or another country.

"Diana," Clarissa said gently, coming close enough for her supersensitive lover to smell her warm skin. "Diana," she said, prying her hands from her face. "Take his body to the graveyard. Then come back to me, as quickly as you can." She performed a small maneuver with her shoulders that pushed the top of her gown down a few crucial inches. Diana stared at her half-bared breasts and felt her teeth descend. "I was so afraid of losing you," Clarissa cried. "Go, go, so you can hurry back to me."

Loading the depleted body into a crypt in a nearby graveyard was quick work. When Diana fed this deeply, there was little left of a body but mushy dry pulp in a collapsed balloon of skin. It would crumble away to nothing on its own. As soon as she got home, she went to the shower and stood naked beneath a warm spray of water, willing herself clean before she went to Clarissa. The blood she had stolen was filling her with vitality, giving her skin a more human texture and providing a little give to her normally rigid flesh. It also meant that the capacity for swelling and moisture returned to her cunt. Without blood, her clitoris could not erect, and she could not enjoy the orgasms that Clarissa's mouth and hands were adept at providing.

Clarissa was a small form in the huge four-poster bed, curled on her side like a croissant. Diana stopped a moment to relish the sight of her. The sound of her breathing filled the vampire with such tenderness, she wanted to swoon. How did she want to be taken tonight? What would best please her?

Diana crept to the side of the bed and settled beside her lover. Clarissa ignored the mattress shifting beneath her sweetheart's weight. Diana stroked her first on top of the satin coverlet, beginning with a touch so gentle that with her eyes closed Clarissa could not have been certain she was actually making contact. Gradually she increased the pressure, using the slick texture of the sheet itself to caress her. Then inch by inch, Diana drew it down her body, being careful to keep each bit of exposed flesh warm with her hands. She wove a seductive pattern of sensation, by turns mild and stern. At just the right moment, she fully exposed Clarissa's breasts, then pinched both nipples. The copper-haired wench finally opened her eyes and gasped.

Then Diana drew the sheet off her completely and covered her instead with her own body, knowing she would enjoy the slight discomfort of taking her full weight. When the submissive began to struggle, Diana lifted herself on her forearms and kissed Clarissa, making sure her tongue entered her mouth slowly and completely. She released her lips and bit her, taking care not to puncture her skin despite the tantalizing way Clarissa moved beneath her. Too much blood was as bad as having none at all, she had learned during one excruciating bout of excess consumption.

"I love you," Clarissa said. "I want you. I love you. I want you. Oh, please."

With her thigh Diana parted her legs, then her hand wandered into the cleft. There were many possibilities there, but she did not neglect her lover's breasts while she counted her other treasures with her fingers. She sucked her nipples until they were as hard as her clit, then loved them some more, until Diana knew Clarissa was aching from her nursing. Her fingers were wet, and Clarissa was a hair's breadth away from jamming her lover's hand into her body. Diana saved her the trouble and went there first, petting all the creases and surfaces inside, looking for each nerve ending and befriending it. Soon she was open, quaking, and Diana knew that to postpone entering Clarissa with her favorite dildo would cause more frustration than ecstasy.

The mortal girl had blushed when they saw the crystal-clear dildo in the shape of a leaping dolphin. So Diana had bought it at once. The animal's body was perfectly curved to fit her lover's body, and its tail had been extended enough to form a convenient handle. So Diana lubricated and then guided this hard, pretty tool into the place that was ready for it. Sometimes Clarissa liked to roll Diana onto her back and ride her strap-on like a pony, tossing her red hair until it stung Diana in the face. But tonight she wanted to be on her back, she needed the security of having Diana over her, between her and the world. Diana knew how to be restrained in her lovemaking, but she was not a withholding butch. If Clarissa wanted to experience her impetuous strength, she would not deny her, even if it meant things were going to get rough. Clarissa moaned as she entered her again and again, and put her own hand between them, to touch the sensitive part that Diana could no longer mind. She came around the crystal dildo, came hard, with no mistake.

Diana shifted her position a bit and continued to go at her, knowing it would not be long before Clarissa's excitement would return, and she would rock her hips up to meet the toy's thrust and beg for a second coming. "I hate you," Clarissa said, hanging on to Diana's shoulders, and the vampire smiled and said, "Thank you." Clarissa dug her nails into the vampire's back, and Diana noticed that she was not being careful about breaking her skin. Diana took her wrists and pinned them above her head, so she would not get vampire blood in her mouth accidentally, and fucked her so hard the bed complained. Clarissa came again. A handheld dildo was no longer enough. Diana lifted Clarissa off the bed, rotated their bodies, held her over her torso, and fit her down upon the thick shaft she had strapped to her hips. The vampire moved her submissive lover up and down as if she were a doll.

"No," Clarissa told Diana. "No!" The rubber cock felt as big as an arm inside her.

"That's right," Diana replied, "just keep saying that, until you—ah—do that, yes, I've got you now, haven't I?"

Clarissa was crying, and Diana licked her wet cheeks, then found the stamina somewhere to continue pumping. The surface of Clarissa's vagina was slightly raised, abraded, but she was still wet, so Diana did not think she was making her too sore. Somehow she located a tube of lubricant and got some on one hand, then cupped it beneath Clarissa's buttocks and filled her other hole with one, two, then three fingers.

Clarissa moved more rapidly than usual through the initial phase of anal penetration, which typically conjured up more ambivalence than anything else. Very soon, she was open enough to enjoy the double fuck. This complete sense of fullness undid her, and she locked her arms and legs around her lover. The orgasm made her hold her breath at first, then she practically shouted as it peaked.

After that, Diana switched on a vibrating egg that

rested in the dildo harness right above her clit. She kept moving, and Clarissa moaned in protest, but began to come again as the slow, relentless thrusting propelled her into another cycle of erotic release. Diana came wrapped in Clarissa's musky heat and crying out in her arms.

The tender mood rapidly gave way to fear and anger. Clarissa hit Diana, pounded her, screamed at her and wept and wept. "Never leave me again," she insisted, kissing her then punching her again. "You must never leave me, never leave my side. I'll go with you when you hunt. I'll guard your back. We must never be separated. Promise me. Promise me."

It was an old fear, and Diana followed their formula. "Yes," she repeated to each of her property's orders. "It will be as you say, my love, my treasure, loving you is the only good thing I have done in my whole life. It will be exactly as you say."

Clarissa fell asleep clutching at her lover and Diana winced, but endured it until Clarissa was so far under that her grip loosened. Then she tucked herself in beside her to watch her sleep. At just the right moment, she slipped into Clarissa's dream and began to pleasure her once more, this time with her mouth and hand, on her knees, while Clarissa stood before her like a goddess.

By now, Clarissa was used to having Diana in her dreams, and happily played this imaginary erotic game with her. Her lover lapped at her and savored her until a shift in the light warned Diana that she was about to be taken down by the day. She eased Clarissa into a deep and dreamless sleep.

Tonight, she would stay by Clarissa's side. They had been up so late dealing with this disaster that her lover would no doubt want to sleep in. Once daylight had rendered Diana immobile, it would be difficult to rouse her, but Clarissa knew how to do so in a crisis, and woe betide the being that stood between the daylight and a freshly woken vampire. The intruder had made her even more conscious of Clarissa's fragility and her own vulnerability. They would, Diana resolved, go to Venice for a while, until this ugliness had faded from Clarissa's mind. It was so dangerous to live this close to the mortal world, to pretend she was one of them. But Diana knew she would never abandon her sweetheart. How many vampires had been lucky enough to reestablish the ancient contract between the blood-drinkers and their willing feeders and slaves? Not many, she was willing to wager. They knew of only one other couple like themselves, and they were lesbians as well. The last time Diana had heard from them, they were living in New York City, a dark-haired, butch leatherdyke with a busty blonde.

She would just have to take additional measures to protect them. That was all. Tomorrow she would find a new place for them to live and search for better technology. Thank the gods for Orpheus and Eurydice, her oracles and bodyguards. Perhaps living beings were a better guarantee of safety than electronic systems and wires. Tomorrow, she would also have to visit Chiquita's apartment and dispose of her body. Now, there was a potential disaster. But Diana had been compelled to return home, to rescue Clarissa, even though the clever wench had not been afraid to immobilize their trespasser.

Diana willfully switched over to thoughts of Clarissa's body and her smile, not wanting dawn to freeze her with a memory of the missionary's crumpled body foremost in her consciousness. She kissed Clarissa's breasts in her imagination, and then—there was nothing at all.

It Takes a Good Boy
(to Make a Good Daddy)

Kip had already signed the waiver and handed over her fifteen dollars in wadded-up bills and change. But when it came time to actually go through the swinging doors into the party, she almost lost her nerve and ran back outside to flag down the cab that had brought her here. It wasn't the idea that she might actually see some of the "sadomasochistic activity between consenting adults" mentioned in the waiver that made her want to flee. The cold type had announced the potential presence of bondage, whipping, verbal abuse, piercing, cutting, branding, water sports—everything, it seemed, except kissing. But Kip had been to S/M play parties before. All that shit (with the possible exception of kissing) didn't faze her. It was just that she was here all alone, and she hated going stag to any social event. Being a bottom without a date was especially grueling.

Kip threw a panicked glance over her shoulder

at Jezebel, the six-foot-tall African American drag queen attired in flawless white and gold leather who was the latest door goddess. The white-bread straight boy who actually ran these parties had cast her in the part of his next mistress. That was probably not going to happen unless he took up serious cross-dressing as well because Jezebel considered herself to be a lesbian. Unfortunately, The Belle had been at the Friday night leather AA meeting where Kip had said (through gritted teeth), "I have to quit isolating so much."

So her smile when Kip appeared at the door had been knowing, kind, and encouraging—a combination that made Kip feel small and exposed instead of loved and supported. "You look so butch tonight," Jezebel had said, openly cruising Kip's fresh auburn flattop, short-and-stocky-but-muscular frame, black 501s, carefully polished but battered combat boots, leather vest, and *California Bear* T-shirt with sleeves neatly rolled up in half-inch increments.

"Thanks," Kip had said, feeling like a fool. Everybody knew Jezebel dreamed of being thrown over the seat of some big, bad dyke's motorcycle and whisked off to submissive femme heaven. It wasn't that Kip didn't know how (or like) to top; she just didn't want to be anybody's full-time top. Just last weekend, Kip had broken off what seemed like a promising fuck-buddy relationship with a girl who pouted every time Kip reminded her that they had originally agreed to switch off every other date. "I just don't understand what went wrong!" Babette had wailed. "You were so perfect for me!"

Now, sensing Kip's fight-or-flight response, Jezebel

stood up, and the seven-inch heels on her thigh-high, gold lamé boots made her look like an outraged goddess. "Get your ass in there," she said impatiently, flipping her platinum hair over her shoulder, and making shooing motions with her big man's hands, incongruously tipped by press-on gold glitter claws.

Kip took a deep breath and repeated the Novice's Creed under her breath: Say please and thank you, always carry cab fare, keep your boots polished, get a haircut every six weeks, don't bleed on the rug. Then she put her shoulder to the French doors and went in sideways, like a crab. If this was a movie, they would be using special effects right now to morph her from Street Kip into Party Kip. Party Kip was a close relation of Nigel the Movie Queen and Shopping Fairy, her mother's favorite companion and confidante. Party Kip had no fear. She smiled at everyone, moved with confidence around the room, and engaged in pleasant, lighthearted banter with people she hated. Party Kip also tended to slip out the back door about sixty minutes after her arrival. In the bad old days, that persona had to be rinsed away with several shots of tequila. Now that she didn't drink anymore, Kip sometimes wondered if her mother's childhood threat—"Your face is going to freeze that way!"—would materialize, and she would have a forced grin welded to her lips and her eyebrows permanently frozen in an arch, questioning position.

The parties were held in the ground-floor flat and basement of a large Victorian. The first floor was where people went to piss and grab a snack or their next trick. There was, as usual, a line for the ladies' toilet and no line for the gents'. *If cross-dressing did not exist,* Kip thought, *we would have to invent it, if only for the sake of our aching bladders.* She edged past the potty queue and bravely sailed through the social area, trying to make it to the kitchen unscathed so she could grab a glass of ginger ale. Even clean-and-sober Party Kip had to prop herself up with a glass full of liquid and ice.

But she didn't quite make it. Chev (whom the Generation Xers had privately dubbed Your Father's Oldsmobile) was holding court in the living room. Her entourage partially blocked the entryway to the kitchen. Chev, who was almost as tall as Jezebel and exactly 180 degrees away from her on the gender scale, always seemed to be surrounded by a bevy of hopeful femmes. These girls in their leather miniskirts, body harnesses, and mascara sometimes got lucky with the equally hopeful baby butches who hovered nearby, eyes riveted to the muscles in Chev's right arm and her broad shoulders. Kip was as impressed by Chev's brutal aura of physical strength as anybody else in the leatherdyke community. Imagine how many cigarettes and shot glasses you'd have to hoist to get that bulked!

"I'm not talking to you," Chev roared, and blocked Kip's way. Silently, Kip cursed leather community mores that made it acceptable for tops to do this to bottoms. She hated feeling cornered. *Call me crazy, call me a fool, call me an incest survivor, but leave me an escape hatch!*

"So I gathered," she shot back, but Chev seemed to be deaf.

"How come you never call me anymore?" she thundered.

"Oh, but I did. Three times. And you never returned any of my messages. So I gave up. I am in the phone book, you know."

Chev produced a series of baffled grunts and puffs of air that made her pilot fish gather in a closer knot about her. Did their leader need CPR? Kip waved ta ta with one hand and slipped around them, covertly feeling the hard cheeks of one of Chev's butch attendants. *That's the most action you're going to get tonight,* she thought meanly, and said out loud, "Meow."

The refreshment table was loaded down with a dozen partially full green plastic bottles of generic soda. The bowl of potato chips looked suspiciously like the same bowl of chips that had sat beside the soda for the last three parties. Kip wondered if they had been glued into place, or if everybody was just smart enough to avoid getting a mouthful of stale grease and salt. There was also an empty plastic tray of Pepperidge Farm cookie crumbs and a wedge of unidentifiable cheese that might have been Swiss or might have been fossilized brie someone had attacked millions of years ago with Neanderthal fingers. Never mind. Fill the glass with ice and flat soda, twirl it about. Lovely clinking noise. Something to hang on to. God knows hope itself was in short supply.

Kip wandered back into the social area (luckily, Chev had vanished, perhaps downstairs to flail away at the newest side of beef in town). *Who isn't me anymore,* Kip thought bitterly. She had been in town less than six weeks when Chev came up to her at a party, introduced herself, hung her on a cross, and took her apart as quickly and systematically as thieves dismantle a stolen car. It had been a good time. A little frantic, perhaps, but in those days Kip didn't expect or need a lot of warm-up. After years of waiting to find somebody who would do all these kinky things to her body, she was hungry enough to provide her own mental and physical foreplay. Back then, all she asked of a top was a mean disposition and a reasonable degree of hand-eye coordination.

After the scene was over, Chev had given Kip her telephone number and told her to call. The possibility of private play was broached. Kip called. And called. And called. Then she had overheard a couple of older and wiser (not!) perverts discussing a long-standing feud between Chev and Kip's roommate. The whole thing had been a grudge match. It made Kip's entire body twist and wrench with shame, to think of being used that way, for petty revenge on somebody she herself didn't much care for. (The roommate never bought her own shampoo, and had once gotten the telephone turned off by "losing" the bill for three months in a row.)

"Blood under the bridge," Kip said out loud. She drained the last of the soda from her glass and balanced it on top of a trash can that somebody really should have emptied. She went down the back stairs, trying not to inhale because that was Tobacco Road, where all the smokers perched, and then she entered the dungeon.

There was a vacant space along one wall, where she would not be occupying any equipment or standing in somebody's backswing. Kip marched over and took it like a McJob. Other people were not so considerate. Some reverent tourists were occupying one of the bondage benches along the far wall. Every time footsteps could be heard on the stairs, they would crane their necks, trying to see who it was, hoping for entertainment.

Master Jack had arrived early and preempted one of the crosses. His boy's limbs were Saran-wrapped to its wooden legs, and his head was covered by a helmet of duct tape over plastic wrap. Only his genitals hung exposed, and Jack was working on his balls with a pair of drumsticks. There was no obvious response, but Kip had watched Jack at work before, and knew he would be content to labor over this boy for several hours, gradually escalating his torments until he was rewarded with one piercing scream. Then, as if by magic, the toys would fly back into the bag, the bandage scissors would separate the boy from Saint Andrew's relic, and they would disappear into the night. Kip found them soothing. Reassuring, even. At least somebody in this community was going home with the same person night after night.

To the delight of the voyeurs, Mistress Electra came clomping down, dragging a rather paunchy man along by a leash. His hands were cuffed behind his back, and he shuffled along with his head down, as if he knew he was no credit to his trainer. Kip was relieved when they disappeared into another room in the dungeon. She was in no mood to watch his inept body worship while Electra stared hungrily at the bottoms who were getting thrashed or caged beneath a rain of hot wax or dressed in fans of clothespin finery. Some of the bench warmers, not so fussy, followed the domme and her slave with anticipatory giggles. Master Jack lost a few members of his fan club as well.

Kip had never known Electra to appear with any equipment besides the collar and leash. Perhaps she should organize a benefit to get the domme some nice toys for Christmas. *We could call it Toys for Tops! Oh, I am too young to be so cynical,* Kip thought, and shifted weight to her other boot. Not for the first time, she wondered what she was doing at a mixed party. This really was no place for a dyke. But there wouldn't be another women's party for another three months, and they were held in a foul, chilly little cellar that made this mildewed basement with its sticky walls and floors look like a palace. Although the food was better. Dykes like to eat. Kip patted her own stomach.

Then a piece of shadow detached itself from the opposite wall and walked toward her, frowning at its gold pocket watch. Kip's heart did an involuntary flip, like a playful dolphin. It was Doyle, whose first name was presumably too feminine to be disclosed to anybody, although Kip had heard a rumor it was Heloise. Every time Kip saw Doyle, she was surprised by the fact that she was shorter than Kip and about fifteen pounds lighter. Why was it that you always remembered tops as being taller and heavier than they really were?

Doyle was wearing a pleated and starched white tuxedo shirt with black leather pants. Kip knew without looking that she would also be wearing her trademark opal cufflinks. She had shaved her head three months ago, and then let it grow out, so it was past the velvet stage, but still looked very petable. Kip's hand hurt just thinking about touching Doyle without permission. Didn't tops ever get lonely inside that self-imposed envelope of empty air, the armor of isolation that they wore as if it made them God's gift to the world?

Doyle hadn't seen her. If she took another four steps, she would run smack into Kip. Kip resisted the temptation to let the collision take place, and cleared her throat. Doyle stopped, looked up from the watch, and said, "Late again."

"Me?" Kip squeaked. Then realized that was ridiculous. Doyle was complaining about somebody else.

"As if you'd be late for anything," Doyle said, giving Kip a slight smile.

Kip blushed as if she'd suddenly discovered she'd forgotten to put her pants on. Doyle had noticed something about her, the fact that she tried to be meticulous and punctual. Were there dark smudges of exhaustion under Doyle's eyes? That ear cuff was new, wasn't it, jet and silver poised above the three rings in her left ear? Then she was furious with herself. Who gave a shit what Doyle thought?

"My subject," Doyle explained, "is late. Again. We were to meet here five minutes ago. I have been reserving this equipment." She indicated a low table. "It's the only place in the dungeon where I can beat somebody without throwing my back out." Kip repressed the urge to give Doyle her chiropractor's telephone number and prescribe ice packs every twenty minutes and six-hundred milligrams of Advil four times a day. Doyle was still talking. "If you are not otherwise engaged, could I trouble you to keep an eye on my bag and notify anyone who is looking for a space to play that the table will soon be in use?"

"No, I'm not otherwise engaged," Kip muttered. How did Doyle get away with talking like that? Any other top would have been branded effeminate and laughed out of town. But Doyle made a living selling handmade daggers and other weapons. She had a booth at flea markets and craft fairs where she sold her work and sharpened knives. She was about as foppish as an Elizabethan dandy with a rapier looking for a duel. Probably wrote sonnets while she was sitting on the toilet.

Doyle said, "I thank you," and went up the stairs without looking back to see if Kip had assumed her post.

Kip did her best to stroll over casually to the abandoned toy bag and massage table, feeling ridiculous. Nobody was looking at her. Nobody cared about a bottom sent on a top's errand, whether it was done quickly or slowly, with grace or ill will. Nevertheless, she stood in front of the table in "at ease" posture, hands crossed behind her back. Doyle had apparently been looking for something in her duffel bag. It was unzipped, and some of the whips were spilling out of it like strange flora. Doyle did not own any black whips. She had purple, red, gold, blue, green, and brown-and-white ones, but nothing in your basic absence-of-color. She was also known to burst out singing "Somewhere Over the Rainbow" in the middle of a particularly happy flogging.

Kip knew this was true because she had actually heard it one night. The memory made her grin. Doyle was weird. She did not act her age, which had to be past thirty-five, maybe even forty. But weren't you supposed to have gray hair by that time? Maybe she did, if you got to look at her up close and personal. Perverts that age were supposed to be giving lectures on proper technique, holding office in the National Leather Association, and judging the Ms. Hidebound San Francisco contest. But Doyle did not give programs, and she did not run for election. The thought of her draping a titleholder's sash over a twentysomething's shoulders tickled Kip's tonsils.

More people were trickling into the dungeon. It was starting to get a little crowded. Master Jack worked stolidly on, but because of the crowd he had to keep his elbows a little closer to his body. He wrapped a Brillo pad around the base of his boy's dick and hooked it up to a small, black electrical box. The onlookers yawned and chatted, oblivious to the fury about to be unleashed from two small batteries through a couple of alligator clips and a copper scouring pad. Kip shuddered and told the eighteenth person, "I'm sorry, Sir or Madam, this table is taken."

There was a flurry of noise from the head of the stairs. The atmosphere in the dungeon changed slightly. It had been placid, almost lazy, down there among the bathtubs, racks, bondage platforms, dust bunnies, and spiderwebs. If she had been outside, Kip would have sniffed the air for impending rain and thunder.

Someone slid down the last few stairs. She made a

lot of noise, but landed on her feet. Then she grabbed the banister and shook it, which made the rickety stairs complain. Kip tried unsuccessfully to keep her face from tightening with distaste. Doyle was apparently still going out with Rudy. "Hey, watch out, you could really hurt me!" Rudy yelled. Her voice was full of genuine-sounding rage. Kip contemplated taking a walk to the back of the dungeon, then decided to hold her post. Rudy was not the one who had asked her to keep watch here.

Doyle's knee-high riding boots were the first that Kip could see of her. The rest of her followed at a leisurely pace. "But you aren't hurt, really, are you?" Doyle said, as if she did not care much about the answer. "You must expect a little rough treatment if I have to go and fetch you. It's much wiser to simply turn yourself in."

"You embarrassed me up there," Rudy hissed. "I was talking to my friends. How dare you interrupt us and throw me down the stairs?" She was far too close to Kip, who braced herself to toss the other woman across the room if she stepped on her toes. It would be a pleasure, in fact. Rudy was cute, with her tousled blue dreads. In bicycle shorts, her little butt was as round as a perfect scoop of ice cream. But she had a nasty mouth and a foul attitude.

"You embarrassed yourself," Doyle replied. "I did you the favor of reminding you of our appointment. Now, will you make yourself available?"

A sly look of calculation crossed Rudy's face. Kip despised her for letting it show, and she despised Doyle because she tolerated it. "Maybe," Rudy said coyly, laughing. "Maybe I will and maybe I won't. Come and make me."

Doyle did not respond. She stood at the foot of the stairs, waiting. Her facial expression did not change. She did not so much as tap her toe.

"I hate you!" Rudy exploded. "You're the worst daddy I ever had. You can tell I'm feeling small and you won't help me. I can't make all these decisions all by myself. I'm not big enough! Why won't you make me behave? I hate you."

Doyle moved a little then, just enough to allow Rudy access to the stairs. The message was plain: make yourself available, or leave. But instead of making good on her implied threat, Rudy plopped her body onto the low wooden table hard enough to make it walk two inches away from the wall. "Oh, let's get it over with," she snapped. She grudgingly reached down and lowered her spandex shorts. "There, now you've got what you want," she sneered.

Doyle went to the table, cutting through the small knot of people who had been attracted by the sounds of conflict. She reached out and took her cane from Kip's hands. Kip had not realized she had taken the implement from Doyle's bag, and she was horrified at her own temerity. But Doyle seemed to take its presence in Kip's grasp for granted.

Rudy recoiled like a rattlesnake that's just been stepped on. "Don't you fucking dare to cane me!" she howled in a murderous tone of voice. "I'm just a little boy, do you hear me? Just a little boy, and you don't cane little children! That's punishment, and I don't play punishment games. Especially not in public!

What the hell is the matter with you?"

Kip wondered, *Did I just hear something break?* Then she realized it was the sound of the last straw, hitting the camel's back. Doyle brushed by her to slip the cane back among its fellows. She murmured, "It would be a great favor to me if you could endeavor to forget what you have seen and heard here tonight. My apologies." Then she took Rudy by the upper arm, hoisted her to her feet, and said, "Cover yourself. I am taking you home."

Rudy guffawed and broke away from Doyle. She scampered up the stairs, oblivious to the disapproving looks thrown her way by scandalized spectators. The small crowd dispersed quickly, disappointed by the fight that had not materialized. Kip realized she was the only one present who seemed to be upset about what had just happened. "Are you really leaving?" she dared to ask.

"I really think we'd better," Doyle replied. "It's a mistake for me to play when I've lost my temper." She looked at the heavy bag of equipment, packed and dragged here for nothing. A crease appeared between her eyebrows.

Cursing herself for being a codependent monster, Kip said, "Here, let me get that for you." Doyle demurred, but couldn't stop her because she was so close to the bag. Kip knelt, gently tucked the unused weaponry back into its container, and sealed the zipper. From her place on the floor, she could see that Doyle's boots were looking dry and dusty. The sight made her fists clench with fury. Her own boots cost less than a hundred dollars, and she took meticulous care of them. Doyle's boots looked custom-made. They must have been four or five hundred dollars. And nobody was loving them, or even maintaining them.

But Doyle had turned her back, and was waiting for Kip so she could climb the stairs. It felt like a funeral procession. They passed Rudy, who was talking loudly to a group of women who did not seem very pleased to have her speed-rapping company. "I'm telling you, this project is going to take off. Nobody's ever heard of anything like it. It'll make a million dollars! I'll be a celebrity. I've got serious backing, Hollywood boys with megabucks, and they've given me complete control." Doyle ignored her.

Kip ducked into the foyer and used the telephone to call Yellow Cab. She also fetched Doyle's leather trench coat. Then she stood outside by Doyle, waiting for the taxi. Just as the driver pulled up and honked, Rudy came running out, went between them, bumped them apart, and dove into the cab. Doyle turned to take her bag. "Thank you for your timely assistance," she said, and gave Kip another one of her barely-a-smiles.

"You're welcome," Kip said. She was surprised by how angry it made her to be pushed away from Doyle. It had been a nice five minutes, standing in the cool evening air with their shoulders almost touching. "But tell me something, Doyle. Do you really have to be an asshole to get any attention in this community?"

Doyle flinched as if she had been asked to clean out a refrigerator. "I would certainly hope not," she said courteously. But she paused after tossing her duffel bag into the cab, and turned to give Kip a long and thoughtful look. Kip missed it because she was heading back inside by then. She collected her own jacket and called her sponsor, who told her to wait there; she would come and take Kip out for breakfast and then home.

Several weeks later, Kip saw Rudy at Hello Kitty, a dyke bar in the red-light district downtown. Kip had gone there because the bar was hosting a benefit strip show for the Women's Cancer Education Project. It was nice to be raising money for a new disease for a change. Rudy was so drunk she could hardly stagger up to the stage. She leaned against the runway, weeping and stuffing tips in the dancers' garters. The third time she almost knocked a stripper off her high-heeled shoes, the girls started dancing on the other side of the runway. Rudy just stood there bawling like a hungry baby calf, waving money in the air that nobody would come and take off of her. It was such a dreadful spectacle, Kip knew she shouldn't gloat. At least Rudy hadn't thrown up on anybody like some other people we could mention. Oh, dear. Maybe it was time to sign up for that fourth-step workshop at the Dry Dock. *Time for another Calistoga, anyway. Did I ever really have fun in these places?*

She scanned the crowd, but she didn't see Doyle anywhere. That was interesting. Rudy and Doyle weren't living together, and Doyle wasn't known for her pub-crawling or lesbian merge. But if Rudy was that broken up, maybe the two of them had broken up. A girl could dream, couldn't she?

The very next night, she ran into Doyle at Friends of Dorothy, a queer bookstore that always had

Drummer in stock. The ACT UP survivors behind the cash register didn't curl their lips at girls who bought *Mach* or *Bear* magazine. How could they? They were too busy reading *On Our Backs*. Kip was flipping through a copy of *Powerplay* and wondering if they would run her ad when she felt a familiar presence just behind her.

"Anything here for acute insomnia?" Doyle asked. Her voice was just strained enough to make Kip believe it was not a joke. She reached for a copy of *Daddy* and handed it over. Doyle made a little face that would have been a moue if she'd had more hair. Kip had a brief flash of what that angular Celtic face might look like if Doyle was getting fucked blind, deaf, and stupid, and the vision made her look down as if she had a guilty secret. "I can't account for this daddy craze," Doyle complained. "I suppose I should be a bit more stringent in preventing anyone from employing that honorific with me. Because I simply don't comprehend it, I really don't."

"Well, I don't wish to be disrespectful," Kip replied, hoping she did not sound as if she was mimicking Doyle, "but you sure seem like good daddy material to me."

"How so?" Doyle had put *Daddy* back on the rack and was looking at the centerfold in *Bear*, running her thumbnail up and down the furry butt-crack of the model, Eric the Red, who had spread himself wide enough to accommodate Odin's spear as well as Thor's great hammer.

"You aren't exactly the mommy type," Kip said sarcastically. "You don't go waving your dick around like a riot cop with a red-hot baton, but I've seen you packing. You don't line people up and knock them down like bowling pins either. From the outside anyway, it looks like you want a relationship with a bottom. And if you're going to have a relationship with a bottom, why not have one with somebody who wants to show you how good they can be? Instead of being a royal pain in the rear? Not every bottom in town is a rebel or a do-me queen, Doyle. I get so fucking sick of these girls who think being a bottom means being a selfish, egotistical, whining, snot-nosed, rude, difficult, lying, lazy little sod. And God knows you deserve to have a boy at home who would look after you a little, Doyle. Your boots look like shit."

Kip realized to her horror that this speech had gotten quite passionate, and as she talked, she had gotten closer and closer to Doyle, until she was literally in her face. The boys who had been trying to share the magazine rack with them had moved over to the other half of it, and were trying to find some consolation in *Curve* and *Girljock*. Had she really told Doyle—Doyle!—that her boots looked like shit?

But the object of Kip's lecture was simply examining her own heels and toes. "Yes, I suppose they do look rather ratty," she mused. "But what possible purpose could a top have in connection with such a paragon, Kip? You don't seem to think much of the disciplinary or pedagogical aspects of sadism."

Kip shook her head. Where else was she ever going to meet somebody who could use the word *pedagogical* in a complete sentence? "That's not true," she said slowly. "There's still a role for discipline between a daddy and a boy. And training. Every daddy wants something a little different. Or a lot different. I don't know! But it's a lot more fun to teach somebody who wants to learn, Doyle. What's the point in punishing somebody who likes to be bad? All you do is reinforce their rude behavior. I think that must get awfully boring. And lonely."

"Hmm. Well, they say the proof is in the pudding. I'm dining by myself this Saturday next. Why don't you pop 'round?" She wiggled her eyebrows hopefully.

"I don't know," Kip said. "I don't really see myself as the dessert course, Doyle. I'm a big boy. More of an entrée." *What are you doing?* her libido shrieked. *Trying to talk yourself out of the date of a lifetime? You ninny!*

Doyle glanced at the substantial biceps that protruded from the arms of Kip's tight, white T-shirt. "Mmm," she said. "Well, I'm sure we can fit you on the menu somewhere." She produced an engraved, white business card with pristine corners. "My address. Seven-thirty will be fine."

Does this mean I get to call you Daddy? Kip wanted to say. But Doyle had gone, her insomnia apparently cured without the benefit of printed matter. Kip grimly put all the fag rags back on the shelf and decided to go home too. It would take more than beating off over a picture of this year's Drummer Boy getting his frenum pierced to make her sleep tonight.

Kip could not remember a single thing that happened to her at work that week. She was so exhausted by anxiety that she overslept on Saturday and woke up in a sweat. She spent the rest of the day frantically oiling and polishing every piece of leather she owned. When she found herself cleaning off a pair of loafers she hadn't worn since the last time her parents flew into town for a weekend, she threw them back into the closet and put herself in a bathtub full of the hottest possible water. It was the week before payday, so she didn't have much money for food, let alone cabs. She gobbled a peanut butter sandwich before catching the bus to Doyle's neighborhood. The bus was late, of course, but she ran all the way uphill to Doyle's address, so it was two minutes before seven thirty when she stood on the doorstep, breathlessly reciting the Novice's Creed. *Say freeze and fuck you, always carry a haircut, keep your boots bloody for six weeks, don't carry away the rug!*

Nobody answered the doorbell. Oh, God. What should she do now? Turn and walk away? No, the very thought made her suicidal! Kip raised her fist to hammer on the door. It opened suddenly, and she fell forward. Doyle caught her and drew her inside. Kip almost fainted. Their bodies were pressed together in a full embrace. She wasn't used to having that much physical contact with the women she played with. Doyle was wearing a leather uniform shirt neatly tucked into leather fatigues. Kip had worn a tank top with her 501s, and the buttery-soft leather of the shirt made her exposed skin purr. She could swear, judging by Doyle's grin, that the minx could feel her nipples getting hard.

Doyle's face moved closer, and Kip turned her head wildly from side to side, in a heated state of panic. "What's this?" Doyle said ironically, catching

Kip's chin in her gloved hand. "Resistance already?" Then she kissed her.

Doyle's mouth was small and neat, her teeth wolfishly sharp. Kip wriggled, but Doyle's arms simply held her more tightly. She could not breathe. Doyle wasn't wearing any perfume or aftershave, but the smell of her was clouding Kip's brain. She couldn't let that tongue into her mouth. It would smother her!

Thank God, Doyle's lips came away from hers, and Kip took a deep, sobbing breath. *I hate you,* she thought, then blushed when she remembered the last time she had heard that sentence spoken aloud.

"I think I'll do that again. Just so you know I can," Doyle said firmly, and once again took Kip's mouth. This was a different kiss. Ravishing. Mouth-raping. Oh, Kip knew her underwear was just a mess.

"Well?" Doyle said, breaking away again. "I thought you were going to show me how good you could be." Then she once again bent her head, and Kip knew this was all it would ever take for Doyle to master her. No studded collar, no slap in the face could ever be as effective as this. She was utterly defeated by her own response to Doyle's lips, teeth, and agile tongue. And Doyle knew. There was no hiding it. So Kip shrugged her shoulders and let her own tongue explore Doyle's mouth. It wasn't much, really, just a shy response to all the thrilling attention she was getting. But it satisfied Doyle, apparently, because she let Kip go and preceded her into the house.

They walked through a living room (one navy blue couch, three marmalade cats, a television and CD player in a pine cabinet, magazines lined up with the corners of a maple-and-glass coffee table). Beyond that was a dining room, and beyond that (apparently) the kitchen. But Doyle halted by a round mahogany table. "Dinner's made already," she said. "I thought I would let you serve it." Kip looked around wildly. Doyle drummed her fingers on the tabletop. Kip took the hint and pulled out a chair. "Thank you," Doyle said, and graciously accepted its support, as Kip carefully inserted it beneath her hips.

"Excuse me," Kip said, out of breath, and went into the kitchen. A hallway tantalized her, but she refused to yield to the temptation to explore. Doyle had not invited her into the rest of the house. She stowed her backpack in the pantry.

A breakfront held china and crystal glasses. Surely the drawers beneath would... Yes! Silverware, a tablecloth, napkins, even napkin rings. *This is okay,* Kip thought. *I come from an entire generation of food service workers. I can do this.* She took a tray and piled her treasures upon it. It did not even occur to her to take down a second cream-colored plate (decorated only with a thin band of gold) and glass or remove a second set of flatware from the blue-velvet-lined drawer. She went back into the dining room and set the table, forcing herself to move slowly, doing one thing at a time. When the job was done, Kip gave Doyle one furious glance, certain she was smiling at her, but Doyle was only studying her fingernails.

Then it was back into the kitchen. Doyle had said dinner was already made. Where would it be? She found a large bowl of salad crisping in the refrigerator. *Hmm.* No, Doyle would eat her salad after the main course. She uncovered the pots on the stove. One contained a creamy soup. Kip filled the china tureen, found a ladle, sliced bread, and at the last minute remembered to add butter to her tray. For a miracle, she got the tureen into the dining room and soup into Doyle's bowl without spilling anything. She was feeling rather cocky as she turned to go back into the kitchen.

But Doyle cleared her throat. Kip spun on her heel, and soup slopped onto the tray. *Don't panic,* she told herself. *Doyle can't see it.*

"Just water would be fine," said Doyle, and sketched a figure eight with her empty crystal goblet. "There's a carafe in the refrigerator."

Cursing herself, Kip fled in search of the beverage, and only at the last minute remembered to serve it from the right. As she turned to leave, Doyle cleared her throat again. What now?

"A bit more skin, if you please, upon your return," Doyle said.

Kip took a deep breath and did not let it out until she was safely between the kitchen sink and the stove. Okay…a bit more skin. She had to think. She was not going to serve Doyle with her tits flopping in the Bernaise sauce. Kip bent to unlace her boots, yanked them off, and removed her 501s. Underneath them she was wearing a hunter green jockstrap. She had brought her harness and dick, but she wasn't wearing them. That would be hubris. Would the tank top, jock, and her boots give satisfaction?

She jacked the laces around their little cleats, grunting and sweating. It was one of the drawbacks of wearing combat boots. You couldn't just kick them off. She folded her jeans and stashed them with her backpack.

The well-appointed kitchen calmed her down. She forgot about her partial nudity. Any utensil or dish she needed was available, right where it should be. Kip filled casserole dishes with rice, chicken pieces in a cream sauce, and steamed carrots. This was a lot of food for one person. Apparently she wasn't the only person who had spent all day preparing for this date. Her stomach growled, and she said out loud, "Be quiet, for God's sake." The peanut butter sandwich wasn't going to hold her for too much longer. She looked longingly at the delicious-smelling sauce, but didn't so much as put the tip of her finger in it. She had not been given permission to eat yet.

Kip removed Doyle's soup bowl from the left, simultaneously pouring her more water. Ice splashed into the glass, but no water got on Doyle or her plate. *Good, good.* Helping Doyle to the main and side dishes, she felt a warm, slender hand on the inside of her thigh. Doyle was sampling her skin. Kip held perfectly still, balancing the heavy tray. The hand went around her body, briefly touching the back of her legs, then smoothing out the bare skin of her ass, exposed by the wide elastic straps of the jockstrap.

"Delightful," Doyle murmured. "I'd like you to remain in case I need anything else. Please stand by that chair over there." Kip took the assigned post, wishing the room was just a little warmer. There was a small stand to receive the tray. Doyle ate at a leisurely pace, not wasting any motion or touching her food with anything except utensils. Lulled by the sight of her chewing, Kip jumped when Doyle said, "Please recite something."

"What? I'm sorry—I mean, I beg your pardon?"

Doyle gave her a quizzical look, as if she thought Kip had suddenly stopped understanding English. "I like to hear a little poetry while I dine," she explained, speaking a little more slowly than usual, to aid Kip's comprehension. "Anything will do. Anything you remember, perhaps one of your favorites from school?"

Kip was horrified. This was not one of the many of the skills, talents, and abilities she anticipated having a top demand of her.

"Would a little water help to loosen your voice?" Doyle asked politely. There was a slight edge to her voice, like the burr on a dull knife.

"Thank you, no," Kip said, and suddenly found herself declaiming, "Others, I am not the first, / Have willed more mischief than they durst: / If in the breathless night I too / Shiver now, 'tis nothing new."

"Housman," Doyle murmured with deep satisfaction. "Charming. Please continue."

No one was more surprised than Kip when she remembered the whole thing. But Doyle was still cutting up her meat, dabbing it delicately with sauce, and consuming it with tiny spoonfuls of rice. Something longer was required. Kip resolutely launched into "Complacencies of the peignoir, and late / Coffee and oranges in a sunny chair."

" 'Sunday Morning,' " Doyle said admiringly. "I thought Wallace Stevens had fallen out of favor in literature courses these days."

Kip's hands were sweating. Not just her palms, her entire hands. But she thought she did not do too badly, especially with her favorite verse, which began, "She says, 'But in contentment I still feel / The need of some imperishable bliss.' / Death is the mother of beauty; hence from her, / Alone, shall come fulfillment to our dreams / And our desires." Doyle did not say anything when she was through, so she was racking her brain to see how much she could remember of Robert Graves's "To Juan at the Winter Solstice." She could only remember "Water to water, ark again to ark, / From woman back to woman: / So each new victim treads unfalteringly / The never altered circuit of his fate, / Bringing twelve peers as witness / Both to his starry rise and starry fall." But what came in between that and "Fear in your heart cries to the loving-cup: / Sorrow to sorrow as the sparks fly upward. / The log groans and confesses: / There is one story and one story only. / Dwell on her graciousness, dwell on her smiling, / Do not forget what flowers / The great boar trampled down in ivy time. / Her brow was creamy as the long ninth wave, / Her sea-blue eyes were wild / But nothing promised that is not performed."?

"Very nicely done," Doyle said a little too loudly, and Kip suspected she had done it just to make her jump and flex her buttcheeks. "Come here," Doyle said, and indicated the floor. Kip gave it a dubious look, then decided, *What the hell. What difference can it possibly make? You've already fallen into her arms and served her dinner with your gluteus maximus glowing like a lighthouse. She has probably already guessed you're half in love with her and ready to do anything she wants.*

Doyle was shredding a piece of chicken. The sight of food making contact with those immaculate fingers made Kip gape. Then Doyle was pushing warm strips of gooey food into her mouth. "We can't have the help passing out from hunger." Kip closed her lips quickly enough to taste a little bit of Doyle's fingers along with the chicken. "No nipping," Doyle said, smiling with half of her mouth. And fed her another mouthful. Doyle even made her drink from her own glass. Kip was mad with longing. *No matter what else happens tonight,* she thought, *this is good. This part is very good.*

Doyle erupted from her chair, took Kip by her forearm, and hauled her through the kitchen so fast, she didn't have time to make sure the stove was turned off and the cupboards were shut. In a trice, she was bootless, jockless, tank topless, and neatly strapped to a hard bed. "We'll have coffee and dessert later," Doyle explained, and brought a strap down upon her butt.

Because the first blow was hard and quick, Kip tried to steel herself for a whirlwind whipping, the kind that made you feel like you were a cord of wood being chopped up for winter. But Doyle did not continue at that level. In fact, she immediately switched to something soft and heavy that coaxed Kip's ass up off the bed in an attempt to bring it back. Doyle applied each stroke with so much care, Kip felt like a three-layer cake getting a professional icing. Then Doyle gave her a few alternating blows with a small plastic flail, and that was like the roses coming out of the pastry tube in neat red petals of pain. Then, like most metaphors, it collapsed under its own weight and the weight of a blackjack, used in moderation as a surprisingly satisfying paddle.

"Why aren't you fighting me, boy?" Doyle asked.

The question surprised Kip so much she barely felt the next three blows. "Because I want it," she explained, as if to an idiot.

"I see," Doyle replied, but did she?

Kip tried again, although Doyle was using a braided quirt, and she could only get enough breath to speak in between lashes. "My job is to accept the pain, *umph*, presumably because you like giving it to me. *Uh*. I get pissed off sometimes, but it's my job to deal with that. *Oof*. I asked you to do this. *Yow*. So it's up to me to—*hey*! Meet me halfway on this, okay?"

"You can stop talking now," Doyle said, and lavished a rabbit-fur mitt across her inflamed hindquarters and shoulders. "I think I get your drift. We tops get smarter when you play with us, you know. I like the difference. I feel as if I could be much meaner to you, but somehow I'm not being mean at all. Interesting, isn't it?"

Kip threw up her hands as far as the bondage allowed and choked out an agreement.

Every inch, every inch, Doyle seemed to want to touch every inch of her with every whip she owned. And she was not stingy with her hands, either. Kip was caressed, smacked, punched, scratched, slapped, and fondled. She lost track of how many times Doyle had turned her over, or how many different toys had

222

come off the wall and connected with her flesh. She was close to tears from the dizzy pleasure of it, so much of what she wanted, from someone she didn't have to watch with the eyes in the back of her head, and in a warm and private place, no slivers or sticky patches of old lube to overlook, no need to resolutely ignore the ex-lover lurking in the corner, licking her lips, or the suburbanites agog with the discovery that most real dykes did not look like Vanessa Williams or Nina Hartley.

Then the whipping stopped, and Doyle was kneeling behind her on the bed. She felt bare skin against her own thighs, and sneaked a look over her shoulder. Doyle was wearing nothing but an undershirt and a condom. Her breasts beneath the thin white cotton looked bigger than they had seemed beneath her formal evening wear and uniform shirts. The hands that had bruised Kip's butt were playing now with something harder to give up. Because it did not hurt. Because it was intimate. And wet, and Kip realized that she hated needing this, was terrified to move against Doyle's tool even though there was very little chance that it would be withdrawn.

"You have been a good boy," Doyle admitted. "I'm very, very pleased with you. Are you ready for your reward?" And that made it even worse. Kip was not used to praise, much less sex, after a scene. This was when you were supposed to get up, dust yourself off, find your clothing, make a joke, and disappear. She wanted to sink into the flannel comforter on the bed and vanish beneath the mattress.

Still, it took the presence of a fingertip within her

anus to make her speak. "Please, sir, not that," she said, and meant it.

The greasy worm of pleasure and discomfort vanished instantly. "Why?" Doyle whispered.

"I don't know, sir, I just...it's, I can't."

"Then shall we do this instead?" The piece was just substantial enough to make Kip want to encounter it again, nudging her cervix. "Better say yes or no, boy," Doyle prompted.

"Yes, sir!" Kip said fervently, rocking. "Oh, more, sir, please."

"Sir," Doyle repeated. "Not Daddy? Not even now?"

Kip was going to come already. She wanted to say the forbidden word. Giving in to the desire to say it out loud would make her orgasm more intense. But she could not. She wound up screaming silently, jamming her face into the pillow as if she were actually making a noise that had to be hidden. The wave of pleasure did not crest as high, but Doyle had taken her further than anyone had for years, and was still lodged firmly in place, apparently prepared to continue the ride.

"Well, if you won't say it, I will," Doyle said firmly. "Your daddy is going to fuck you now, Kip. Hold on to the ropes. I'm going to fuck you really hard."

"Noooooo," Kip wailed, but Doyle had the good sense to ignore her. "This is what good boys get," Doyle said, and showed Kip what she meant. Kip thought she probably could have beaten Doyle in a wrestling match, but this was not a fair fight, and the other woman made her come again and again, even succeeded in getting the silent scream to turn into an audible groan or two.

The bed was a mess, and both of them were sweating freely. Doyle collapsed on her back and unsnapped her harness. Kip rolled onto her side, feeling her internal organs settling back into place. Her knees were wobbly, but she forced herself up anyway and skedaddled for the pantry. She put her 501s on so fast, they might have been backward for all she knew. No time to do up the boots, so she just took them under her left arm. Thank God she hadn't unpacked her knapsack. She hauled one of the straps onto her shoulder and sprinted for the front door. The buses had to be running still, they must be, it couldn't be that late.

But Doyle was blocking her exit. God damn it. Did tops think they owned every door in the world? "Where do you think you're going?" she asked. She must have been really angry. Kip had never heard her speak so rapidly and loudly.

"Home. I'm going home." Her own voice sounded thick and confused. Kip loathed herself for being so hoarse and disorganized.

Doyle held out her hand. Kip looked at it, confused, and realized she could not quite see the hand or anything around it. Her vision was blurred by tears. "Dummy," Doyle said fondly, mushing a handkerchief into her face. "I can't let crying women flee my house at all hours of the morning. What will the neighbors think, you stupid boy?"

"Screw the neighbors!" Kip said, blubbering into the hanky.

"No, thank you. I was having a much better time

with you," Doyle replied. "Come on, now, boychick, don't be so distressed." She had somehow managed to get her arms around Kip and was turning her back toward the bedroom. "It's cold out here, no wonder you're so unhappy. And probably hungry too. I shouldn't wonder at all if you were ravenous. Come on, come with me, it's okay, I'm not mad at you."

Kip made a fist and halfheartedly slammed it into Doyle's chest. "Yes, I know you're mad at me," she soothed. "That wasn't very nice, what I pulled on you back there, was it? But you have to expect that, yes you do, because I am a sadist, you see, and we like to hurt people. But I will pay for it now, yes I will, my little man, just let me make sure you are okay, and if you still want to go home I will give you a ride."

Kip found herself back on the bed. Doyle didn't try to take off her clothes, but she did pry the boots from Kip's frozen fingers and sit close to her, with her arm over her shoulders. They sat that way in silence for a few long minutes.

Then Doyle said simply, "Please stay."

That brought on a bout of more crying. God, Kip hated breaking down in front of other people. It was hideous. But Doyle took it in stride, patting her gently, not saying anything stupid, just handing her a hanky from time to time. They all seemed to be freshly washed and pressed. Was she pulling them out of thin air, like a magician's silk scarves, gold coins, bouquets, and bunny rabbits?

"I have to go home," Kip finally made herself wail.

"Why?" Doyle said, gripping her shoulders a little more firmly.

"Because you asked me to dinner, and that's all, and I had a very nice time, but you never said anything about spending the night so I don't have any clean underwear and besides I'm not sure I want to sleep with you, that's very different from having sex with you, and anyway—"

"But you haven't had sex with me," Doyle said.

"Huh?" Kip said, giving her a bleary look. She had about six soggy handkerchiefs wadded up in both of her fists. Doyle took them away and tossed them into a corner of the room. They landed on her boots, which Kip thought looked as if they were going to crack in half if somebody didn't oil them immediately. But this was probably not a good time to take the edge dressing and sooty silk stocking out of her bag.

"I was about to ask you if you thought you had been good enough to fuck me," Doyle said patiently.

"Well, I think so," Kip bristled. "How many other boys do you know who can recite that much fucking poetry at the drop of a hat?"

"I agree," Doyle said gravely. "Well, good, then, that's all settled." She dragged Kip's backpack over to her feet. "I believe you might need this." Then she flipped the covers on the bed back, took off all her clothes, and lay down.

Kip found that her tears and hiccups had disappeared. Her face was dry, as if by magic, although it probably still looked a little swollen. Doyle was waiting with one eyebrow and one knee cocked. It would be really rude to walk out now. So she stood up, took off her jeans, and dug the necessary out of her pack.

Kip planted her hands on either side of Doyle's

head and settled her hips between Doyle's legs. She looked really different from this perspective, kind of feline and fragile, awfully much like a girl. Her lips were thin but so dark red they looked extremely sensual. Would it be all right, she wondered, if she bit Doyle's neck?

"You'd better call me Daddy now," Doyle said, putting arms and legs around Kip and taking her full weight.

Making Honey

My friend Horace is all right. *He* can jump. When he first came around, he wanted to be down with the boys in the 'hood. He was wearing his pants baggy and puttin' his baseball cap on backward. First thing I did for that white boy was to change his name. Can you imagine going through life with a name like Horace? What's your nickname gonna be? Uh-huh, you don't have to say it! Well, I don't know why I befriended him, except that he was trying so hard and there wasn't any meanness or pretentiousness in him, he was just looking for a posse to join like any of New York City's children. In my life, I have been in many places where I was made to feel like I did not belong. He gave me a big old grin when I told him none of the daughters of the African diaspora were going to dance with him because he looked like a heavy metal has-been. He let me cut that stupid bleached-blond ponytail of his off with my highly illegal double-edged dagger, which I usually keep hung upside down in a quick-draw sheath inside my leather jacket. So he's just Ace now, and if he keeps on doin' good he might get to be Aces High or Aces Wild. You know how that goes. That's how we do things around here.

My girlfriend liked Ace pretty good too. She's a tall, long-legged woman created by the love of many nations poured into the perfect vessel of her body. She's got eyes like a Japanese girl and long, black hair like one too, but her skin is golden-brown suede and to kiss her lips is to kiss our mother, Africa, herself. I caught that little honeybee of mine making eyes at him a time or two, and it made me laugh up my sleeve. Because that's her name, her name is Bea, although when we have finished one of our leisurely Sunday afternoon fucks, when she has put all the man back into me and I have shown her all the woman that she can be, I call her Beatrice, pronounced like they do in Italy, Bay-ah-trish-ah. The sun falling across our bed feels to me like we have arrived in a new land where anything could happen, and all of it would be good. Beatrice. Sounds like the name of a queen. And she is the queen of my heart, even if she comes into the bedroom most times on all fours, with a riding crop in her mouth. That's how she likes it, and if you want to be in her neighborhood, you play the lady's game. So I guess you could call me a player, but only in the sense that I have my eye on the prize, which is her.

If she wants to have her birthday two or three times a year, I guess Ace can be a present on the table of my brown-eyed lioness, but he's got to understand that Bea is the one who likes to get gift wrapped nice and tight. You could say it's my birthday every damn day because I don't know which part of the process I have come to enjoy more: wrapping the sister up, or unwrapping her. Either way, she just gets sweeter the longer I touch her, and I'm not ashamed to say I'll kiss her everywhere. If the bee makes honey, wouldn't a man be a fool to refuse to lick it off his fingers? Oh, yeah. That's what I'm talking about.

You may think I'm a fool anyway, because I'm putting my sweetheart in the position to be had by another man. But you can't tell a bee to land on only one flower, and I'd rather be there when she gets her fill of the sweet stuff. She has proved to me that her body and soul belong to me, and I'm not afraid that she'll find some other big black man who will love her like I do. And if she was gonna do that, Ace wouldn't be the one, now would he? Not hardly.

So we went to a party or rather I went to a party and then Bea met me there. I was already talking to Ace and his date, who was so polite it was obvious that she was terrified. Everybody was watching her to see if she would chill, but when Ace tried to get her to eat some egg rolls and whatnot that were laid out, she jumped like he had tried to give her typhoid. So I didn't feel too bad about putting her on the spot. We had gotten there late enough that a few people were already starting to leave, so I suggested we go back to my place for a drink, and face to face with me, she couldn't hardly refuse. You'd think she could just say no if it was something that she didn't want to do, but white people are weird that way.

Once at my apartment, I got everybody a beer, and

then I told Bea to stand up in front of me. I was sitting on my favorite big soft chair. I ran my hand up her leg under her skirt and said, "Girl, you're in trouble now. Didn't I tell you not to leave the house if you're gonna see me unless you took off your panties? Look at these!"

I tugged them off of her right then and there, and tossed them aside, trying to make it look accidental that they landed on Ace's lap. His date was trying to stand up, looking slightly scandalized, and then I grabbed Bee by the wrist and dragged her into the bathroom. Once we were in there, I bent her over the sink and spanked her good. She cried a lot, she loves to do that, and told me she was going to be a good girl and started describing the princely blowjob I was going to get as soon as I was done chastising her ass. It's not a very big apartment, and we made sure that we were overheard. When the door slammed, I got Bea fixed up for the next act of our little play and dragged her out of the bathroom.

Ace was on his feet, torn between goin' after his lady friend and getting a better look at Bea's womanly treasures. I got myself and her bare, red ass in between him and the door and told him, "Feel that booty, brother, and tell me if I laid on enough strokes to teach this bitch what's right."

He reached out like he was getting to touch something holy and ran his fingers down the nearest cheek. "It feels so hot," he said, wondering, then swiveled his body to look at Bea's face. "Are you okay?"

She was smiling through her tears. "I will be as soon as I do what I need to do," she told him. She tossed her head to straighten her hair out, and it made the blonde stripes in her black mane ripple like gold flames in the darkness: a guiding light, a beacon, my wealth that was stored up where nothing could corrupt it.

I was back in my overstuffed leather easy chair, and she came to me. Ace was following her like a puppy, eyes crazy-glued to her luscious form. "Barbara was really mad," he said. "She didn't want to hear—"

Bea wasn't having any of that. She never apologized for who or what she was. "Hear what, baby? Hear a woman get what she needs? What she thought no man in the world would ever be brave enough to give her? Hush, now. I have an obligation to meet."

Smiling up at me, my girl tugged my zipper down with one hand while she grabbed my stuff with the other hand, giving me a good, firm squeeze. By the time she got me out of my pants I was ready for her, and she commenced to kiss the bright pink head of my cock with her soft, sexy mouth. Her tongue felt so good. I just wanted to melt into her. But she was working my dark brown foreskin back and forth, showing me my own manhood, so we both understood how much we wanted each other. I love lookin' at my own dick, those contrasting colors, and felt grateful that God gave me something very pleasing to my lover girl. I was leaking worse than the faucet in the bathroom. She licked up my pre-come with naughty kitten laps, making porn-star faces for me.

But I could at least pretend to be angry. "Stop playin'," I said. "You've been a very bad girl, Bumble Bee. Time to turn naughty into nice."

"You never like it nice," she said, and swallowed a third of my cock. Like having somebody step on the gas, hard, before you get your seat belt on! I just about folded in half, and all the air went out of my lungs. While she sucked me, her tongue never stopped moving. If you could have told me that the underside of my dick would be as sensitive as the head of my cock, I would have told you that you didn't know shit about anatomy. But that was before I freaked out with Bea. That girl could suck ice cubes through a straw, and I do mean without waiting for them to melt first.

"Doesn't she look delightful?" I asked Ace, who was standing with his hands in his pockets, probably wishing they had holes in them so he could grab somethin' other than cloth.

"Oh," was all he could muster. "I just, it's...oh. Bea. You're so beautiful. So free." It made me proud to know I had a woman who deserved that much admiration, and the respectful but horny way he was with her made me glad he was my friend.

All on his own, he knelt down beside her and pushed her skirt up to her waist. She was working her way further down my cock now, and couldn't have said yes or no, but she stuck her ass out further so he could get the message that it was okay to touch her.

"Come on, Ace," I said, taking my prized possession by the back of her head so I could fuck in and out of her mouth. "Give her a little slap for me. Don't pretend you're like Barbara. You stayed around to listen. So help me out. Takes more than one spanking to teach this girl a lesson."

"Spank? Bea? Oh. Oh." He drew his hand back,

then hesitated. I could tell he was afraid to do it wrong, to be too wimpy or too hard.

"Come on, man, just hit her. She likes it any way you dish it out. Just spank her." I let Bea come up off my dick enough to add her own soft words of encouragement. She wagged her rear end at him, butted up against his hand. "Oh, I wish you would," she pleaded. "Spank me, honey, I've wanted you to spank me for such a long time. Spank me for my papa, Ace."

He didn't hesitate anymore. I let him whack her half a dozen times on each side, then I said, "Run your finger down her slit, Ace. Just so you don't doubt the truth of what she says. Suck harder, Bea. Oh, yeah, baby, you got a mouth the Dalai Lama himself could not resist."

"What's this?" Ace asked, puzzled by what he had found already inside of her—the plastic rim that hung between her inner lips.

"That's what they call a female condom," I explained. "But you can tell her nature is coming down all around it. Check it out." Then she played some kind of trick on me, contracting her cheeks and twisting her mouth up then back down the full length of me. "Oh—my. Take me down, Bea. All the way down. You got glory for me in that throat of yours. Take me to glory and glory over me. I love you, yes I do, oh, baptize that dick, girl. Wash me clean."

Ace was fondling her pussy, almost as happy as if he had his dick up against her. "She's so wet," he hissed. "Watching the two of you, it's so amazing, I feel like I'm going to die or I must be dead already and in heaven. I never saw anything so hot. My dick is climbin' out of my shorts, banging on my belt buckle. I'm so hard it hurts me, man."

"You want to fuck her, don't you?"

I said it in a kind and open tone of voice, but he froze. We were really good friends, but there are certain things you just don't say or do. We had talked about every kind of sex thing from how we first learned to jerk off to the fucked-up circumstances in which we both had our first woman. But you don't usually tell your best friend you want to push wood into his girlfriend. You might hope you'll get a chance to do it, but you keep it on the down low. But I knew Ace was a man because he knelt there beside my girlfriend, watching her blow me, with his hand on her ass, and owned up. He took a chance and said, "Oh, yes, Willis. I do. I do want to fuck her."

"Show her your cock."

Ace stood up long enough to shuck his pants and briefs. The cock that he presented us with was thicker at the base than at the tip, perfect for the ride I had planned. I pulled Bea off my cock by her hair and got her busy on him. She slicked him up good, and he got a little rough with her, just enough to make sure she was extra-juicy in her other hole. But before he could make a mistake and come in her mouth, I took her back for myself and told him to get behind her. "Stick it up in the air nice, now, for Ace," I told Bea. "Roll that fine ass for this white boy you been craving for so long. He's going to fuck you from behind and get so far into you, you'll be able to taste it."

Somehow, even with my dick in her mouth, she managed to add her pleas to the conversation. We were cheerleaders for sexual license, seducing my studly assistant into joining us in our kinky, healing magic act.

He slid into her and gasped when he got that pussy filled all the way to the top. "Sweet," he said, backing up to buck into her again. "Oh, you feel so good." We had loaded that condom with a lot of lube, so he wasn't feeling at all deprived by the lack of skin-to-skin contact. If I was going to let him do this, I wanted him to get the whole show, no holding back. "We're going to have to call you Ace in the Hole now," I joked, and everybody giggled.

Bea's lips rolled up and down my cock, massaging me with intimate skill. It was a game we played. I would try to come in her mouth, and she would keep me hard but not let me come because she wanted me to fuck her, and she thought shooting my load in her mouth was a waste. Watching my friend piston her from behind made me think tonight I might win the contest. He had this look on his face like he was studying for a test, but every now and then his real self would break through, and he would just be fucking away without a care in the world, lost in being human, a man being received by a willing woman, being built up and pleasured by her while he gave her what she needed so, so bad. We were all making a lot of noise, cries of joy that they can never get right on the sound track of an X-rated movie.

"Did it make your dick hard to spank her?" I asked.

"Yeah," he panted. "It made me real hard. I wanted to do it some more."

"So do it," I instructed. "I want to see if you can do two things at once. Isn't that supposed to be good for your brain? Maybe it'll stave off Alzheimer's."

Bea moaned and twisted. The sounds she was trying to make felt good against my cock. The head of my dick was so far down her throat it was like getting a vibrator put on me. She rolled her eyes at me, begging, and I said, "You want to come, baby girl?" With a mouth full of me, she nodded, barely able to move her head. "Ace!" I said. "This little bee wants to give you some of her honey. Can you take it, man?"

"Yeah," he said, humping hard. "Tell her to come, Willis. I want to see her lose it while I pump her cunt."

"She knows the rules, Ace. She can't come unless she's tied up, can you, Bea?"

She stopped moving on his big dick and gave me a scared look. This was a rule I had just made up so she wasn't due any extra punishment. (As if Bea would let me spring a "punishment" on her by surprise, anyway!) I dug a short piece of rope out from the cushion of my chair and handed it to Ace. "Tie her hands together," I said. "Then she won't be able to cheat no more, keepin' her hand wrapped around my johnson. I'll deep-throat her then. For sure."

He grabbed her hands and bound them, improvising rather well, I thought. It's good to have a friend who can think on his feet—or should I say, on his knees with his dick out. "Now let's do her nice and slow," I suggested. Me and Ace started moving in synch, in and out, teasing our girl. She was slurping on my whole cock, giving me head with all her might, and Ace wiggled in deep then slid out an inch at a time, making it last. She thrust out her bound hands in frustration and her whole body was strung tight, waiting for us to let her testify. We picked up speed together, looking into each other's eyes, and it was like we just knew what to do, together; I felt so close to him in my heart and knew it was a good thing. The girl was panting; I eased up a little because I didn't want to get bit, and gave him the signal. Then he went at her from behind like he was mad, and I just kept a little cock in her mouth so she would remember who her master was.

She danced for us, the very picture of pure female energy, more beautiful than an angel, and I realized I had better put the rest of our plan into motion, because I couldn't hold back much longer myself. As soon as her hips slowed down—"Fuck her in the ass," I told Ace, no-nonsense. But once again he hesitated, afraid to take what was free right in front of him. "I done it to her lots of times," I reassured him. "She can take what you got. Slide it in. Now, Bea, don't you come till I tell you."

Shiny-wet, his dick came out of her pussy and he aimed higher up, hand around the base of his cock, keeping on target. She took the head of his cock easily, but as he slid in further, Bea let him know she could definitely feel it. He was gentle with her at first, rocking her carefully, until he somehow knew that she was ready and willing for more. They were going to go off together, I could tell.

"Now fuck her in the cunt again," I ordered.

By now, Ace was deep into his groove, and he

didn't even blink, he just moved his cock down and screwed it into her socket. The female condom would keep her pussy nice and clean. She gasped from the shock of all these new sensations, and I came out of her mouth so she could talk to him. "Please," she was singing. "A woman needs to come when her time is on her, don't be mean to me, baby, Ace, you tell him, oh, your cock is so big, I need to let go, please, Papa, I've been so good. Let me. Oh, please let me."

"Fuck her in the ass," I snapped, although I was pleased with both of them and how they looked slamming together. This time he went into her ass more quickly, and she got with him fast, too, not allowing any of this slow in-and-out messing around. She was saying, "Fuck me hard," over and over again.

I made them switch holes until we were all crazy, then slid my dick down Bea's throat again and told her this time she was going to drink all of my cream. With Ace giving it to her alternately in the cunt and the ass, one stroke in each, two strokes in each, not letting her predict what would happen next, which hole would be full, she was confused and delighted, excited beyond measure, and I suspected she had snuck in an orgasm or two without telling me.

"Suck," I said, giving her face a little slap. "Pay attention, now." Her face said, *How can I?* But I didn't care. She had gotten fucked by the man she was curious about; now I was going to get what was coming to me. "Nobody comes until I do," I pronounced, and papa got some sugar then. She licked up and down my dick, chewed on my foreskin, sucked the sweat off my balls, swallowed me down and gave me such ardent attention, I was soon grabbing her head with both of my hands, using her mouth frantically, as if I was the one who needed more air. "Soon," I hissed. "Get ready. I'm close. Oh, God, lord above, woman, you send me to paradise. I love you crazy. Come for me, Bea, Ace, I'm spurting. It's a flood of hot cream. Come—swallow me, Bea, you worked hard for that good stuff, girl, now drink it down. That's your man loving you. So take it for your own and savor it. Don't I taste like somethin' special? Better than liquor but it will get you just as high."

Despite the way I was talking, Bea didn't need any encouragement. She was wailing on Ace's fuck stick, coming like a wild woman, and he was saying her name. Women love it when you do that. Like all of a sudden you realized there was a person wrapped around that booty. "Come in the condom, Ace," I reminded him severely, but he was already there and doing what God made him to do. Planting his seed. Celebrating her beauty with the overflowing tribute of his masculinity. I'm a preacher's kid, but I don't have any problem with women who pour their juices out with other women or men who need to do their sex trips with another man. But this is how I like it, her smell and mine blended into the worshipful perfume of fertility. Now Ace was mixed in with us, rewriting Genesis, two Adams and one Eve, arriving at a place of union and innocence despite all the things that had happened in our lives to make us cynical, bitter, or suspicious. I would have told Ace I loved him, but you kinda trust your best friend, when you are a guy, to not embarrass you by spelling it out like that. We exchanged a look of mutual congratulation, and he knew.

Bea slumped down between us, wrung out. "Get us something to drink and some warm wet towels," I said. She slowly levered herself to her feet and went to do her job, with hands still tied behind her back. So she wasn't very fast. Ace moved toward her as if to untie her, but saw me shake my head, and sank onto the couch, forgetting to put his cock away. "Part of the fun is watching her do stuff like this," I said. "She's pretty ingenious."

Eventually we each got a cold beer and she brought us warm, wet cloths that we could wipe ourselves off with. I untied her then. She took some extra time cleaning up Ace's cock and gave it a little kiss before he pulled his briefs up. Without being told, she kept on her knees mostly, giving us a little floor show, dancing like a submissive stripper who's found a client who really turns her on. I told her to go get her jewelry, and she came back with the nipple clamps, which I carefully put on her soft, swollen tits. Her breasts were each the size of half a cantaloupe, and sometimes when I nuzzled her, I could swear I smelled that ripe musky sweetness. I wanted to go again later, and the clamps would keep Bea's mind on sex. Once I got her nipples fixed up I sent her over to give Ace a lap dance, and told him it was okay to handle her. He squeezed her proud, full breasts as if he'd never grabbed a jug of milk before. Made Bea squeal when he tugged on the tit clamps, then put his mouth around them to suck hard on her nipples. I guessed that he was probably getting hard again.

"So, Ace," I said, clearing my throat to get their attention. "Do you think you want a girl like this of your own? Somebody who'll get on her knees and beg for a spanking, like butter wouldn't melt in her mouth?"

"Geez, Willis," he said, running his hand through his short blond hair. "I don't know if I'm ready for that." His honest face was a puzzle, and there was a lump in the front of his boxers.

"Well, then, you'll just have to share Bea with me for a spell, till we get you ready to subdue your own woman. Likely she'll find you when you are ready to take her. The universe brings us together that way, I believe."

"Yeah, right. Somebody like Barbara. Not!"

"You never know, Ace. You never know. Barbara saw some things tonight I bet she never saw before. It was kinda mean of us. She's probably turning it all over in her mind right now. And she's going to want to talk to you again 'cause she'll expect you to apologize for stayin' over after she left. She'll want to know what all went on."

"I don't think so. She's not that kind of girl."

Bea laughed. "Don't look so sad, honey. Barbara wasn't so bad. She had such a cute little butt. I could have spanked her myself."

We were both shocked into silence by this unfamiliar assertion of a dominant streak in Bea. I pondered it as I finished my beer. Life with my woman was never boring, but sometimes I wondered if it was good for me to think so much. Well—I trusted her to take me to good places. She had never steered me wrong so far.

"Come on, Willis," I said, taking hold of the slender chain between Bea's breasts. She came to her feet behind me, gasping. Ace had helped her stand up. "This time I get to grab her ass, and you get to grab her by the hair."

"I'm tired of sucking dick," she complained. "What about double penetration? I always had a fantasy about two cocks moving inside me at the same time. Don't you think that would feel good, Papa?"

"Another country heard from," I said. She was rubbing her decorated nipples against my back, the best ambassadors she could have sent to plead her case. "This ain't the United Nations."

"No," she said, laughing at her own joke before she even made it. "It's a banana republic, and I'm the Head Banana."

"Har-har," Ace said, putting on his West Virginia white trash accent. "I gotcher banana right here, baybee."

Giggling, we trailed into the bedroom, Ace trying to feed Bea some of his beer as we walked, and spilling most of it across her face and breasts. Soon she would be wearing a pearl necklace of his come, and I would be fast asleep, but only after my cock was too sore and limp to fuck her anymore. But I would wake up, I knew, still craving honey.

Tamping the Dirt Down

"Your father is dead."

It was my grandmother's bitter voice, message number three on Wednesday's voice mail. How had she tracked me down? My family had disowned me after that terrible day at school when I took my shirt off to force my guidance counselor to admit that I had been burned with an iron and then beaten with its cord. Before I was whisked away to foster care, my father's mother told me it was my fault that the family had been broken up and disgraced, and I'd never hear from them again.

It made me cry, but they were tears of relief. There was only one person in my family I would miss, and it wasn't her or my father.

No—wait—come back from the past. She was telling me when and where the funeral would be. Another person took over my fingers, picked up the pen, and wrote down the facts she recited. The message ended with the sharp sound of her phone, banged down into its cradle. She hadn't greeted me by name, and she didn't say good-bye.

Was I in shock? She said the prostate cancer had finally gotten him. So he had been eaten alive from the asshole up, I thought with grim relish. That had to hurt. I wondered what it was like for someone who was so good at inflicting pain to be trapped with a lot of it, unrelenting, day and night. And the terror of death.

I knew what that felt like. And I'd had to hustle my own medication for the agony. No doctor was going to write me a prescription. Because children are so resilient, don't you know. They forget, and outgrow trauma as easily as they grow out of shoes and T-shirts.

The only thing I forgot was why the hell I packed my best courtroom suit and bought a plane ticket immediately, so I could arrive in time for the viewing. That maxed out my only valid credit card. No price break since I wasn't purchasing my ticket thirty days in advance, and I wasn't going to a major city, either. I would have to change planes three times to get there, rent a car, and drive for an hour and a half. I must have slept, called my boss, gotten someone to feed the cat and water the plants. But I was on autopilot. My memories had claimed me, and I was sleepwalking through both day and night.

But I snapped to, wide awake, at the front door of the mortuary. The world was full of bright colors; infused with heavy, damp Southern heat and the smell of hundreds of rapidly dying flowers. Someone had opened the door, tamping a cigarette out of its pack, and he looked surprised and happy to see me. The cigarettes went back into the inside pocket of his leather jacket.

It was my older brother, Joshua. I saw his lips form the first letter of my name and almost whinnied in terror. For no reason at all, I had the irrational fear that he would call me Nelly. But that was my dad's slur, his excuse for hurting me. My brother saw me only as a man, my masculinity equal to his own. He made sure of that. To all intents and purposes, he was the one who raised me, who taught me to be a man.

"Ned," he breathed excitedly, and took my hand. Instead of shaking it and letting go, he drew me across the threshold and into his arms. There was too much fabric and leather between our hearts, not to mention history. But I could smell his sweat mingled with the lime deodorant he had been using since high school. It was the smell of safety. He looked nothing like our father. I am the short, dark-haired son. Joshua was tall and blond. We had been told he took after a deceased uncle, but I always suspected he resembled the mother who ran off when I was too little to remember her. I never saw a picture of her, and we were rigorously kept away from her side of the family.

I held my brother tight, as if he was the mast of a ship and I was a sailor caught in the rigging by a sudden storm. He held me too, gently and tenderly. There was no squeeze or pat on the back to let me know it was time to disengage. Instead, he held me patiently, and I relaxed into him, trusting his love. I was the one who finally pulled away, afraid we would attract too much attention. But as I looked up, past his leather-clad shoulder, I saw that they were all keeping their distance, and no one was looking at us. So when he drew me close again, I went willingly, because he was my only ally in this sedate but vicious mob.

"I know why you came," he whispered in my ear. His voice was as intimate as a kiss. "He really is dead. Come and see so you can rest easy."

We went arm in arm to the coffin and stared at its contents for a long time. The other mourners held back or circled around us. That was my old man, all right. Even in death he looked dangerous. No amount of putty or makeup could erase the lines around his mouth and between his eyes that made him look angry with the world. He didn't look like he was asleep. He looked like he had just closed his eyes for a second because he was exasperated with me. His eyes would open and his hand would come up—

I realized I was flinching away from the gruesome figure in the ornate metal box. "Lean over and give him a good hard poke," Joshua whispered in my ear, like a miniature devil in a cartoon. "I had to. Just to make sure. Go on—it'll look like you're kissing him good-bye."

So I leaned over, put my face into a harsh bath of embalmer's chemicals and cosmetics, and stuck my forefinger into my sire's chest. A split second before I actually touched him, I sensed that I would encounter nothing but inanimate matter. But I shoved him anyway, a minute savagery, and he did not react. I was suddenly so happy and dizzy I might have tumbled face-first into the coffin if Joshua hadn't grabbed me. As if Dad would ever let me be on top.

"Steady there, Ned, steady," he said, as if he were talking to a hand-shy dog. He led me to an alcove where there was a blue velvet loveseat shielded by two palm trees and a braided ficus in a faux Chinese pot. But I didn't let him sit down. I pressed him to the wall and burst into tears.

We both cried. Loud, unmanly tears. Little-boy wails. If Grandma saw us, she probably thought we were repenting of our wicked ways, the ruination of her favorite son. But we were sharing a childhood full of humiliation and fear, and giving vent to everything we had to hide so we could live among normal people and pretend to be as careless as them.

Joshua had one hand around the back of my neck, and the way he stroked my hair felt incredibly good. What a rebel he was to come to a wake in a leather jacket, jeans, and boots. He looked like a modern Viking, while I looked incongruous—like an auto mechanic who has dressed up for church. He smelled like a strong, healthy man who needs to get laid. I always notice what men smell like. I've spent enough time nosing around in the dark to get good at it. Joshua leaned forward, scorning all discretion, and licked the tears from my face. Between us, even through a layer of underwear and my wool slacks, I felt his cock twitch, then slowly thicken.

"All these people knew what was happening to us," he said, holding my head in both of his hands and turning my face this way and that so he could look at me and lick the tears on the other cheek. Oh, that indiscreet whisper, the soft puff of air that made me long for his imperious lips upon my own. My knees felt weak. "They knew then, they know now, and yet they'll put him in his grave as if he was a good man who deserved their tears and their prayers. And they'll to go their own graves denying that he's a twisted psychopath who tortured his own children, punched them and put cigarettes out on them, and put them to bed with tears on their faces and his thick, stinking spunk in their butts."

He pushed his hips forward. I gasped, but I didn't move away. I had, after all, been taught not to try to escape. Maybe it was perverse of us to get excited as we discussed the wrongs our father had inflicted on us. But if we could get any pleasure out of the past, so what? That was our business. Reparations.

"Fuck them all!" Joshua said, loud enough to be overheard. A passing cousin flinched but rapidly re-arranged her face and hurried away from our niche.

"I already got a room for us," Joshua told me, as if he had known, without talking to me for all of these years, that I'd be here, and I would need him to shelter me. We left the funeral parlor holding hands. Grief gives men permission to break the usual rules about not touching one another, and Southern men are more prone to emotional breakdowns and grabbing one another than Yankees, but we were pushing the boundaries of what could be justified by crazed grief.

He was driving a vintage Mustang convertible that he'd restored himself. There was a new fifth of Jack in the car, and I unscrewed the cap and tilted it to his lips and then my own. The bottle's slick glass stem reminded me of a slim cock, barely breaching my mouth. The liquor burned like a hot poker going down my throat, so I had to have some more, to dull the pain of the first slug. Joshua kept his right hand on my knee as he drove. We fell into our old pattern. I shifted, he steered. We drove to his motel through the dark streets of the hellish little town that had robbed both of us of our belief in any hell hereafter.

We were laughing and drinking and breaking the speed limit so blatantly that we were lucky the police didn't pull us over. But there weren't many cops, I guess. This was a town were people still didn't lock their doors at night—unless they were locking a kid into the shed. Spiders like sheds.

But there were no spiders in Joshua's Eezy-Breezy Motel cottage, which consisted of a room barely big enough to house the bed, a bathroom with a shower and no tub, and a small kitchen. He said he was hungry so I went to the refrigerator and found our staples: eggs and frozen potatoes, butter and cheese. I made him a big plate of scrambled eggs and fried potatoes, and it was so good to see him put food that I had cooked into his mouth that I ate some myself. Then I tried to claim the bottle again, but he wanted it first, and so we had to wrestle for the next drink.

Joshua made me wait to get pinned. I wasn't quite drunk enough to have an excuse or the courage to just beg for his dick. So I struggled with him, honestly pitting my strength against his. He seemed to have a counter for any move I made. My hands couldn't get a grip on him. They just slid over his muscles and betrayed me by wanting to linger there, holding on to his biceps or his ass. I was out of breath and hard as a teenager who just went to second base. Joshua had me down on the bed with my legs spread and my hands pinned over my head. "You want a drink?" he asked, hoisting the bottle with his free hand.

"Yes, you fucker!" I said, laughing.

He took a pull on the bottle, then held his face over mine. His raised eyebrow asked me a question. I felt a change come over my face as I melted into submission. My mouth fell open and he covered my lips with his own. We kissed around the whisky, sucking it off one another's tongues. The feel of his probing tongue and his hand tugging at my zipper made me squirm. My breath came out in short gasping whines. He got his hand into my fly, that competent hand that had shielded me from schoolyard bullies, from every hostile force except our father. What he found there made him shake his head at me and grin. "You want more than some Jack," he said.

"Yes," I told him. "I want Joshua."

He played with me, working my cock with his hand while we kissed again. "If you let my hands go, I'll unbutton my shirt," I whispered. He rolled to one side, and I sat up and tore my shirt off, hunched awkwardly out of my pants. They would get wrinkled, and I needed to wear them to the funeral tomorrow. But let them lay on the floor. I had something more important to do.

Joshua was sitting on the edge of the bed. While I was getting naked, he had taken his dick out. I wondered how many places it had been, that proud rascal. Well, I had no grounds for jealousy. I had gotten busy as well. Sex doesn't fill the hole in my spirit, but it mercifully turns my vision away from it for a while.

Maybe I had learned a trick or two that would make Joshua even happier to see me.

He poured some whisky into his hand and worked his cock. That had to burn his pisshole, I thought, but he didn't seem to care. Maybe there was so much precome that it kept the alcohol away from his slit. "I don't have to slap you to get you to suck my dick, do I?" he asked gravely.

I stiffened, surprised by this phrase from the past. The night before I had gone to the guidance counselor and demanded that she report my father, he had gone crazy on me. When he came into my room, I had gotten some weird freakish fag courage from somewhere, and I told him, "You don't have to slap me to get me to suck your dick, old man."

"No, Joshua," I whispered, kneeling and tonguing the head of his cock. "You don't have to slap me. But I'll probably do a better job of sucking your dick if you do."

He hit me without any hesitation. That's how you know when someone really wants to hit you, when they go after you as soon as they have permission. Sadists must walk around with a perpetual mental hard-on, seeing potential victims where other people see strangers or coworkers or friends. Joshua had once been a very angry young man, and I was used to being hit. I liked it when it came from him. I could comfort him by siphoning off his rage so it didn't get him in trouble outside our house.

"You know I used to listen to him working you over," he said. As lust filled him up, his Southern accent came out. I was only listening with half an ear.

I had a third of his cock in my mouth, and it tasted so good I wanted to bolt down the rest of it. But I teased both of us, sliding his shaft in and out of my throat, giving him only partial access. He kept on talking, caressing my head. I wished it was shaved so I could feel every callus on his fingertips. "I used to feel so guilty because I'd get turned on listening to him hit you with that belt. I would try to keep my hands off my cock, sit on them, bite them, until my balls were blue. But I'd always lose. I'd jack off when you'd start to cry. And I'd make myself come before he let you go, so you wouldn't see me do such a sick thing."

I let his dick slide far enough out of my mouth to allow me to say a few words. "But one night your timing was off," I reminded him.

Joshua's hand moved to my neck and he forced me forward, taking charge of the blowjob. "Things have never been the same since then, have they?" he mused. His cock fucked my throat, and the further it went into me, the harder my own dick got, until I knew exactly what he meant when he said it was impossible to keep his hands off his own cock. But I didn't touch myself. I knew the rules. I was the one who had made them up in the first place.

"You want to jack off, don't you?" he teased. His voice had just the right derisive edge. He was aroused by his power over me, my willing surrender, and the humiliating evidence my body gave him of how much I enjoyed it. I gasped or grunted some affirmative response, feeling tears start to flow down my face. He would allow me to suck and lick at him for several minutes, then he would push past my ability to caress him with my tongue and deliberately make me gag. I didn't care what happened to me, if my throat got raw or I choked on him. I just wanted the taste of his dick ground into my mouth, so I would never be able to get it out, so I would always be able to taste him there.

"Show me your cock, little brother," he ordered. I put both hands at the base of my dick and tipped it up so he could see its ruddy rigidity. "Nice," he complimented me, hips swaying as he fucked my face. "Do yourself while I watch," he gasped, close to coming himself. My fist moved slowly. I had to hold myself back. It was hard to monitor my own body when his sex had taken over. I wanted all of me to be absorbed in servicing him, as if there were only one cock between us.

"Are you going to come with your big brother?" he asked. I nodded, made slobbery pig noises, begged him with my eyes. "Don't you dare shoot until I tell you," he warned. "Oh, suck me!" He grabbed my neck with both hands and screwed me roughly, sharp deep thrusts that I felt in the pit of my stomach. My cock was so ready to come that I had to stop stroking it. I could feel the moisture leaking from the head of my cock, imagined it running down the shaft to coat the crack of my ass with its slickness.

"Do it good. Do it like a big boy. I want to see my little brother shoot," he commanded, speaking in short, harsh phrases. We were both out of breath. His salty cream flooded the back of my palate, and I aimed my dick at myself, leaving white spatters all over one nipple.

Joshua slid out of me. He put his hand on the top

of my head and tilted my torso back. With an index finger, he scooped come off my chest and fed it to me. "See how much good stuff you've got in that little pecker of yours?" he asked. God, how weird is it to be turned on when somebody talks about your dick being small? But I was. I sucked come off his fingers as if they were extra cocks, and I could make them shoot. He laughed at me, pleased with himself and with me, and when my chest was clean he gave me a drink, took one himself, and then dragged me up onto the bed.

We slept. My body was more relaxed than it had ever been. I hadn't seen Joshua after that day in school. I got sent to a foster home, and he was placed in a group house. There were so many times I had wondered where he was. If I had really tried I probably could have tracked him down. After all, my grandmother had managed to find me. But I had been afraid that this would happen even though I had never stopped playing these games. I was afraid he would call me a freak and turn away from me in disgust. I was equally afraid he would put me on my knees and dominate me again. Hell, I didn't even know if Joshua was gay, like me! But my body didn't care about any of this bullshit now. I slept cradled in the hollow of his shoulder, curled up against my brother's clean and sexy self. We were like two wolves safe in their underground den.

The next morning we started to fuck again as soon as we woke up. This time he tied me up with cords he cut from the blinds, and teased me with his hands and mouth until I was beside myself, ready to say or do anything if only he would let me come. But once more, I was not allowed to orgasm until he had his cock deep down my throat, and I was gulping down his load. He had pinched and bitten my nipples until they were painfully alert, and I felt both shame and exultation when he fondled my chest and I got hard once more. I would have been a girl for him. A dog. An alien. Anything he wanted, any place, any time. He was that good, he knew me that well.

I felt like I was being trained. But training implies an ongoing relationship. That had never happened for me, and it certainly was not a possibility with Joshua. But a boundary like that was hard to remember when he pushed me into the shower, aimed his cock at me, and pissed all over me, then made me kneel to jack off with his piss and swallow the bitter remnants from his softening meat. It was impossible to hold any part of myself back from him when he shoved his boots in my face and made me lick them, my ass in the air, groveling and weeping to make him believe that I really did belong to him.

Then he slid the belt out of the loops of his jeans, doubled it over, and made me kiss it. "I thought you might like this," he said easily, hitching up his pants. The first hit almost flattened me. But I'd been told to keep my butt up for this belting. I tried every trick I had learned long ago to get me through the pain: panting, holding back my screams, letting my screams go. But it didn't stop what was happening, and I couldn't take it. I couldn't take it, but I had no choice, it wasn't going to stop.

That was when I found a door I hadn't seen for many years. I opened it up and fell through it to the other side. There were the same amazing colors, the music, the sensation of dancing on air while being filled with boundless serenity. The longer I was suspended in this place, the better it felt to be there. When I cried out, it was because my human body could not contain so much ecstasy. My mind was not schooled to feel so much joy.

So Joshua came to get me. Pushed his arm through the door, grabbed me by the scruff of my neck, and hauled me back to his room. I lay facedown on the bed, sighing while he fondled my welts. "I think we might have missed the funeral," he said.

"Shit," I replied.

"Do you care if we miss the rest of it?"

I thought about it. Seeing the monster's corpse laid out, frozen by time's justice, had done me a world of good. But he was still above ground, and while he was in the world, he might still have the capacity to do harm. "I think I need to see him buried," I whispered.

Joshua nodded. "Okay," he said. "Let's go." He offered me a hand. We quickly showered and dressed, then climbed into his car, ignoring the maid who had been trying to get into the room to change the towels all day. She glared at us as we drove off. I wondered what she would think about the mess we had made in the room—the piss on the bathroom floor, faint lines of blood on the sheets from where I had rolled over after he belted me, come on the pillowcases. I became silently fierce with the need and righteous power to defend us.

"What the hell are you grinding your teeth about?" Joshua asked. I didn't reply. He sighed and put my hand on the gearshift. Sliding across the seat to get closer to him, I felt much better. I was so far under that I didn't question where we were going. He seemed to know what he was doing, and I didn't want to worry about it. All I could really think about was his cock. When would I see it again? When would I taste it again? He had used me hard, and it only made me want him more. Was I one of those horrible bottoms who becomes a black hole sucking the life out of any top within arm's reach? Or was this just one of the masochistic joys of slavery, to have your need brought to the fore and kept in consciousness, with no ability to sate it? It certainly made me attentive to him. For example, I had brought the whisky along. There wasn't much left in the bottle, but we downed it before we made it to the graveyard.

The Mustang ground out a place for herself in the gravel parking lot. Dust hung in the air like the aftermath of a bombing. It was getting late. Soon the sun would go down and insects would begin to bite.

There was no gatekeeper or overseer to give us directions. But it wasn't a very big cemetery. We went hand in hand up a grassy hill, and sighted our kinfolk not far off, gathered around a red granite tablet that was half as tall as I was, thick as a loaf of bread, and as wide as my outstretched arms. Now we knew where the estate's funds had been invested. I guessed no money had been put in trust for me to pay for therapy. I told Joshua what I was thinking, but he didn't laugh, just looked at me queerly, as if I had gotten too much sun.

Nobody acknowledged us, but we made a place

for ourselves among them. I gave Grandmother a little wave, and she pointedly turned her head away from me. Why had she called me? Did she invite me to come home just so she could shun me? My father's cruelty had to come from somewhere. Or someone.

The closed casket was lowered into the ground with slings and an automated hoist. When it hit the bottom of the grave, the slings were dragged out from underneath it. Everyone took turns throwing a handful of dirt onto the coffin lid. I hurled mine like a baseball. *Don't tell me I throw like a girl, you bastard.* Never again. I'll never hear those taunts again. Nelly. Sissy. Fag.

But I'll always have to wonder how much he has to do with what I have become.

The mourners drifted away, leaving the coffin still exposed in its pit. Joshua and I lingered. A white-haired man in overalls and a black man in brown pants with stained cuffs were going to shovel the dirt in. There was a roll of sod to lay over the disturbed earth. "We'll take care of it," Joshua told them, and put a shovel in my hand. "We're part of his immediate family."

The two workmen shrugged and gave up their tools. "Guess we get to go home early," one of them said. They bummed a cigarette apiece off of Joshua, then trundled off to the parking lot, where I had seen a pickup truck and a van parked side by side.

"Put your back into it," he ordered me, and I dug into the first chunk of brown soil. It was heavy with clay, and I twisted my shoulder heaving it into the hole. "No," Joshua said, correcting my posture with a hand on my shoulder and another on my hip. "Put the weight here. Then pivot. I don't want you to hurt yourself."

We were high enough from having sex to giggle together at that one. Then we went to work, unable to talk much. An evening breeze had come up that threatened to blow dirt back into our mouths. I felt a quiet happiness, the way I used to feel when Joshua and I managed to sneak off together to play ball or go fishing. The more bizarre aspect of what we were doing I forced beneath the surface of my awareness. Besides, it was hard work; it takes an amazing amount of dirt to fill a grave.

Once we were done, Joshua took my hand and put his other hand on my waist. "Shall we dance?" he asked, and stepped onto the grave. I followed his lead without thinking. "We have to tamp the dirt down," he explained, and kissed me on the forehead. Up and down we went, I think we were waltzing, but I don't know anything about ballroom dancing. Or disco, for that matter. I pirouetted; Joshua let me go, and bowed to me. I wasn't even tempted to drop a curtsy. I bowed as well. Then he motioned for me to help him shift the huge roll of turf and position it properly over the bare ground. We somehow managed to shove it into place and then unroll it. The dirt hadn't settled yet, so it wasn't level with the rest of the sward. It looked like a green toupee.

Looking around, I realized it was completely dark, and we had no flashlight. Would we trip over headstones as we walked back to the car? I jumped when Joshua's hands found me. He caressed my back and chest, then began to peel off my T-shirt. I resisted, and he grabbed me and bit me on the neck, hard. "If somebody shivers when you walk on his grave, what do you think he does when you fuck on it?" he hissed.

If I had fought with him before giving him that first blowjob in the motel, it was child's play compared to the combat we engaged in now. I swung at him, clawed and kicked, bit and poked at his eye, pulled his hair, had no compunction about using any dirty trick I could think of to get away from him. But he was bigger and stronger than me, and he was my older brother. He had been the one I ran to when I needed ice on a burn or a bandage on a bleeding wound. He had let me sleep in his bed. He had given me my first *Playboy* magazine, seen my first ejaculation, and been the first one to show me how to take away the pain of degradation and turn it into pride and pleasure. Pride in my ability to give him pleasure. Delight in cheating my father by letting Joshua do the same things that he did, but letting him willingly, with love.

Bit by bit he got my clothes off. Hold by hold he took me down to the ground and pinned my hands at my sides, sitting on my stomach. He had kept my necktie and used it to bind my wrists together; put it once around my neck, then around my hands, so they were held up under my chin, and I could barely breathe. Then he slapped me, once with the flat of his hand, then backhand. Even in the dark he knew how to find my vulnerable face, twisted with tears, aching for his approval. My face rang like the hollow bowl of a Tibetan bell. I wished that he would hit me again.

"Don't fuck with me," he warned me. Then he

said in a softer tone of voice, "Because I'm going to be fucking you."

The grass tickled my bare back so much that I wanted to shriek. Joshua's weight on me was almost welcome because it forced the blades of grass to lay flat and stop flicking my sensitive skin. "On your back where you belong," he recited. "Now you say it. Say the words, Ned."

I was weeping. "No," I choked. "Stop this. I won't. I don't want to."

"We have to," he said. "Don't you understand? We have to, or it will never be over."

Then he was quiet, and perhaps because I can never stand a long silence, I broke its ominous spell. "I am on my back," I said, pronouncing each word with difficulty. "Where I belong."

He parted my legs and lifted them, bent my knees. He was holding on to my ankles. His cock brushed the crack of my ass. I shivered, grateful for the warmth of the night and its rural depth. There were no house lights, streetlamps, or passing cars to break up our camouflage and expose us. His cock bobbed up and down, moving as he swayed his hips, maneuvering the hard shaft, keeping it near my asshole.

"I'm going to rape you, Ned," he told me. "Come on, little bro, it's not like you never had anything up your ass before."

I gasped. He had used one of the words that triggered both ambivalence and desire in me. Rape. Did I want to be raped? If I wanted it, was it rape? What if I didn't want it when it began, but did want it when it ended? Lust began to tinge my fear, like two watercolors mingled in the same brushstroke. His cock was slippery. Had he managed to spread some lubricant on himself? I wouldn't have been surprised; he was still fully clothed, still wearing his leather jacket, his fly open. Only his cock was naked, while I was bare-assed, stripped, tied, and spread wide.

He used the tips of his fingers to push the head of his dick down, where it would find an opening. He moved forward. I moaned when the cock head grazed my hole. "See?" he whispered huskily. "You do like it. Why shouldn't I fuck you, Ned? Everybody else does, don't they?"

"No!" I replied, even though it was a lie. I couldn't count the number of men I'd bent over for or crouched above, hoping the frantic motions of their cocks would erase my misery.

"Got you," he said when the head of his dick made it past the first sphincter. I twisted, trying to break away, but he held me fast. His hard thighs made contact with the bruises on my ass, and I opened to the pain and opened to his cock. He sailed forward, then grunted as he hit bottom. I was plugged. My breath raspy. It's a sensation you can never quite remember when you're jacking off, and even a dildo in your butt doesn't replicate it. It wasn't just his size, although that was nothing to take lightly. It's the man's presence behind the cock that moves me so much, the feeling of his need inside me, his intention to possess me.

"Oh, Joshua," I said, longing to touch his face, his arms. Straining to embrace him and straining to escape made every muscle in my body pop out. He fondled me, especially my tits, reminding me that he could elicit whimpers and pleading when he twisted and tugged my nipples. He kept his cock hard yet barely moved inside of me. I think we both enjoyed prolonging that moment of first contact, the break-in. But he finally had to threaten to take his thick rod away from me, make me cry to think it would be gone, convince me he was going to let me go, before he plunged back in, laughing at my resistance and surrender.

He leaned forward and put his face close to mine. "We're tamping the dirt down, Ned," he said, his cock stirring my ass and heating it. "I'm going to fuck the shit out of you. All of it. We're going to leave it right here."

And that is what he did. I have no idea how long he tormented me. It seemed to last for hours. I raged, I screamed, I cried, and I laughed hysterically. Through it all his cock kept him connected to me, abided with me, schooled and tended me. Was this how the man possessed by evil spirits felt when Jesus chased them all away? For years I had run away from my feelings. Now there was no way that I could escape them, no matter how terrible they were. And Joshua didn't care if it hurt me. In fact, that was what kept him hard. He loved healing me because it meant he got to put his hand inside the torn and bloody places and explore them as much as he pleased. I had no idea why anybody would want to know that much about me. But he did, and I clung to him mentally, since I could not use my poor numb hands to reach him. For a miracle, he did not leave me.

I felt light enough to lay my heart on the scales of the afterworld, with a feather resting in the other pan.

The house of my existence was empty but clean. I told my brother so. I thanked him with eloquent incoherence. He grinned, or was he biting his lips?

I hissed, "No!" when he lifted his weight from my body, backing away from me and leaving me empty and himself unsatisfied. But he was not finished with me or with the shadowy trench in his own psyche.

Joshua untied my hands and flipped me over. I could barely feel my fingers, and I knew I would have a ligature mark around my neck that would be hard to hide from airport security. The perfect cock, a cock I had grown up with, a cock I had envied as a small boy and now coveted, edged back into my body and then swayed confidently within me. How could I have forgotten its length and circumference, the fact that his cock got so much bigger at its base, how the huge knot of his cock head compressed my prostate, the kinks and eventual smoothing out of my own passageway?

There was no more teasing. We fucked as hard and fast as we could without losing the bridge of flesh between us. Joshua seemed to swell inside of me, and I knew my ass was raw, and didn't care. I would trade the integrity of my skin for Joshua's release. This tall, blond man, stranger/brother and witness to my ruin, had made me as untroubled and insubstantial as the air. I would die to make him fly with me. So I reached for him with my words, binding him to me as he had merged with me. "Please take me," I said at last, exhausted but happier than mortals should be. "It's all I can give you, Joshua. But you've got it. All that I am. All that I ever was."

"And all that you ever shall be," he said through

gritted teeth, and made those small quick motions that sometimes herald a fountain of jizz. "Come on his face," Joshua urged me. "Shoot all over the dirty bastard. Make him take your load."

The indecency of it was inspiring, but I had waited so long to come, it was hard to bring myself off. The urgency of Joshua's thrusts had me facedown on the unrooted grass of my father's grave. I knew a smothering moment of terror as those green shoots brushed against my face. I expected something evil and insubstantial to come out of the ground and enter me, pollute and occupy me, dethrone me from control over my own flesh and blood. But all I could sense was the quiet decency of earthworms and beetles. There was no one here but two brothers, master and slave, equals and survivors. We had nothing but each other and the precious moment that was about to pass forever, the moment of our union.

Impatient with my delayed spurt, if only because it meant he had to delay his own climax, Joshua finally spit in his hand, wrapped it around my cock, and made me shoot with just a few expert strokes. "Take that," he whispered as the white jets left my body. "Drown in it. Lick it up. Tell me you like it!" After all the come we had milked out of one another, I don't know how much cream he had left in his balls, but his orgasm was a long one. I took his load with my head bowed, honored to be soiled by it, wishing it could go on forever.

Some moments passed that I can't remember. Eventually I realized I was no longer in Joshua's embrace. I was panting from the huge energy drain that follows coming. I felt like I could fall down on the ground and sleep right there. But Joshua still needed me. He was beside me, on his knees, bent over, pounding the grass. "Tell me you like it!" he shouted. "Tell me!"

This was no time to crawl around in the dark, patting the ground to locate my underwear. But I did find my pants and a shirt and yanked them on. I went to Joshua, knelt beside him, and put my hand on his shoulder. "There's nobody here but me," I whispered. Then my voice got more confident. "Us. But I'll tell you how much I like it." I leaned over to nuzzle the blond whiskers on his cheeks. "I'll always be here to tell you I love it. And you."

Then I led him away.

The Mustang had a full tank of gas. We would need every mile we could wring out of it.

About the Author

Patrick Califia is the most outspoken and prolific sex writer working today. He is the author of twenty books, including four previous collections of BDSM fiction, *Macho Sluts, Melting Point, No Mercy,* and *Hard Men;* a novel, *Mortal Companion;* and the classic introduction to BDSM, *Sensuous Magic: A Guide for Adventurous Couples.* He is the author of the seminal texts on sex and gender politics *Speaking Sex to Power: The Politics of Queer Sex, Public Sex: The Culture of Radical Sex,* and *Sex Changes: Transgender Politics.* He lives in San Francisco.